FEELS LIKE HOME

JO COX

1

"Hello, monster," Jess growled as she stepped into the entrance hall and a set of podgy fingers dug at her leg.

She hauled Grace over her shoulder and took the stairs two at a time, then launched the toddler at her bed with a bit too much enthusiasm. Jess winced and clasped a hand over her mouth when she realised she'd also almost sworn, but her shoulders dropped again as Grace giggled. She was a lot sturdier than she seemed, thank God.

"What are you looking so worried about?" V appeared in the doorway, clutching a clean nappy and frowning as she leant sideways against the frame.

Jess left Grace to sprawl out on the duvet while she opened the wardrobe, shrugging and trying to remain casual. "Nothing, just picking something to wear for my dad's barbecue."

She held out a black T-shirt but then let it hang limp by her side as Grace bounced on the mattress, sending pillows crashing to the floor. She screeched and bashed the headboard against the wall, which was a lot more action than the bed had become accustomed to of late.

"Why do you insist on dressing like a vampire? It's summer, go wild and try colour."

Jess let out a long low grumble, returning the rejected top. "Go on, take over."

V nudged her out of the way and flicked through the hangers, sucking her teeth. "Yellow suits you, not everyone can pull it off. You don't own any, though, so it looks like red will have to suffice." She inclined her head as she held up and surveyed a fresh T-shirt. "Not helping on the vampire front. Sorry."

"Anything to get out of these clothes, I'm melting. You'd think we could spring for a fan in the office."

It would be Jess's first act of mercy when she took charge on Monday. Her dad was on holiday for four weeks, which meant she was managing his letting agency and the company credit card. She had every intention of exploiting her new powers to buy three and stick them all on full blast.

V handed over the T-shirt she'd selected and closed the wardrobe. "Complain all you like, but it was your choice to work on a Saturday rather than coming to the park with us."

"Oh, lovely," Jess mumbled. "I'm glad I can always rely on you for a bit of sympathy after a hard day."

"If that's what you're after, you've come to the wrong place. I might stretch to making you a cup of tea, but that's the limit."

Jess was about to say she'd also show less compassion when Grace next threw a tantrum but stopped herself. It was an insensitive comment to make to your best friend, given she hadn't made a deliberate decision to get pregnant in the last year of her degree. Considering it had also resulted in her losing a teacher training place, any remark was ill-advised, and she returned the conversation to safer ground.

"Well, my day wasn't a waste. I tied up three flats while you two were enjoying yourselves, which means a nice chunk of commission."

She lobbed her phone at the bed and peeled off her trousers while V nodded, gathering the discarded clothing with her free hand and tossing it at the washing basket.

"Impressive. That'll keep us in new shoes for a while."

"Does Grace need shoes?" Jess paused with her fingers on the buttons of her shirt. "Take some money from the kitchen jar for essentials. I know it's meant for food, but I don't mind."

V laughed and drew her into a hug, the nappy crinkling as she adjusted her grip. "No, it was a joke, but I understand it's been so long since I've attempted one that it might not have landed. Thank you, though."

Jess tried to dial down her smile as she hopped into a pair of denim shorts from the floor. She didn't want to scare away V's glimmer of a positive mood, but couldn't restrain the grin anymore when her phone vibrated and she leant over to read the message.

"I'm determined to get us in matching Converse," she murmured, still distracted and itching to reply. "It's my mission in life."

"Yeah, but the lesbian urge to merge thing only applies to girlfriends." V dipped her head, attempting to snoop at the screen, then relented and slumped back against the wardrobe. "Speaking of which, who keeps putting that goofy look on your face? If you've started seeing someone and haven't told me there will be hell to pay. I require immediate access to all gossip."

There wasn't much to tell. Between work and adapting to having two extra people in the house, romance had fallen to the bottom of the priority list. The large, inappropriate crush Jess had been trying to quash for months hadn't helped. Not that she'd even call it a crush. She knew it was more than that, but minimising her feelings was sometimes the only way to deal with them.

"I wish, but she's way off limits. In fact, so far off limits this isn't worth talking about." She tapped out a quick response, tucked the phone in her pocket, and folded her arms in an attempt to regain control. "Now, about these shoes. Are you sure I can't treat her just this once? It's for my benefit more than Grace's, after all."

"No, but you can buy them for her birthday if you're desperate. You'll spoil her, otherwise."

That was the idea. Grace had been through her parents splitting, several disastrous weeks living with her grandparents, and countless other upheavals. A bit of spoiling seemed long overdue, and it wasn't like Jess had anyone else to fuss.

She continued unbuttoning her shirt and went in for another try. "Isn't it a key requirement in the fun auntie job description? It's right next to reading bedtime stories and sneaking her chocolate biscuits."

"I'm sure that's correct but since you're not her aunt, I guess it doesn't matter. Sorry."

"What? I thought you'd made me an honorary aunt?"

V rolled her eyes, but as she smiled Jess knew she would get her way. "Fine, if having a title is so important to you."

"If I have to share my hobnob supply, I should receive one as a standard courtesy."

They were sharing more than just biscuits. After four years living alone, her two-bed terrace was overflowing with all the crap required to feed and entertain a nineteen-month-old kid. The lounge doubled up as a play area with boxes of toys everywhere and walking through was like tackling an assault course. Her kitchen was also being used to store a highchair, pushchair and various other bits they couldn't cram into V's room. The only space that remained sacrosanct was Jess's bedroom, and even that was being infiltrated.

She finished dressing and caught hold of Grace, tipping her upside down and tickling her tummy as they all wandered downstairs. "Presume I still can't tempt you to join me this evening? There'll be free booze and cake."

"And your dad. No thanks." V followed them into the kitchen, still brandishing the nappy. "Can you stop? I need to change her. That's why I'm carrying this thing."

"Oh, sorry." She set Grace on the lawn, then stood back until they could resume the fun part of parenting. "Don't think we've changed the subject, though."

V knelt and tugged Grace's shorts as she squirmed, clawing for her sandpit. "Why? He hates me, he hasn't invited us, and it'll just be uncomfortable. Leave it."

"He invited you," Jess protested, replaying the scene and feeling less convinced. She shrugged, and this time when she spoke her voice carried less certainty. "Well, I asked if you could come and he agreed. I'm choosing to believe they're the same things."

"That's not an invitation. It's more of a concession, so he doesn't look like an asshole. Do you see the distinction?"

She almost argued on a technicality but knew asking V to sit through an evening with her dad was unfair. He'd been objecting over their living situation for months, and she felt bad enough.

"At least let me bring home dinner."

V pulled up Grace's shorts and released her to scramble away. "Oh yeah, food poisoning will fix this. Great idea." She stood, straightening out her dress and wiping a hand across the sweat beading on her forehead. "Sorry, but I'm sick of talking about your dad. I long for the days when he was just a casual annoyance."

She wasn't the only one. Somehow, helping a friend had launched World War Three. It'd be bearable, except there was no escape. People warned against working with family, but Jess had found it a breeze until now. She never guessed arguing over her spare room would be the thing to cause friction.

"I know, and I promise not to mention him at all for the next four weeks. When he comes back from holiday, he'll have loosened up a bit. You'll see."

V huffed as she perched on the edge of the sandpit. "I hope so. I hate making you argue when you've always been so close. If there were anywhere else for us to live, I wouldn't put you through it."

Her features softened again as she stroked her daughter's blonde curls. Where they'd come from no one knew because V's hair was a lustrous red that turned a hundred or more colours in the sun. At least it would, when it wasn't run through with grease, but she'd had a worse week than usual.

Jess squeezed her shoulder. "I can tough it out with Dad, he'll get over this."

"Fingers crossed, because I'm not sure how much longer I'll survive being public enemy number one."

* * *

Half an hour later Jess crunched up the drive of her dad's cottage through a thick billow of smoke. He could never barbecue without at least one of his neighbours peering from a window, wondering if he'd incinerate the entire village.

"Is there anyone you haven't invited to this bloody thing?" She frowned, scanning the garden. "You are sure this is a holiday rather than a permanent move?"

There were people everywhere, laid across picnic blankets or sat in fold out chairs on the lawn and patio. Even his accountant was over by the pergola, flicking fag ash into a plant pot.

"Come one, come all," David declared, snapping his tongs.

Jess reached into her back pocket and pulled out a folded piece of paper, heavy with paint and sagging in the middle. "Grace made you a card at nursery. Well, sort of. She hasn't quite progressed that far yet."

It was a blatant ploy to win him over, but she wasn't above trying. Since common sense and reason hadn't worked, anything was worth a try.

"Nursery?" His eyes shot up from the barbecue and he dropped a burger. "Who's paying for that?"

Jess rubbed a hand along her face with exasperation. They'd agreed not to tell him, but it'd slipped out. "Not me, don't panic. If it goes well, V wants to find a job."

"Shouldn't that money go towards giving you some rent? Food, water, and electricity might also be helpful, unless they're free now and I've missed a memo."

Next time they should stick to less incendiary topics like politics or religion, and Jess gritted her teeth for another argument. "I don't want her to do that until she's back on her feet. Besides, it's a breach of my contract to sublet. You should know better, given you wrote it."

"For Christ's sake," David scoffed. "Rachel's your landlady. You could burn the entire place to the ground and she'd still forgive you, tenancy agreement or not."

It wasn't the point. Rachel was her godmother and his best friend, which was even more reason not to take the piss.

"We've done this conversation to death, can't you let it drop and enjoy your holiday?" Jess took a deep breath, trying to steel herself. "Please, for everyone's sake."

David huffed and as another puff of smoke blew off the barbecue, he looked like an old dragon. It provided a little light relief in the middle of an otherwise tense exchange, and she struggled not to laugh.

"No. I'm your dad and it comes with the territory. The same as it's V's job to care for Grace, not yours. I sympathise with her, I do. Life's tough when you're a single parent, but she can't rely on other people forever."

"And you never had a helping hand?" Jess pointed at him with the painting, back to feeling nothing but frustration. It didn't have the same threat value as a searing hot cooking utensil, though, so she let it flap by her side again. "Because I remember spending a lot of my childhood at Rachel's house when you were working. After school, occasional Saturdays, and most of the holidays, in fact. One summer, she set up the spare bedroom for me and had done with it."

He hooked his tongs over the handle of the barbecue, reaching out to her shoulder, and she experienced an impulse to ram them somewhere. It was a shame his travel insurance didn't cover acts of violence brought on by overzealous parenting.

"You weren't living with them. It's not the same thing."

"How do you figure that? When Mum left, you wouldn't have coped without support. It never did us any harm, though, did it?"

"No, true." David nodded, seeming to concede the point. He scratched across the greying stubble on his chin, then waved at another arrival. "Rachel loves you like a daughter."

"So why is it one rule for you and something different for me? I care as much about V and Grace."

He mumbled, eying her with suspicion. "That's the other thing worrying me. Are you sure nothing's going on between you two?"

"Don't even go there."

They'd split when they were eighteen and both been in other relationships. Neither were pining over a sixth form romance and the idea was ridiculous.

"We'll see. It might appear platonic right now but soon you're cuddled up on the sofa of an evening with one too many glasses of wine and nostalgia kicks in." He lowered his gaze, drawing her in as if he had something important to add. "Be careful."

Jess struggled to hold in a laugh again. It wasn't even that funny, but exhaustion was doing strange things to her. As if living with a screaming toddler was conducive to romance. Grace woke them at five every morning and Peppa Pig was seeping into Jess's nightmares.

"You've been watching too much television, old man. I know you believe they've written it into law somewhere that you can never move on from a breakup, but it is possible to be friends with an ex."

"Now that's not fair." David returned to jabbing his tongs. "I'm letting go of my grief with your mother, although it's taken a while."

"Eighteen years."

"Okay, I conceded it'd been some time, but I've done as you asked and got a life."

He'd added air quotes to the last bit, and Jess grunted out a laugh. "Not sure I worded it quite like that."

"No, you were far more brutal. I heard the phrase 'sad old twat' more than once, but come to mention it, that may have been Rachel."

"Expect so, we both know she's got you pegged." Jess wiped tears from her eyes as they stung with smoke. "I take it your girlfriend isn't here?"

The secrecy surrounding his new romance verged on MI6 level, and no one understood how he'd started a relationship with a woman from Devon. They lived in rural Oxfordshire, which was a three-hour drive even in good traffic. Everyone had taken a shot at getting him to release the details. Her name might be a start.

David shrugged as he flipped a burger. "Wasn't worth her making the trek when I'm heading there on Monday. She'd only have spent most of the weekend on the M5, it's always a nightmare when the weather's nice like this."

"Convenient. She couldn't put up with a few hours on the motorway to meet your only daughter?"

He ignored that question and focussed on his barbecue, not even bothering to forge an excuse this time. Jess had already heard them all, anyway.

"I'm nervous about this holiday," David whispered as he leant towards her, his features creasing with a concerned frown. "A cruise ship isn't something you can leave if things don't go well."

"What's up, are you worried she'll throw herself overboard? I'd watch out if you packed those awful Hawaiian shirts."

David picked up a sausage but grimaced as it left a smear of black across his lips. "Thanks for the support." He tossed it in with the coals and licked his fingers clean. "Any tips I can use, or are you only here to torture me?"

"Can't help, I don't think. Middle-aged women aren't my forte."

"Are any women your forte?"

"Ouch, that burned." Jess rubbed her arm, then tapped him with Grace's painting. "I'm adding this to the wall of fame before you turn on me again."

She wandered into the kitchen and found a slither of space above the Aga, then stood back to admire her work. It looked a right mess—the entire room did—but she loved it. Her dad, whose life was so neat and ordered, let everything fall out here. There were baby pictures and birthday parties in black frames nestled against random snaps in modern chrome frames, and none of them matched much in his nineteenth century cottage.

Even before the divorce, Rachel took centre stage in every picture. She'd always treated Jess like a third child, and it was hard to understand David's point of view with V and Grace, given the complete double standard. He'd been more than happy to enlist help and even now encouraged them to have a close relationship but couldn't see his own hypocrisy.

Rachel waved as Jess stepped onto the patio, lifting the sunglasses from her face and setting them atop her head. "Hello, my darling." She leant back, demure as ever in a flowing skirt and white blouse that showed off her tan. "Come and sit so I can ask a favour."

Jess crouched to kiss her cheek, glad to receive a warmer

welcome, then toppled and reclined on the blanket. "Do I need to worry?"

"Don't be silly, I'd just like you to give my wayward daughter a bit of encouragement."

In that case, she needed a stronger word for what she should be feeling. When Rachel and Melissa started going at each other, you got as far away as possible and hoped not to become speared on any flying shrapnel.

"What do you want me to do?"

"Only have a quick chat. She's more likely to listen to you than anyone else." Rachel paused, waiting for further probing. "I'm cutting her off," she continued when Jess didn't bite. "No more degrees. Someone has to convince her to join the real world and put them to use."

"Oh, perfect. I've heard it's nice there," Jess muttered. This was another argument that'd been raging since Christmas, and it wouldn't end until Melissa found a job which met with her mum's approval. "I'm sure she'll start applying now the dissertation meltdown's over. The past few months have been stressful."

"Mm. Has she told you about this book blog?"

Jess frowned. Rachel knew they spoke every day, and she felt positive this was a trap. "Yeah, what's wrong with that?"

"Nothing. I don't have a problem with her taking on a new hobby, but the fact she's been hiding it speaks volumes."

That was a stretch. Melissa had been posting to social media for over a year and telling anyone who'd listen. The trouble was, Rachel wasn't interested. If it didn't involve world domination in the more traditional sense, she never wanted to know.

"It isn't a national secret." Jess reached for her phone to pull up the positive comments in the hope it might appeal to

Rachel's competitive nature. "Lots of people have already viewed the website."

"I don't doubt it. I only want to ensure she's not focussing on this side project to the detriment of everything else."

It was unlikely. Melissa got fixated on things, but she'd never let it interfere with her studies. She had a first-class bachelor's degree, was at the end of a master's degree, and worked through both of them.

"I'll have a word with her," Jess conceded, knowing she'd need to compromise somewhere. "But only to check she won't be in your spare room for the rest of her life. Okay?"

"It's all I ask." Rachel leant across to whisper. "But remember, she mustn't know this conversation happened."

Jess sent Melissa a quick warning message, then tapped a finger on the side of her nose. "Covert ops. Got it."

She smiled at the stream of emojis flashing up in reply and tucked the phone back in her pocket. It was one thing having V catch her out earlier, but on an awkwardness scale of nought to one hundred, letting Rachel see how gooey eyed she went over her daughter was somewhere close to a million.

"Did I detect things becoming heated with David again?"

Jess ripped out a handful of grass. "Yep. He's leaving in forty-eight hours and still won't let it drop. I don't know what to do. V's stressed and miserable, Dad's driving me mad. Any advice?"

"He'll calm down, stick with it. V's a lovely girl and you can see he has a soft spot for Grace." Rachel draped an arm across Jess's shoulder and dropped a kiss on her temple. "It'll be fine, my darling. Bring them both over some time. If he sees we get along, it may help."

Jess laughed to herself, forever perplexed how Rachel

could be so supportive of V when her own daughter got nothing but earache. "They'd enjoy that, thanks."

"Well, it's also selfish. I'm eager for the practice with Grace. Now my son has his act together, we're hoping for some grandchildren." Rachel rolled to her knees in one fluid movement, stretching her shoulders and yawning. "Speaking of which, I should eject my family from David's spare room. They're all playing Xbox, being antisocial as per and Melissa no doubt the ringleader."

Jess jerked upright with a mix of excitement and pure terror, sending blood rushing to her head so it burst with colour. "Melissa's here? I thought she wasn't coming back until next weekend?"

"There was no point staying, so she packed up and left Cardiff first thing this morning." Rachel sighed as she straightened out her skirt. "Another week with her, lucky us."

2

Jess braced herself to keep from tumbling into the flower border as Melissa sprinted across the garden. When she landed, her arms flung around Jess's neck, legs squeezed her middle, and a tangle of blonde hair almost resulted in asphyxiation.

"I missed you so much," Melissa whispered, straightening up as two hands wrapped under her knees to hold her in place. "Did you miss me?"

Jess tried to laugh off how much she was enjoying having their bodies welded together after four months apart and hoped it was convincing. "Couldn't care less." She released her grip and Melissa slid to the ground. "Who are you again?"

"Liar. I know you were desperate to see me."

It was true, but she wouldn't admit anything, and more warning might have been nice. Time to prepare adequate excuses for the blushing, averted gazes, and other signs of her raging hormones. She struggled to breathe whenever Melissa was within a hundred metres.

Rachel glared at her daughter, chewing a thumbnail

with her head still buried in Jess's chest. "I thought the varnish was to discourage you from biting your nails?"

"And so it begins," Jess muttered.

Melissa held out her hand, the hot pink polish chipped and broken, then tucked it into her back pocket. "Yeah, and it was working until today. Right now, I'm not even sure coating my fingers with cyanide would stop me." She released her grip on Jess's waist, but only to take hold of her arm. "Show me your new tattoo?"

Jess hitched up her T-shirt sleeve to unveil the full jungle scene. "What's the verdict?"

Melissa ran her thumb from the jaguar that took pride of place at the top, through the trees, sloths, snakes, and other animals until they ended at her wrist. "I love it, but the bit by your armpit looks painful. I wouldn't cope with that." She tickled the soft flesh before turning, tugging her T-shirt and holding her hair up to show a small Welsh dragon. "What do you think of mine?"

"Very understated." Jess ran her fingers over the outline, smiling as goose bumps rose on Melissa's skin. "Better than in the pictures."

She'd provided a virtual hand hold during the appointment a few weeks ago. Melissa wanted something to mark the end of her degree and she'd always loved Jess's tattoos, so it seemed a natural choice.

Rachel stood, taking hold of her daughter's neck in an altogether rougher manner. "Oh, you haven't. The nose ring was one thing, but this is permanent. You understand that, don't you?"

"Calm down, it's covered by my hair most of the time." Melissa swatted her mum's hand away and adjusted her T-shirt. "Nan and Pops like it. They thought it was sweet to get a Welsh tattoo for them." She dropped onto the blanket, considering the matter closed, and reached to grab a paperback. "Are you on my glasses?"

Rachel grunted as she sat, searching under her skirt and pulling out a pair of thick plastic frames. "You should be more careful, they're expensive."

"You're the one who sat on them." Melissa wiped the lenses with her T-shirt and perched them on her nose, peering over the top. "Now all I'm missing is my pillow."

"I presume you mean me." Jess crouched to study the peppering of freckles across the bridge of her nose and then lay down before she looked like a weirdo who'd never seen a pair of glasses. They were also a new addition so far only seen in a photo, but in person the new look was far more alluring. Of course, she could have come home dressed in a bin bag with a patch over her eye and still have had the same effect on Jess's heart rate.

Melissa smiled and scrunched her nose, repositioning herself a few times before getting settled and propping the book on her stomach. "Are you comfy? I can move."

"Mhm," Jess murmured, shuffling but not wanting her to go anywhere. She stroked the hair that fell along her side, taking out the knots with her fingers. "Not sure when you started worrying whether I was comfortable, it's never bothered you before."

"How true, there's a chance I'm maturing."

"Turning twenty-three was pivotal, I see."

Melissa ran a finger across the page to keep up the pretence she was reading. "Oh, you remember me having a birthday. That's good, I thought it'd dropped out of your calendar."

"You know I remembered, I sent you a massive gift card." Jess flicked at the book to make her point. "I already apologised for not visiting."

"And I'm still working on forgiving you."

Jess laughed to mask her unease for the second time. What was she supposed to say, though? "Sorry I didn't visit but I can't sleep in a bed with you anymore because it turns me on," wouldn't wash, even if it was the truth. Melissa had never guessed her feelings, and she didn't plan on embarrassing or ostracising herself by spelling them out.

"What have you done with your dad and brother?" Rachel lobbed a sandal and knocked the book from Melissa's hand. "I thought they were coming out with you."

She glared at her mum, trying to straighten out the creases. "Nothing, they were boring David over this wedding last I heard."

After two years of planning, everyone was sick of venues, cakes, and dresses. A month to go and it couldn't come soon enough, so they could move on to more stimulating subjects of conversation.

Rachel rolled to face Jess and chucked her sandals onto the grass. "Have you decided if you'll bring Grace? She's more than welcome."

She only wanted Grace there to put pressure on her son, but she was out of luck because Jess had made sure it was a toddler free zone. V needed to relax, and a weekend at a fancy spa hotel was the perfect opportunity.

"Thanks for the offer but she won't be here. Dad has donated us his suite and we're making the most of it."

Melissa lowered her book. "Hang on, aren't you staying with me?"

"Oh, no. Sorry, change of plans."

David booked the room a year ago, intending to stay the whole weekend. Now he could only make the Saturday Jess had taken the reservation and planned to enjoy every single perk at his expense. The knowledge that V benefited gave her an extra shot of satisfaction, after the grief he'd caused.

"You want to watch out, I'll take offence." Melissa frowned and raised her book again. "You've dumped me at my brother's wedding."

"I haven't dumped you, I just thought you'd be more comfortable having the room to yourself if I've got somewhere else to sleep."

Melissa shuffled to push her head into the bottom of Jess's ribs. "Sorry, did that hurt you?"

"We'll still have fun together." Jess winced, then reached to pull Melissa's cheeks into a smile with her thumb and finger. "Don't sulk, I didn't think you'd mind. If V's coming as my plus one it makes sense for us to share a room."

"I'm not sulking. So what if Mum hates my tattoo, I can't get a job, and now you want to share with someone else? Doesn't mean I've got any reason to complain."

Jess began to argue the toss, but David cut her off when he wandered over to join them. "I can help you out with one of those. We'll be short-staffed while I'm away, so why don't you work in the agency for a few weeks? You've done it before and not much has changed."

"Hang on," Jess murmured, shuffling onto her elbows. "Shouldn't I get a say? The other day you were giving me a lecture about how I'm a company director now and should take more responsibility."

Melissa dropped the book and folded her arms. "Oh great, you don't want me working with you either. Thanks a lot."

"It's not that, I just didn't think you'd enjoy it. If you want the job, take it. Don't moan to me when you're bored, though."

David beamed, puffing out his chest as if he'd just won

Mastermind. "That's settled, then. Let's make it a three-month contract, give you something proper to put on your CV. I dare say I'll be back and forth to Devon all summer."

That long? Jess tripped over his last comment. They hadn't talked through what was happening when he came home from the cruise, and the realisation that he might move to Devon was like a tonne weight crushing her chest.

Melissa stood and hugged him, but even with her gone the ache in the centre of Jess's rib cage persisted. She rubbed on her sternum, trying to soothe the guilt and apprehension. It was hard not to feel nostalgic for their earlier argument now. At least she knew she was right about that, but the rest was far less clear cut.

"Thanks, David." Melissa dug her hands into the pockets of her jeans and kicked Jess's foot. "I'll do whatever she says, and I won't let her down. Promise."

Jess rolled over, groaning and wishing that were true. "Great, looking forward to it."

"Can we go to your house?"

"Now? I only arrived twenty minutes ago, and I haven't eaten yet."

"That's okay, I'll get you some food to take." Melissa strode across the garden, pushing past anyone who stood in her path. "Come on."

She went ahead in her own car, packed to the roof with boxes and suitcases. Everyone had warned it might be wise to drop them at home first, but as Jess pulled into her parking space, Melissa was waiting on the doorstep.

When the front door opened, she crept through the

lounge and into the kitchen as if she were hunting for wildlife. "Do you think Grace will remember me?"

"I don't know. She always remembers your mum and you're a miniature version, so that might help."

Melissa stopped and fixed Jess with a death stare. "That's the most hurtful thing you've ever said to me."

At least she'd only morph into an older form of her current self—short, blonde, and covered in freckles. In the photos on David's wall, it was hard to distinguish whether you were looking at a young Rachel or her daughter. Jess was the one with genuine problems. Her dark hair was likely to go grey and start falling out by the time she turned thirty, if her dad was any indication.

"I'd take it as a compliment," V yelled from the garden. She crouched on the edge of Grace's sandpit, tapping the top of a sandcastle bucket. "Rachel's gorgeous."

Melissa retched, setting the bowls next to the cooker. "Gross," she called back. "If you find judgemental old snobs so attractive, you're welcome to her. I don't suppose my dad would care, he's too busy playing golf."

"I do as it happens. She's got this whole hard on the outside, soft on the inside thing going on. It's very sexy."

"Don't continue or I'll be sick." Melissa buried her face in her hands as she groaned, then grasped for Jess's waist, pulling her into a loose cuddle. "Mum is a living nightmare, not a sex symbol. Please make this stop."

Jess squirmed with discomfort at the buzz of her skin wherever they touched. Being so attracted to Melissa when she resembled Rachel was too weird.

"Why don't you explain to me what you're doing here," she suggested, trying to wriggle out of the embrace. "You should have told me so I could prepare. I'm not sure we've got enough biscuits until the shopping's delivered."

"Are you asking why I've given up a week enjoying the beach when I can be here getting abuse from my mum?" Melissa laughed, helping herself to a cookie from a tin on the side and hauling herself onto the work surface. "I wanted to surprise you. Figured I may as well come home for David's party."

"I'm sure he appreciated you putting his games room to use."

"Don't doubt it. Are we playing later? I've got extra controllers in my car if V wants to join us."

That was unlikely. It drove her up the wall how much time they spent talking to each other via headset in front of the television. Jess had often decamped to her dad's house, to avoid an argument.

"She's not into games, unless you count board games, mind games and hockey. But we can play when Grace goes to sleep."

"Can I stay tonight if we're up late? I promise to be quiet."

"Sure. You can't disturb Grace, though. No banging about in the bathroom or moaning when you get woken up early."

Melissa smirked, bashing her hands together to dislodge the biscuit crumbs. "I'm not even allowed to moan? Come on, give me something, we are catching up." Then she scratched the back of her neck, and it turned to a frown. "Although I've got that stuff in my car, guess I should go home tonight."

"Oh no, that's a shame. Another night."

Jess wandered across the patio. It was only half five and warm sunlight bathed their little garden. At the end of the lawn, Grace was still playing in her sandpit, and Jess crossed her legs as she sat on the grass next to her.

"You weren't at your dad's long. Did you murder him?" V batted away a swinging shovel, trying to save her sandcastle from destruction.

"Yeah, problem solved. We brought some food home for you. Well, anything that seemed edible, by which I mean cake."

Grace's eyes lit up at the mention of dessert, and she tugged on her mum's dress. It wasn't helping that Melissa had moved on from biscuits and stood in the doorway with a bowlful, licking buttercream from her hand.

"Can I give her some?"

V lifted Grace over the lip of the sandpit. "Yeah but not too much."

Melissa sat and held out a chunk, but Grace only watched, her fingers curling into V's shoulder. She'd become suspicious of anyone getting near Jess over the past few months, which was both sweet and terrifying. Giving them a home was one thing, but sometimes the thought of how reliant Grace had become was daunting.

"It's okay. I know she's strange, but you'll get used to her," Jess whispered, stroking back the hair from Melissa's shoulders. The action generated a waft of vanilla scent which made her stomach flip. "See, like one of the guide dogs we saw at the supermarket. Do you remember?"

Melissa snapped her head around. "Did you just call me a Labrador?"

"Yeah, and I stand by it." Jess slid the phone from her pocket and swiped through to her photo gallery, pulling up a picture of Grace playing with the puppies. "Don't worry, it's a compliment. She was so upset when I tried to tear her away, the security guard thought I was kidnapping her."

Grace inched forward with encouragement from V and reached out for Jess's hand as if she might not make the journey unassisted. She climbed onto her lap, as far from Melissa as she could be without falling off and clutched at her neck.

"Why does she hate me?"

"She doesn't. Toddlers reserve those extremes of emotion for broccoli, or if you look at their toys the wrong way."

"Don't worry," Melissa whispered, still trying to coax Grace out with a chunk of chocolate sponge. She shuffled across Jess's lap, taking the piece of cake and stuffing it into her mouth, then wiped her fingers on her shorts.

Jess pulled a tissue out of her pocket like a seasoned pro and wiped away a blob of errant icing. "You need to get used to her, monster. She'll be over all the time now she's back, eating our food and driving me up the wall."

Every time she came home it was the same, although in the past it had always been the two of them. She slept in the spare bedroom when she stayed over, and Jess's guts gave a little twist when she remembered that was no longer possible.

"I'll win her over with some books."

"You've got something in common there, besides your appalling table manners and aversion to brushing your hair."

Jess tucked the tissue back in her pocket and ruffled the mess of blonde locks. After a few moments Grace joined in, giggling and then patting Melissa like a dog.

"Rude. Both of you." She scowled, rubbing a streak of buttercream along Jess's chin. "I wanted to take you some-where for your birthday but now I'm reconsidering."

Jess licked it off with a smile. "When? I have a very busy social calendar that weekend."

"Saturday night."

"Ah, then I can't. It's V's hockey club social."

"We don't have to go." V waved a hand and scooted backwards to lean against the fence. "It's no big deal, spend the evening together."

For weeks she'd needed a push out of the door to training and this was the excuse she wanted. She wasn't getting out of it, though, or she'd turn into a hermit.

"Theatre, then?" Melissa looked satisfied and pulled out her phone, sucking her fingers clean and wiping them on her shorts before scrolling. "Where would you like me to book for dinner?"

"Do you want a drink?" Jess gestured towards the kitchen as she stood.

"No, I'm fine."

"Make everyone else one, then. It's the least you can do if you're planning on gate-crashing."

Melissa frowned but allowed Jess to cajole her into the kitchen. She filled the kettle and flicked it on, pulled out three mugs, dropped in tea bags, then stood back and folded her arms. "There, happy?"

"Very, thanks." Jess heaved herself onto the work surface, picking up the other bowl of cake they'd brought home and lowering her voice. "I need to go to the hockey social, but I couldn't say in front of V. I know she won't leave the house unless I drag her out."

"Oh. Sure okay. Well, that's fine. Another time." Melissa turned and leant on the cooker, fiddling with her nails again. "Can I come?"

"To The Crown? Of course."

They would have invited her, but it wasn't Melissa's scene. She didn't drink and only went to the pub with her grandparents when they were buying fish and chips on a Friday night.

"It isn't, but I'm not above compromising. If we want to spend the evening together, it doesn't look like I have much choice."

"Sorry, I wish we could go to the theatre, but it might be fun." Jess bit twirls of milk chocolate from her cake, and Melissa smiled. "What?"

She stroked a thumb across Jess's lip, holding it up to show the cream and then licking it away. "You're not the only one who makes a mess when they eat."

Jess laughed, sucking where Melissa had touched and feeling another pulse of arousal. "We're also having a party on the Friday evening, before Grace goes to her dad's. Do you want to come? It won't be very exciting, so it might be more your speed."

"How sweet that you think I'll be anywhere other than here, invitation or not."

3

After a thorough hand over from David on Sunday, Jess arrived at the office early on Monday morning to give her newest employee an induction. They'd agreed Melissa would handle viewings, having done it as a summer job two years ago, but she still needed a refresher. At least, Jess wanted to give her one, but it had only resulted in eye rolling and moans because they were covering old ground. Twenty minutes in and she'd decided it was a lost cause.

"If we're working together for three months, these are the ground rules." Jess held up her index finger and leant across the desk. "First, don't use my mug." Then she added another. "And second, you will address me only as your highness or your majesty. Got that?"

Melissa crossed her arms, leaning back in the swivel chair she'd been whizzing across the office in since they arrived. "Sod off."

"I thought you were ready to do whatever I say, or was that only for my dad's benefit?"

The chair glided into Jess's desk, stopping with a thump.

"I will, so long as it's reasonable and in line with how you treat all other members of staff."

"Great, because they don't use my tea mug either."

Jess tapped out a quick email, then hit print on their itinerary. She'd rejigged a few appointments so they could spend the day together, reallocating her valuations to someone else.

Melissa peered across the desk, narrowing her eyes through her glasses, and blew in Jess's face. "When are we doing some actual work? I'm bored."

"Soon. I'm taking you for a drive through the new estates before our first appointment, then we've got five viewings back to back."

"No need. I live on one, remember?"

Jess creaked back in her chair. "You can locate every shop, playground, and school?"

"Yes. I visited our shop yesterday. It was very nice. Clean and modern. Friendly staff, too."

The house her parents moved to a few months ago was on one of the newest builds in the town, and the local amenities were still a mark on a plan. Even the roads remained unfinished and she'd overplayed her hand.

"Impressive given it isn't open yet. Did you stumble across the world's first invisible Tesco?"

Melissa's lip twitched as she tried to hide a smile. "Must have been another shop altogether. Not sure where I ended up."

"Nice try. Study a map while I get the keys and don't lie to me about anything other than how amazing I am."

Jess got up and wandered out to the back office. This was a first-floor unit with secure entry, but they still kept valuables locked away out of sight. David had a desk in there, too, so he could create the illusion he was important.

Melissa laughed, rolling into the doorway. "Calm down, I'm only teasing. You know I'll be serious about this job." She pursed her lips for a moment of consideration. "Speaking of which, we shouldn't be too friendly. I don't want anyone to assume you're giving me preferential treatment. We need to be model professionals when we're with other people."

Jess opened the cabinet and grabbed five sets of keys, marking them on the signing out sheet. "I'm positive I can handle that. Any other rules, or is that everything?"

"No, that's it for now. I'll inform you if any further points occur to me during the day."

"Fantastic, I look forward to it. Are you ready to go?"

Melissa used the frame to push herself the entire length of the office. "We're leaving already? Aren't you going to introduce me?"

That treat could wait until later. Rachel wasn't easy to handle and telling everyone their favourite client's daughter was working with them would be fun.

"No, we haven't got time." Jess tucked the keys into her pockets and grabbed her wallet from the desk drawer. "I've emailed with the brief gist. We'll save the joy of meeting you until this afternoon."

Melissa sprung from the chair. "Lucky them. Do I need anything?"

"You mean besides some tape for your mouth? No, we're set."

"Very funny." She pulled the door open and let it slam in Jess's face as she ducked through to the landing. "I hope you never speak to anyone else in that manner, or you may find yourself in serious trouble."

Jess laughed as she wrenched it open again and they descended the stairs. It wasn't even nine yet, and she was delirious. By the end of Friday, she'd be a basket case. "Don't worry, it's reserved for you. I'm getting all these comments out now, so they don't eat me up later when I have to act like your boss."

"How loud are they, these employees of yours? I'm concerned six people in that small office has the potential to become noisy." Melissa dug a finger into her ear, stopping in the entrance hall. "Am I allowed to bring earplugs or headphones?"

"No, but you'll get used to it."

"Doubtful, but if you say so."

Jess took a deep breath and leant a hand against the wall next to Melissa's head. If tape wasn't appropriate, could she shut her up with a kiss? Wild sex in the car? A quickie over the filing cabinet? She sighed and kept her mouth shut. Work would have to do.

* * *

They drove out to an estate on the edge of the ring road for their first viewing, pulling up in front of a one-bed terrace. It was empty, which made it ideal for a practice run. Tenants weren't always great at remembering there was someone coming, or cleaning up, and it was also an extra person to manage.

"You ready for this?" Jess slammed the car door and jiggled the keys in her pocket as they wandered along the path.

Melissa looked up at the house, shielding her eyes from the bright sunlight streaming over the pile of red brick. "Shouldn't I be?"

"No, I was only being pleasant. Sorry, I thought I could do that when we're alone. It seems I was wrong."

A waft of cool air and the smell of fresh paint hit them as they stepped onto the laminate floor, and Jess walked straight through to the living room. She hadn't been in since the valuation and wanted to familiarise herself, given one house merged into another when you looked at enough.

"It's depressing, isn't it?" Melissa ran her hand along the magnolia wall and then busied herself switching off the plug sockets. "Like a hutch for humans."

It was a dig at her parents' choice of house more than this one. Most people would have considered the brand new five bedroom detached a dream home, but they hadn't told her until a week before completion. Needless to say, it hadn't gone down well.

"And that, ladies and gentlemen, is exactly the type of comment you shouldn't make in front of a potential tenant. Boring has its benefits. If you're busy, you might prefer functional and low maintenance."

"I guess. When I grow up, I want an old cottage like your dad's. Wonky walls and an enormous fireplace."

Jess laughed, sliding open the back doors and stepping into the garden. It was only a small square of grass, not even big enough to house a rabbit, but she wouldn't admit to agreeing. "When you grow up?"

"You know what I mean. I wouldn't mind his car, either. When did he get that?"

"When he got the girlfriend. He's been using it to visit her. I don't understand why he didn't buy a newer one, it's costing him a fortune in fuel. He'll end up spending whatever he's saved."

Everyone thought David was experiencing a mid-life crisis when he bought an old Jag that guzzled more diesel than a tractor. According to Rachel, though, he'd always wanted one. They'd gone to pick it up together, reliving their youth.

"It's romantic. I can picture him whizzing about in the countryside, stopping for walks and picnics along the coast."

"Romantic? Do me a favour, it's insecurity. She'll be twenty-three with killer legs and a thing for older men who have money and cars. It's why he hasn't introduced us: shame."

Melissa shoved hard on Jess's shoulder as she let out a long groaning noise. "Shut up, I'm twenty-three."

"With killer legs, yeah I know."

Jess pushed her back and then walked out to stand on the path and wait. Their nine-forty-five was due, and she wanted to check they weren't loitering somewhere. She'd lost track of the times people had sat in their car for twenty minutes before realising they might need to get out.

When Melissa rubbed a hand over her tattoo again, Jess jumped and unrolled her shirt sleeves to cover them. As soon as he'd seen them, David had made it company policy that they couldn't be on display in front of clients, but with the distractions she'd forgotten.

"What are you doing? You'll roast," Melissa cautioned, trying to re-roll one.

"Have to hide my arms." Jess batted both hands away and fumbled over her buttons again. "That's why I wear a heavy black shirt. They should tell people about stuff like this before they draw jungle animals all over them."

"Thought you were the boss, or was that empty talk?"

She was, but this was unlikely to hit the top of her priority list. They'd never gone so long without David and she'd vowed not to contact him unless it was life or death.

"Core changes to policy are not my department and I haven't got time to think about it."

Melissa relented and stepped back, staring at her own outfit. "I should go shopping at some point. Is this okay for now?"

"You look gorgeous." Jess straightened the blouse, feeling sure it'd come out of Rachel's wardrobe.

"I was going for professional."

"Okay, you look professional. Either way, what you're wearing is fine. That tape for your mouth would be handy, though. Wonder if Dad would write it into a policy."

Melissa glowered, but then let out a grunt of laughter. "Jokes aside, do you miss him?"

"He only left yesterday. I'm sure by twenty-four I should be able to go that many hours without seeing my dad."

"Yeah, but you see him every day. I appreciate the upside is you get to see me instead, that will have softened the blow, but you'll miss him."

"Will I? Reckon I'll be too busy to notice."

That was the new party line, anyway. It'd had consideration since Saturday and she knew if they were serious enough to take a holiday, David would move closer to his girlfriend at some point. Jess was treating this as a chance to flex her executive muscles, clothing policy aside.

Melissa squinted down the road and tried to straighten out the to let sign as a car approached. "What do you want me to do?"

"Nothing. I'll take this viewing, just follow my lead."

"Boring. You realise I've done this before?"

"Yes, but it was years ago." Jess waved to the couple they were meeting as they got out of their car, then leant across to whisper so they couldn't hear her. "I'm still not seeing much of you doing whatever I say and being serious about this. Is that coming later?"

Melissa smiled, pulling the glasses from her jacket pocket. "It's coming now, brace yourself."

By the fifth appointment, Melissa was insisting on taking the lead and Jess had given up trying to stop her. She'd been right, turning on the charm when required and behaving like a mature adult. Together they'd let two of the five properties, with someone coming back for a second viewing later in the week, and it'd put Jess in a generous mood.

"What do you want for lunch?" She grabbed her wallet from the glove box as they pulled up in the supermarket car park. "First day treat."

"Can I have..." Melissa trailed off, and she scrunched her nose.

"Why don't you pick for yourself? I'll take you to the deli at the other end of town."

"Yes, I like it there. They have a five-star hygiene rating."

Jess laughed, shaking her head as she led them past the office and out onto the High Street. She knew it was coming but still enjoyed these quirks.

"Is there anyone you don't know?" Melissa gripped Jess's arm as people nodded and tried to stop them for a chat. "You're like a local celebrity."

"If you think this is bad, try going through town with my dad. When I was a kid, it'd take half an hour to walk the three hundred metres from the supermarket at one end of this street to the church at the other."

Even now, she'd get people coming up to her saying they remembered her as a four-year-old or a nine-year-old and she didn't have the faintest clue who they were. It was always best to keep on walking with purpose and nod hello to everyone.

Melissa swerved as they reached the independent bookshop next to The Crown, tugging on Jess's wrist and dragging her towards the door. "Please, five minutes. I promise I'll be so good for the rest of the afternoon."

She pouted and batted her eyelids, and Jess tried to keep a stony expression. This wouldn't take five minutes, it never did. Every penny she'd earned today would end up spent, and they'd go hungry.

"Your mum won't be happy. You're supposed to be using your lunch break to look for a permanent job."

"Best not tell her, then. Please."

Jess felt what little resolve she might have had disappear. Saying no to her was like refusing a puppy who wanted one last ear scratch, and she knew it.

"Fine, but I want to eat so watch the time. I mean it, don't start reading in the shop." She held onto the door handle, making sure Melissa understood before allowing her inside the store. "Buy the book, so we're able to leave."

"Yeah, yeah. Got it."

A bell dinged as they stepped inside, and a woman in a summer dress patterned with bright pink flamingos backed out from between two boxes of books.

"Grab me if I can help," she mumbled, squinting at a clipboard.

Melissa's eyes searched the room in wonder, as if she'd never seen a book shop. It was the same way Grace looked when you pulled out a pot of chocolate pudding.

"Hi, Kat," Jess called, thumbing the pages of a signed hardback.

There was a bookcase full of them by the entrance, followed by rows of fiction. In the middle of the store, shelving units held non-fiction and biography, then in the far corner was a carpeted area with coloured beanbags and toys.

"Oh, it's you." Kat shook her head and smiled as she turned. "Sorry, lost in trying to figure out this order. How are you doing?"

"I'm great. Did those events ever take off? I've seen a few of them advertised but haven't had the chance to come."

Jess smiled, noting that Melissa was giggling at her for proving her own point. They only knew each other because Kat played hockey with V, though.

Kat wandered to the rear of the store and pulled a glossy leaflet from under a pile of bookmarks on the counter. "Not too bad, they're getting some traction." She passed it to Jess and fiddled with the star pendant around her neck. "I've added kids' story time on a Saturday morning. You should bring Grace, if you're ever free."

Jess folded the flyer and tucked it into her pocket. "Cool, I'll tell V. She's playing hockey this Saturday and I've got Grace, so we'll come along."

This was their weekly routine now. Jess had committed to watching Grace on a Thursday evening and Saturday morning so V could keep her one remaining vestige of social interaction with people over the age of two.

"How is she? We missed her last week. I meant to text and check but haven't had a chance, it's been so busy."

"What? Wasn't she at training?"

Jess had stepped away from the counter so she could keep Melissa in check but found herself drawn back. V left the house in her kit on Thursday evening and came home at the normal time.

"No, she didn't turn up. I'm glad it sounds like nothing

bad happened to her. Do you know if she's coming to the social next week?"

"Yeah, I said I'd go with her. She's been having a rough time, I hoped it'd cheer her up."

"She has seemed a bit off, so I'm glad you're trying to drag her along. Wouldn't want to disappoint an entire hockey team."

Melissa slapped two books between them. One was a paperback, and the other was a picture book with dogs on the front cover. Jess laughed, but Melissa only shrugged, sneaking an arm around Jess's middle and attempting to steal the wallet from her back pocket.

"V's that popular, is she?" Jess looked over the illustrations and reached to grasp Melissa's wrist before she bankrupted her. "I'll tell her you said that."

"I meant you, but it was only a joke, don't worry." Kat glanced up as she scanned their books into the till. "No one's after your girlfriend."

Jess relented and pulled out her wallet, knowing full well she would need to pay. "You're barking up the wrong tree there. She's not my girlfriend, she's my... pain in the neck? Person who bleeds me dry?"

"All the above. It's like having all the benefits of a girlfriend, but she doesn't have to sleep with me." Melissa clung even tighter around Jess's waist and tickled her side. "Aren't you lucky?"

Jess punched in her pin number before her mind could dwell on them sleeping together for too long. "So lucky."

"I'm working with her for a few months, but we've known each other forever. My mum's her godmother and we grew up together."

Kat squinted with concentration as she packaged the

books into a pink paper bag. "Which makes you what, her god sister?"

"That isn't a thing." Jess had never seen her as a sister and prayed it was mutual.

Kat laughed, and they exchanged complicit glances as she slid the bag across the counter. "Let's not mention it again, then."

Jess mouthed a quick "thank you" and then returned her attention to Melissa, who'd taken the books and was gravitating towards a shelf full of paperbacks. If Jess didn't cut it off soon, she'd lose her for good.

"I'm impressed with how fast you did that, there's still time for sandwiches." She took Melissa's hand and guided her towards the door. "It also means I can award you a bonus."

Melissa narrowed her eyes, and the paper rustled as she clutched it tight. "Oh no, what?"

"You've got thirty whole minutes left to look at jobs before our next appointment. Now who's the lucky one?"

4

Three days later there had been precious little career hunting, but Melissa was true to her word at work. Between appointments, she'd drafted content for the new website and taken over the company's social media accounts. They'd also resolved an issue with the board erection company in a manner that would make Rachel proud. All Jess worried about now was whether she may be after her job and that was why she wasn't bothering to look for others.

Even leaving early enough to watch Grace on Thursday evening had been less of a hassle. Melissa was waiting by the door with her stuff packed dead on six and marched them to the car park with a pre-made lasagne from the supermarket. She was insistent on helping babysit, not that Jess would have tried to change her mind.

"Sorted," Melissa declared, sliding it into the oven as soon as they'd changed. She set the timer and stood back, bashing her palms together before pulling herself onto the work surface. "You make everything harder than you need to. It's the same at work, there are tonnes of ways to streamline your diary."

Jess rest a hand on either side of Melissa's legs and fixed her with a stare. "Less than a week and you already know better, huh?"

"About some things, yes." She squeezed Jess's shoulders, then guided her to turn and wound both legs around her middle. "For example, if you booked consecutive viewings for the same property you wouldn't spend so much time driving between them."

"That's fine for us, but what if potential tenants can't make the times we set? We'll miss out on letting a property because we're too inflexible."

"True, but you're not short of applicants." Melissa began kneading the knots tied across Jess's shoulders, grunting as she dug in with her fingers. "One thing I'm certain of is you need to take care of yourself."

"You know we're supposed to be looking after Grace, not leaving her to play on her own?"

Jess didn't disagree with a massage, but having Melissa rub her anywhere, even through a layer of cotton, wasn't relaxing. Arousing and pleasurable, yes, which was more reason to stop. She moved to step away, but the legs only gripped her tighter.

"I'm like one of those finger trap things," Melissa whispered, pressing her mouth to an ear. "The more you resist, the worse it gets. Best to submit now."

The tickle of her breath sent a shiver of excitement in all directions that proved Jess's point. She realised she needed to get out of this embrace even more than the massage and held up her hands in submission.

"Okay, but not for long. We still need to watch Grace, and the food."

Melissa laughed and unwound her legs. "Yes, captain

sensible. I'm coming back to this later, though. Don't like to leave a job half finished."

She'd be leaving one job half finished. Jess was melting into the massage with alarming ease, closing her eyes and enjoying the fingertips raking up her neck and into the base of her skull. She imagined how it would feel, in a tight grip between her legs and clutching handfuls of hair as they kissed.

"Am I interrupting something?" V dropped her kit bag on the kitchen floor with a loud clatter and Jess's eyes snapped open. "I can go now if you like."

Jess cleared her throat and tried to step away but ended up with Melissa clung to her back. She wrapped both hands under her knees and adjusted the weight, then carried her out to the garden and set her on the patio. "Why don't you play with Grace for a bit while I finish dinner and have a chat with V? Or take her to the shop and buy ice cream."

At the mention of pudding Grace looked up from the sandpit and dropped her spade. Melissa reached out her hand and Grace stepped over the lip, muttering something and trying to pull her towards the kitchen.

"Don't worry, we realise when we're not wanted." Melissa encouraged Grace across the patio, pouting for a moment but then laughing as they disappeared through the side gate.

V was scrolling through her phone at the table when Jess returned to the kitchen and pulled out a chair. "Are you okay?"

"Yeah. Any fun plans tonight?"

"Force feeding vegetables to a toddler and a twenty-three-year-old." Jess grimaced, already imagining how that would end. "Then I'll give one of them a bath while the other causes mischief."

"Sounds exciting."

V managed a smile, but it wasn't convincing. She looked as if she was off to prison rather than to play hockey with her friends, and Jess wanted to know why training had become such an issue but worried she might land Kat in trouble.

"Are you looking forward to the game on Saturday?" She hoped it was an indirect route to the same answer.

"Should be an easy win. Are you still okay to have Grace?"

"Of course. We're taking her to the book shop. Melissa's more excited about it than we are."

She'd made it her mission to get Grace to like her, insisting on reading stories and playing with her every evening before bed. It was sweet, and Jess tried hard to keep a neutral expression that wouldn't give away how much the thought made her heart swell.

"That's good, thanks. Would it be a problem if I was home a little later than usual?" V pushed the chair back and refilled her water bottle from the tap.

"Not at all. We could take Grace to Rachel's if you want some time to yourself."

Melissa might not enjoy spending the afternoon with her mum, but Rachel would love having them. It was suiting everyone well that she was so desperate for grandchildren. In the meantime, she was lavishing her attention on Grace.

"Lucky her," V teased, perking up with a lascivious smile. She turned to lean against the worktop. "I need to call in and chat with Mum."

"Everything okay?"

"Yeah, it will be. We had a bit of an argument last week. She phoned when I was on my way to training and I ended up missing the entire session talking to her in the leisure centre car park."

Jess nodded, relieved no one had mugged her, and she hadn't fallen foul of some other calamity. "What did you argue about?"

"My brother's buying a house with his girlfriend and they'll have a spare room. She says I should take it, so they can help look after Grace."

Jess scraped a foot along the floor as a knot formed in her stomach. It might have started as a favour, but now the thought of them moving out made her guts churn.

"Are you going to?"

"I'd rather not, given how it went when we stayed with them earlier in the year. They both work shifts and it'd cause a lot of friction. Plus the room is tiny, and it'd be even more crowded than living here."

"Great." Jess let out a sigh and slumped forward to rest her head on her arms. "You had me worried for a minute."

V laughed. "Did I?"

"Of course. I want you to live here."

It wasn't until now that she realised how much. It was exhausting, and difficult, and she'd lost control of every-thing, including her sleep routine. The enjoyable parts always outweighed the bad, though. An empty house would be lonely now.

"That's a relief, because it worried me you might want us to go, now we have somewhere else to live." V moved but then stopped and chewed her bottom lip. "You should check Melissa doesn't have an issue with this."

"Melissa?" Jess straightened, her face contorting into a confused frown. "What's she got to do with where you live?"

"You don't think she might want that spare bedroom?"

Even if she did, it wasn't happening. Spending time with her was great but living with her was another matter.

"No, don't worry about that. I told you the room was yours and I won't change my mind. If Melissa's having problems with Rachel, she needs to sort them out."

"Okay." V smiled, then let out a huff. "So long as it doesn't become an issue. I already feel like we're in your way. I get you two are close and you want to spend time together."

"We do, we are. If it's ever too much, I want you to tell me."

Jess pushed the chair back and checked on their lasagne, steeling herself for another tough conversation later. If they were only four days in and V was worrying, she needed to have a chat with Melissa after they put Grace to bed.

* * *

Once they'd eaten, Melissa had even done the washing up. She'd completed the task without complaint, to Jess's surprise, but it was a different story when the thing she had to wash wriggled.

"Come on, aren't you ready yet?" Jess banged her head on the bathtub. "It'll be cold by the time you're done."

Melissa growled as Grace clouted her across the cheek, giggling and writhing with her T-shirt half over her head. "You could help me, you know."

"No way, this is far more fun."

She removed the last piece of clothing and dumped a squealing Grace in the water, then clutched her own ears. "Where's the volume control?"

"She'll calm down in a minute, you got her too worked up." Jess lathered the soap and washed away a streak of ice cream on Grace's chin, then rinsed her hand in the bath water. "Still happy to do this? You can get her book ready if you want."

"Get her book ready? What does that mean, open it and stare at the pages for twenty minutes?"

"Okay, grumpy."

Melissa knelt and flicked water, then Grace joined in, splattering her T-shirt with bubbles. When she responded by hurling a full cup it only made things worse because Grace picked up another and threw the entire contents with a wide grin.

"Right, that's it," Melissa declared, pulling herself up on the side of the bath, ripping her socks off and throwing them onto the floor. She stepped over the edge and squatted next to Grace, who looked at her as though she'd lost her mind. "Not so fun now, is it?"

"What the hell are you doing?" Jess grasped the sink and creased over laughing as Melissa crossed her arms in defiance. She lowered herself, her shorts soaked and the water inching up her shirt, so it clung tighter and tighter.

"I'm playing dirty."

So was Jess's imagination, not that she needed much of it. The shirt was translucent around her torso, and it was creeping up towards her bra.

"That's great, but you're wet." Jess tried to look at the bath toys instead.

Grace got over her surprise, picking up the cup again and throwing water in Melissa's face. She spluttered and wiped it away, drops falling down her top and clinging to her hair.

"I'm prepared to admit I didn't think this through and may need to borrow some clothes." Melissa pulled a towel from the rail and dabbed her eyes.

"Oh no, you can live with this." Jess laughed, handing Grace a bigger container. "You've made your bath, now sit in it."

"I'll roll on your bed like this and get it all wet, if you don't help me."

"Promise?"

Jess hoisted herself up and rooted through her drawers in the bedroom, pulling out running shorts and a T-shirt. She hooked them over the towel rail in the bathroom and grabbed a bottle of baby shampoo from the shelf.

"Right then, young lady," Melissa commanded in her best stern voice. "It's payback time."

She dumped a cup of water over Grace and held her hand out so Jess could squeeze a dollop of shampoo in her palm. The toddler turned, so stunned that she dropped her rubber duck and gawped as they lathered her. Melissa tipped Grace's head back, shielding her face with the towel, and rinsed away the bubbles.

"Huh. Do I need to jump in the bath in future?"

"No, you only have to stop the shampoo getting in her eyes." Melissa pulled herself up, a stream of water pouring from the heavy denim of her shorts. Grace stuck her hands in to catch it, delighted by the waterfall. "Can I have a towel, please?"

She pinched the shirt away from her skin and then shimmied out of it, so she was wearing only shorts and a bra. Jess averted her gaze, but not before glimpsing the freckles which ran from her shoulders and into her cleavage.

"Here you go," she murmured, wrapping a towel around with her eyes again fixed on a rubber duck.

Melissa tucked it at the top and then wriggled out of her

shorts, which plopped into the bath. "Thanks. Can I change in your bedroom?"

"Mhm."

She swung a leg over the side and stepped onto the mat, placing a hand on Jess's shoulder for support. "Get her changed so we can read, and then I'll finish that massage."

* * *

Grace now trusted Melissa enough that she could get in the bed, giggling as she cycled through the voices they'd created for each character. Jess leant in the doorway and listened for the fourth night in a row, laughing at the growls and barks until Grace fell quiet and they could creep out.

"I'm sleepy," Melissa whispered, yawning and burying her face in Jess's chest. "Can't believe I'm saying this before seven thirty, but I'll go home soon and get an early night."

Jess kissed her forehead. "Not surprised, you haven't stopped all week."

They'd spent every evening together, on top of work, and she was feeling it too. It was fun, running updates on the blog, playing games, and driving out to run a trail through the fields near David's cottage. Now, though, they needed a rest.

"Let me finish that massage first." Melissa peered up and smiled, before taking Jess's wrist and leading her downstairs. "It'll bug me otherwise."

"Why are you so insistent on this?"

Melissa stopped in the entrance hall. "I only want to check you're okay. It's not like you to stay away for so long, and I'm worried you're burning yourself out."

Jess scratched at the back of her neck. She felt uneasy lying about the reason she hadn't visited, but there wasn't any way to be honest. If she confessed to Melissa and she had a bad reaction or told Rachel, it'd be devastating.

"I'm fine. I am stressed, but you've been great this week." She rubbed a hand into Melissa's shoulder, trying to convey her sincerity, and then they moved into the lounge. "I'm sorry I didn't visit, but I'm glad you're back."

Melissa sat on the sofa and gestured to the floor between her legs. "I could have visited you too. I'm as much to blame."

Jess shuffled into position, resting against the sofa. This was the last chance she'd have to iron out the V issue tonight, and she needed to take it.

"Not the greatest timing, but we need to talk." She winced as a thumb caused something to pop in her shoulder and sent a shooting pain into the top of her skull. "The thing is, I'm loving spending time with you, but I'm not sure it's fair on V for us to hang out here every single night."

"Makes sense. It's her house too."

Jess let out a sigh of relief. "Right. I know you don't want to be at home with your mum, but we could go to Dad's and use his games room or something."

"Fine by me, but can I ask you a question, and will you give me an honest answer?"

Jess squirmed, her heart giving an extra pump to send more adrenaline humming around her system. "Sure, go for it."

Melissa was quiet for a few moments, her grip loosening, and the touches becoming more tender. Then she stopped altogether, looping her arms around Jess's chest. "Is there anything happening between you two? I mean, even if you don't think there is, are you one hundred percent sure it isn't the same for her?"

Jess twisted, resting her hands on Melissa's quads. "Why would you ask that?"

"To check, that's all." She fiddled with her nails, squinting as she scraped away a chunk of polish. "I know you told me it's only friendship for you, but that doesn't mean it's the same for V."

Jess squeezed Melissa's legs, desperate to reiterate her lack of romantic attachment. "There is nothing between us." She shook her head as she made each point. "We don't have sex, there's no tension, we both see other people."

Well, that part wasn't true. V hadn't been with anyone since her relationship ended, and Jess hadn't been on so much as a date in a year. Not because of each other, though.

"Okay. If that changes, will you tell me? I'm worried I'll be in the way."

"It won't. For me, anyway. I'm a done deal, and you'll never be in the way. So long as we don't take over the entire house and keep Grace awake, there's no problem."

Melissa smiled, taking Jess's hands and guiding her to face forward. She trailed her fingers under the T-shirt neck this time, then stopped to tug on the fabric. "This would be easier if you'd remove your top."

It caught Jess off guard, and she let out a shot of laughter. "Not happening."

"Why not? I've seen them before."

Jess was wide-eyed as she spun to face her again. "Them?"

"Your shoulders. What did you think I meant?" Melissa smirked, raising her eyebrows. "Now face forward, I've never had to work so hard to give someone a massage before. Anyone would guess I was trying to torture you."

"Yeah, imagine that."

5

On Saturday morning Jess dropped V off at hockey and met Melissa in the bookshop. There were kids everywhere, screaming and throwing toys at each other, but at least the parents all had handfuls of books. Kat may end up having a nervous breakdown if she did it every week, but she'd make bags of money first.

"That was great, wasn't it, monster?" Jess tried to catch Grace before she smacked a small boy on the head with her new book. They'd quietened during the reading but turned feral again as soon as it finished. Kat hadn't helped matters by laying on a table of treats.

"Do you think?" Kat turned her pendant over in her fingers, stepping aside as a child zoomed past her legs. "I'm not great at speaking in front of a crowd."

"Would never have known."

Grace barrelled headlong into a beanbag and Jess glared at Melissa, who mouthed "sorry" and retrieved her. She would get a world of pain later for giving her sweets at eleven o'clock in the morning, even if they were complimentary.

"I'm sure you're only being nice, but thanks all the same. Will you come again next week?"

Jess rubbed her temples, almost wishing she was at work. "Not next week, Grace is at her dad's, but the weekend after."

"Could I tempt you to read?" Kat squinted as she clutched the pendant tight. "It's so new, and I'm struggling."

"Thanks."

"Oh, no. I didn't mean it like that. You would be great."

Jess waved to Melissa, who had Grace upside down grabbing at a girl's hair. They were giggling, but Jess had a headache brewing with the prospect of explaining to a parent why a grown woman didn't have more sense.

Melissa sat Grace on the counter. "What's up?"

She had another book now, and Jess pushed her wallet hard into her back pocket. "Kat's looking for someone to read to the kids. I'd be shit, but you're great at this. What do you reckon, could you come to an arrangement?"

There was an ulterior motive lurking. She didn't have many local friends, and it'd be good for her to meet people. Kat was an ideal candidate given they both loved books, and she didn't seem much of a party animal.

"It doesn't pay anything, I put these on for free, but I could offer you a discount." Kat scrunched her shoulders and smiled.

Melissa glanced at a stack of new arrivals. "Keep talking."

"Twenty percent?"

"Make it twenty-five and you've got a deal."

Kat let out a brief sigh of relief and shook her hand. "You're a lifesaver, I didn't want to do that again. Can you start next week?"

"Suppose so, it's not like I've got anything better to do

besides reading grown-up books. Are you coming to support me?" Melissa prodded Jess in the stomach.

"I'd love to but I'm working next Saturday. Before you say anything, it's only in the morning and I'll go for a run to unwind."

"Then that is acceptable." Melissa set Grace's books on the counter as Kat rounded it to serve her. "How long have you had the shop?"

"About four years." She laughed at Jess as she gripped her wallet again, her eyes widening. "I'd always wanted to do it, so when I got some redundancy money, I figured it was now or never."

Melissa tried to pull the wallet out but then slapped Jess's pocket, taking out her own phone to pay. "I'm so jealous, I'd love to be here all day."

"You should come to some other events. I'm trying to run at least one author signing a month, and then there's book club."

"That's right up your street." Jess lifted up Grace before she tore something expensive. "She runs a book review blog."

"That's so cool, then we need to talk more." Kat passed Melissa the same leaflet from Monday, and then a small stapled brochure. "Why don't we go for a coffee after you read next week? I have extra staff in on a Saturday so I can often get away."

"Make it tea and I'm there." Melissa took their bag, swinging it over her shoulder.

Jess tickled Grace's tummy, feeling pleased with her work. "Come on, let's get you some proper lunch and see what Rachel's got planned."

"What?" Melissa whacked Jess on the legs with Grace's books.

"Oh, didn't I mention? We're taking Grace to see your mum next." Jess shot her a nonchalant smile and made a move for the door before she attacked again. "Sorry, must have slipped my mind."

"If this is my punishment for the sweets, you're over-reacting."

* * *

After Melissa treated them both to sandwiches from the deli in an attempt to bribe Jess into doing anything else with the afternoon, they dragged her home. Rachel was tending to a plant pot on the front step when they arrived, waving with a trowel.

"This is my lucky day." She crouched to greet Grace as she ran over the tarmac holding out her books and pulled her into a hug. "What's that you've got?"

Melissa stepped past her mum. "It's those evil things I'm always reading instead of doing actual work."

Rachel gave a slight shake of her head but then brushed herself off and took Grace's hand, leading her into the house. "Now don't be angry, but I may have gone overboard."

Jess followed them through to the kitchen, all white gloss units and tiles. It reflected the light pouring in from the open bi-fold doors and the effect was blinding.

"Wouldn't have anything to do with the massive paddling pool that's appeared in your back garden, would it?"

If so, she wasn't angry. It was the level of fuss she was hoping for, and the fact Melissa would enjoy it was a bonus. Fingers crossed she'd go two for two and improve mother-daughter relations as well today.

"Guilty. I was in town this morning and I couldn't resist, it's such a lovely day."

Melissa was in it up to her shins, spinning around and spraying water everywhere, but Grace hadn't noticed yet. She was busy exploring the kitchen, opening and closing the cupboards and leaving mucky fingerprints over the doors.

Jess took her keys and wallet out of her pocket, dropping them on the table, and slipped off her trainers. Then she scooped up Grace, who grumbled before spotting the pool and clawing for freedom.

"Yeah okay, calm down." Jess sat on the grass, trying to get Grace's clothes off before she did a dive. "Stay still for a minute."

"Is auntie Jess being dull again?" Melissa called, still splashing in her shorts and T-shirt. She jumped out and ran up the lawn. "I'm going upstairs to get changed, do you want to borrow a bikini?"

"You think one of your bikinis will fit me? Very funny."

Rachel offered to change Grace and Jess brushed the grass from her shorts, finding Melissa waiting for her by the breakfast bar that divided the kitchen. They bounded up both sets of stairs together, stopping on the third floor outside Melissa's bedroom. It felt separate from the rest of the house, which was a calculated move on Rachel's part to give them space from each other.

Melissa pushed open the door, and it stuck on the thick beige carpet. Jess stepped inside, the familiar scent of vanilla she always associated with Melissa's room flooding her nose. It was neat, with rows of bookcases on one wall, and built-in wardrobes on the other. In the middle a door led to the bathroom, and in the centre of the bedroom stood a pine bedstead.

"Very you." Jess flopped back onto the cotton duvet. "Must be weird coming home to a different house than the one you grew up in."

"A bit. I miss the old place, had lots of good memories there, but I'm coming around to having my own bathroom. Not that Mum needs to know." Melissa opened the wardrobe, crouching to root through a drawer. "It'll feel more like home when I've got my photos from the garage, I haven't had time to put them up yet." She held out handfuls of skimpy bikini tops and frowned. "Do you want the shorts and T-shirt I borrowed on Thursday night? I haven't washed them, but it doesn't matter if they're only getting wet."

She fetched Jess's clothes from the bathroom and chucked them at her face. They smelt of vanilla now, so it was possible they wouldn't get a wash for some time.

"You should cover-up, too," Jess muttered, concerned for her friend's skin and her own heart rate in equal measure.

"You mean you won't smother me in suntan lotion?"

Melissa pulled off her T-shirt and Jess buried her eyes behind the shorts, holding them to her nose for a second and inhaling the scent. She longed for the days at school when girls refused to get changed in front of her, because Melissa had no such qualms.

"No. Wear a T-shirt or get your mum to do it."

She grumbled, taking her bikini into the bathroom to finish changing, and Jess slid her own clothes off while the coast was clear. She was just making a quick adjustment of the running shorts when Melissa re-emerged, tying her hair with a band.

Jess pulled the T-shirt up over her mouth this time, trying to hide as much of her face as possible. She was sure it had gone bright red, and she had no excuse apart from the obvious. "You need to put a top on, your shoulders will burn," she mumbled, praying that'd convince her. "I'm begging you."

Melissa opened the drawer again. "Fine, since you care about my shoulders so much."

Jess felt relief tinged with disappointment as she watched the freckles disappear back under fabric. Then she straightened out her own top and followed Melissa downstairs, to find Rachel stood in the middle of the pool. A naked Grace slipped in her hands, slathered in so much sun cream that she was white from head to toe.

"Think you went over the top, there's a slick of lotion in the pool." Melissa laughed, splashing Grace and then herself to acclimatise to the cold. "It's a health and safety nightmare. Thought you solicitors worried about these things."

Rachel stepped out and ran a hand over her skirt as she sat on the lawn, ignoring her daughter's jibe. "Did you three have fun this morning?"

"Yeah, Melissa's even made a friend." Jess took a seat next to her, picking a blade of grass and trying to whistle with it. "She's going for coffee with the woman who runs the bookshop."

"Oh, good. It wouldn't hurt you to meet some people if you're planning on staying. On that note, how are you getting on with the job search?"

Melissa sighed, lobbing an inflatable ball at the side of the pool. "Must we talk about that now? I only started this job on Monday. Can't I have a bit of space to get used to it and catch up with my friends first?"

"Friends?" Rachel's eyebrows knitted together. "I thought there was only this one?"

"Yes, I have friends. Jess, V... Grace. I'd have more around here if you hadn't sent me to school in Bournemouth, but it's done now."

Except it wasn't. She'd hated the private school her aunt worked in, but Rachel had always remained adamant it was too good an opportunity to miss. Even when Melissa had panic attacks over going back after the summer holidays, Rachel told her to tough it out.

"Let's not start this again, hey?" Jess rest a hand on Rachel's forearm, concerned this was going in the wrong direction.

She relented but wasn't willing to let go of the rest. "I don't understand your resistance to finding a job."

Melissa sat in the middle of the pool and let Grace dump water over her head. "I don't understand how you've decided I'm resistant to work." She shivered as she peeled a wedge of hair off her face. "I've always earned my own money. The real problem isn't with me, it's that you don't approve of any choice I make. You won't be happy until I bore myself to death in a job I hate."

"I'd settle for anything at this point."

Melissa glowered as another bucket of water gushed over her head. "No. You wouldn't."

"She looked at lunchtime the other day." Jess smiled at Melissa, trying to reassure her. "Give her a bit of time."

"She's had an entire year." Rachel's eyes widened, and she leant back on her elbows. "What other reason was there for a second English degree?"

Melissa stood up, looking like someone had punched her in the stomach. "Great, thanks for that." She twisted the bottom of her T-shirt and stepped out of the pool, then jogged back up the garden. "Someone needs to watch Grace."

"Can you? I'll go after her." Jess was halfway towards the

kitchen before Rachel could say any more. There was a trail of footsteps across the tile and she followed it back upstairs. When the bedroom was empty, she tapped on the bathroom door. "Are you in here?"

Melissa appeared in her bikini, rubbing a towel through her hair. "What do you want?"

"To check you're okay."

"Shame you didn't care about that a minute ago." She discarded the towel into the sink and pushed past, grabbing her dry shorts and T-shirt from the bed. "I know you think she can do no wrong, but she's a piece of work sometimes."

Jess gripped the doorframe to steady herself and then turned as Melissa tugged her shorts over the damp bikini, hopping across the floor. "I asked her to stop talking about school and work, what else could I say?"

Melissa straightened and fumbled as she fastened the buttons. "Sometimes I want you to stand up for me and not always try to keep the peace. Her comment about my degree was inexcusable, and you didn't say a word." There was a pause as she dug her fingers into her eyes. "If anyone belittled you, I couldn't hold back. It wouldn't matter who they were. I'm always on your side, and you're always somewhere in the middle when Mum's involved."

"Yeah, I know you would."

"Sometimes I wind her up and I deserve you calling me out on that too. I'm not asking you to take my side when I'm wrong."

Jess let go of the doorframe and the colour drained from her face for once instead of lighting it up like a beacon. "Sorry."

Melissa sat on the edge of the bed, letting out a long sigh as she fell backwards and rubbed the space next to her. "I know why your relationship with Mum is so important, but you're my closest friend. It's tough sometimes when I come second to her."

"You're not second to Rachel." Jess climbed onto the bed and crossed her legs, picking at a loose thread in her shorts. "It's only, sometimes I'm not sure what I'd do without her."

Melissa rolled onto her side and wrapped a hand around Jess's calf. "But you won't be without her because you've pointed out when she's in the wrong. Or is that what you think? That if you disagree, she might not want you around?"

Jess shrugged. She'd never considered it, but Melissa's theory might be correct. Now it seemed like a startling lack of self-awareness.

"It's different for you because she's your mum. It doesn't matter if you disagree, but I guess I don't have that luxury."

Melissa nodded, propping herself on her elbows. "Makes sense, but she sees you the same as me or Robbie. I promise."

That wasn't true. Rachel was harder on Melissa because she was her daughter, even if it felt unfair sometimes. She'd never been so bothered about what Jess did with her life. Including someone and viewing them as an equal for whom you had unconditional love and acceptance were not the same things.

"Disagree with you on that, sorry. She lets me get on with it because she's not as invested."

"Bullshit. Nope." Melissa shook her head, splattering the duvet with water. "The only difference is you've done nothing she disapproves of. You work for your dad, you take care of your friends like she would, and as far as she's concerned, you're the model daughter. It's the same with Robbie. He's done nothing to offend her, either."

Jess tried to protest, opening and closing her mouth a

few times but issuing no words. She slumped forward and lay next to Melissa, knowing she was right, even if she didn't believe it.

"Either way, I'm sorry I hurt you today. I'll try to be more aware of what I say, or don't, around Rachel. I worry about seeming ungrateful, but it'd upset me a lot more if you thought I didn't have your back."

Melissa smiled, dipping her head to kiss Jess's wrist. "I know you do with everyone else. I'm sorry too. Robbie's coming over for a family dinner this evening, and it'll be two more hours of how he's a saint and I'm a massive disappointment. It's made me tetchy."

Jess stroked the damp ribbons of hair from Melissa's face. "Rachel's not disappointed in you."

"She is. I went to the wrong university, to do the wrong degree, and the bottom line is she wants me to be a different person altogether."

"Then you'd disappoint me, because I like you quite a lot as you are."

"I know you do," Melissa whispered.

Jess wished she could say something else to make her feel better. She hated the idea that Melissa might feel inferior, but she also knew it would only get worse if she kept putting off finding work.

"Don't bite my head off, but do you think this might be why you're not applying for jobs? You've been looking, but not hard..."

"I guess. The ads I get excited over and want to apply for get bookmarked then forgotten about. Going to Cardiff was right for me, but even now she won't let it go, and I'm worried the same thing will happen with work."

"I understand why you went to Wales. If I could have been near your nan for four years, I'd have done it too."

Melissa had always been close with Paul's parents. They were warm and loving, and it was the place where she escaped. It was no surprise when she chose Cardiff University, but Rachel was dead against it, wanting her to at least try for Oxford or Cambridge.

"I miss them so much." She took hold of Jess's hand, stroking individual fingers and then entwining them with her own. "The only thing I'm looking forward to about this stupid wedding is that they're staying for the entire weekend." There was quiet for a moment as she wiped the tears away, her eyes puffy from Grace's assault and then her mum's. "Would you come to dinner later?"

"Yes, if you run it past your mum. Consider me your support animal for the evening. I'll try to do a better job this time."

6

By the time Melissa agreed to go back downstairs, Grace was grizzling and tired. Ten minutes more play and she was at the point of no return, sprawled out on a towel wailing as Jess tried to dry her off enough to get home.

Rachel peered over Jess's shoulder. "Do you need some help, darling?"

"I've got it sorted, thanks." Jess hoped not to sound too snippy as she grabbed a fresh nappy from Grace's bag. She got her shorts on over the top but gave up on the T-shirt.

"Are you sure it's wise to come back later? You're more than welcome and the boys would love to catch up, but you look tired, too."

"I'll have a nap when Grace does, it'll be fine."

Jess hoisted Grace off the towel and Rachel slung the bag over her shoulder, following them out to the car. Melissa had disappeared back upstairs, not wanting to hang around once they'd decided it was time to leave, and Jess wondered if she should say something. Her head was pounding, though, and Grace was one wrong move away from a full-on meltdown.

She strapped her into the car seat and waved to Rachel as they pulled out, hoping Grace fell asleep on the drive home. The rumble of the car was likely to get her off, and Jess took the scenic route to maximise her chances of success. It worked, and as they stopped on the drive, she was afraid to cut the engine in case she woke up again.

After extricating Grace from the car seat and carrying her to bed, Jess slumped onto the sofa with a packet of painkillers and curled into a ball. How long she'd been there she wasn't sure, but as she came around the television was on low.

"Hey, sleepyhead." The hair was damp around V's shoulders as she tucked into a banana with her feet up on the other sofa. "Which one of them wore you out?"

Jess straightened up and rubbed her eyes. "All three. I needed to recharge before I go back for another round later. Melissa and Rachel were going at each other this afternoon and I'm having dinner with them this evening."

"Oh. That sounds like a barrel of laughs, what happened?"

"Rachel made a crack about Melissa's degree and she got upset with me for not standing up for her. Before you say a word, I'm aware I was in the wrong."

V let out a laugh and jammed in another chunk of banana. When she'd finished with both, she laid the skin on the floor next to her water bottle. "Steady on. You have your head wedged up her mum's backside most of the time, but I'm sure it's not that bad. Did you work it out with her?"

"Hope so." Jess dug her fingers into her eyes, trying to bring herself back to reality. "Not sure I'd realised how much I avoid confrontation with Rachel. She was out of line earlier and I just sat there." She huffed, drawing her knees up to hug them. "I have a lot of respect for her, but I'm not sure I'd appreciated how much Melissa struggles with her expectations. I guess it's a lot to live up to, when your mum's a high-flying solicitor."

"Yep. I love Rachel, but she's like a freight train that takes no prisoners."

Jess laughed. "Wow, that's quite a mixed metaphor."

"Thanks."

She was right, if ineloquent. The more Jess stewed over Rachel's comments earlier, the crueller and more hurtful they sounded. She'd always known how much of an elitist snob she was sometimes and most of the time laughed it off, but it was a different story when Melissa was sobbing.

"I screwed up, and it's bothering me."

"Mm, I can see." V swung her legs around and leant forwards. "You okay?"

"Yeah. I always thought I was a good friend, though, and now I'm reconsidering."

"You are a good friend."

That was debatable. Good friends didn't lie and create excuses to avoid each other. They realised when the other was struggling and put their stupid crushes aside to be there. Melissa had done everything in her power to make life easier this week, and the one thing she needed in return Jess hadn't delivered.

"I guess."

"Well, I'm sure. Melissa loves you."

That wasn't helping. It was even more reason for Jess to pull her head out of her ass and stop ogling at every opportunity.

"Yeah, well. Not sure I deserve it," she muttered, rubbing circles around her temples. "How did you get on with your mum earlier?"

"Oh, it was fine. We talked it out, and she agreed it was best for us to stay here. Seems like you're stuck with us."

Jess smiled. "I'm glad to have a bit of good news."

"See, and you think you're an awful friend. I'm sure she'll appreciate you being there and know how much you care."

* * *

Jess let herself in through the side gate to find Robbie was tossing a rugby ball with Paul, who was inept but attempting to share his son's interest. Melissa came out of the kitchen doors, carrying a handful of knives and forks, and started laying them on the patio table.

"Hey, Jess!" Robbie yelled, waving with one hand as he caught the ball with the other. "Have you changed your mind about my stag do?"

Jess pulled him into a rough hug, and he lifted her clear of the ground. "Dream on. There's no way in hell I'm coming to that."

He set her down and turned to receive the ball again. "But I told the lads you would. Stephen will be so disappointed."

"What a shame."

Stephen was Robbie's best friend and his best man. He also captained the rugby team, wore shirts that were way too tight, and tried it on with every woman he met.

"How does it feel leaving a stream of disappointed men in your wake?"

"Stream might be overstating it," she called back, wandering up to the table and kissing Melissa's cheek. "Stephen fancies everyone. I'm sure he'll cope."

Melissa smiled at her and slammed a knife onto the

table. "Stephen's an idiot. Even if she wasn't a big lesbian, Jess could do better than any of your friends."

Jess took the rest of the cutlery and started laying it out, concerned it'd bend if she continued. "I'm a big lesbian now. Wow, when did I get an upgrade?"

"Think it was when you got that tattoo on your thigh."

Melissa rubbed her hand over it from behind, and Jess spilled the rest of the forks. She might have to rethink how putting her feelings aside would work, because her body had other ideas.

"Come and join in." Robbie stopped with his arm suspended in the air as they both stepped onto the lawn, looking his sister up and down before tossing it to Paul. "What are you doing? You can't catch."

"Leave her alone, Rob. She can catch." Jess received the ball from Paul and lobbed it at Melissa. "Can't throw, but she can catch." She saw the hurt look forming on Melissa's face and berated herself for failing twice in as many minutes. "I'm only teasing."

Melissa smiled at her and mouthed a quick "I know".

"What are you doing for this stag thing, anyway? I thought you were organising a trip to Poland?"

"Nah." Robbie shook his head. "Plan was a pub crawl, but your dad gave us the keys to his cottage for the night instead."

"He's done what?"

Jess was preparing to launch the ball but clung onto it. David would never let Robbie and his rugby mates loose in his cottage and this had to be a joke. Either that or he was less interested because he wasn't planning on living there for much longer, but she didn't want to think about that explanation.

"Yeah, surprised me too, but he gave me them at the barbecue."

Jess threw the ball back to Paul. "In that case there's no way in hell I'm not coming, someone needs to make sure you don't trash the place. You realise if they harm anything in that house, I will murder you?"

Robbie laughed. "Can I take back that invitation?"

"No."

Jess scowled at him but pitched back as the ball hit her cheek and the left side of her nose. After stumbling for a moment, she righted herself, but there was something warm trickling down her chin.

"Told you she can't throw," Robbie teased.

Jess caught the drips with a hand and jogged up to the kitchen. Then she pulled a handful of tissues from the breakfast bar and thrust them at her top lip.

"Oh shit, sorry." Melissa squinted, cradling Jess's face and guiding her to sit on a stool. "Come here. Are you okay?" She stroked her thumbs across Jess's cheeks, pulling away the loose strands of hair which were getting matted with blood. "I'm so sorry."

"I understand I upset you earlier but that was mean. How am I meant to pull Robbie's rugby mates now?"

Melissa laughed, brushing away the tears. "Still gorgeous."

"For a big lesbian?"

"Yeah, even for one of those. Let me find some ice, and then we'll get you cleaned up in the bathroom."

Jess pulled the tissues away, relieved to find she didn't drip anymore. "It's fine I don't need ice."

She dabbed a few more times but had stopped bleeding. Her nose hurt, and she was struggling to breathe through it, but she'd live.

"Tough guy, huh? Is this a re-run of the massage inci-dent?" Melissa ignored her and pulled out an ice pack from the freezer, then wrapped it in a tea towel.

"That's an incident now? I'm sure you got your way." Jess winced as Melissa held the ice to her face. "Worked look, feel my shoulders."

Melissa squeezed with her free hand. "Very nice, I do excellent work. Tell me if you tense up again, I'll come back."

"You've forgiven me, then? I've only been here five minutes and I've already messed up."

"Because you made a joke with Robbie? I'm not that sensitive, don't worry."

"So long as you know you're my absolute favourite person in the world." Jess took the ice pack from Melissa's hand and dropped it on the breakfast bar, then drew her into a hug without knocking her nose. "Anyone who thinks you're not good enough, Rachel included, is an idiot."

"Have you been drinking?"

Jess pulled back. "No, but I sustained a nasty head injury. It may have made me sentimental."

"Must have. I appreciate you saying it, though."

Ten minutes into dinner, all they'd discussed was Robbie's wedding. Even he looked bored with it, developing an unusual interest in a tub of flowers, and trying to divert the conversation.

"How's work going, Jess? I hope my sister hasn't been giving you too much trouble."

As diversions went, it was a helpful one. He'd handed

her the perfect opportunity to sing Melissa's praises in front of Rachel.

"Imagine my surprise, but she's been a massive help. We even had a new instruction on Thursday from someone who'd seen the testimonials she's started putting out on Instagram."

"Who would have thought being a boring geek was useful?" Robbie's smile was warm, despite the jibe. "Bet you're pleased she's doing so well." He turned to his mum prodding her wrist with his fork. "That's one less thing for you to worry about."

Jess wanted to hug him for that alone. She willed Rachel to say something which showed praise, pride or pleasure.

"I'm glad it's working out." Rachel reached for her wineglass. "It isn't permanent, though." She swirled the contents and took a sip. "I'll be happier once she's settled."

With one hand she gave, and the other took away. They needed to pull it back before this descended into another bloodbath.

Jess gave Melissa's shoulder a gentle shake, and she reached out to reciprocate on her knee. "I'm sure the glowing reference I plan to write will help with that. You'll find something that suits you and smash it."

Rachel went to speak again, but Melissa cut her off before any words issued. "Thanks. I've enjoyed it, and digital marketing is something to explore."

Jess didn't mind after that when Rachel steered their conversation back to the wedding. She was regaling them with her oft-told story of how she asked to sample chocolate cake, but they gave her red velvet and she ended up picking it. She'd taken it as proof that things happen for a reason. Even Melissa got into it, making jokes about her awful bridesmaid dress, and teasing Robbie when he knew so little of what was going on at his own wedding.

When they'd finished eating and enjoyed another glass of wine on the patio, Rachel let them get their own back by setting up the Xbox in the living room. She even tried to join in for a short while before finding more booze and squinting as she tried to work out the appeal.

"It might be bedtime," she suggested as it approached midnight, drawing the curtains against the dark and trying to wrestle a controller from Paul's hand. "Will you stay tonight, my darling? I don't want you walking home on your own."

Jess checked her watch. "Shit, how did it get so late?"

They'd been playing for over three hours, which wasn't a surprise. Often, she'd be up doing this until the early hours of the morning.

"I've already made up the spare bedroom, and there are new toothbrushes in the bathroom cabinet." Rachel collected their empty glasses and tapped Paul, rousing him this time. "Good night."

Jess stretched and rubbed her eyes. "Guess the boss has spoken and I'm staying."

She didn't mind. It warmed her knowing someone cared, and that Rachel always had a room for her. Being with them tonight, eating dinner, and playing games, had been like old times.

"Notice how there isn't a room for me," Robbie teased, grunting as he parted himself from the armchair and brushed tortilla crumbs off his lap. "She never worries about me getting mugged on my way home."

"Be fair now, you're the size of a bear. You can hold your own well enough to cycle the ten minutes to your house." Jess got up and hugged him, her arms not long enough to stretch around his torso. "Guess I'll see you at this stag party. Do I need to bring anything?"

"No." He started towards the door but paused as he reached out for the handle. "Well, unless you wanted to make me some of those chocolate brownies. The ones you baked at Christmas."

"I'll see what I can do."

"Awesome. Right, I'm going now. Happy birthday for next weekend, Mum's got your card. Night."

Jess laughed and stretched again, then switched off the console while Melissa gathered up the controllers. They turned off the lights before trudging upstairs, stopping on the first-floor landing.

"Good night," Melissa whispered, as Jess pushed open the bathroom door.

"Good night."

Jess took a toothbrush from the cabinet and brushed her teeth, then wandered through to the bedroom, flicking on the side lamp and removing her shorts and bra. The smell shouldn't be too bad if she slept in her T-shirt tonight and showered when she got home in the morning.

The sheets were crisp as she slipped into them, and there was a chill in the air from the open window which still didn't remove the lingering stench of paint. It wasn't warm and inviting like Melissa's room, but it was a relief not to have to worry about errant limbs.

Jess had just started to drift off, trying to visualise what she might put on a dating profile, when the door creaked and she shot up, pulling the covers aside. Footsteps padded across the carpet, and the mattress dipped.

"Only me," Melissa whispered. She shuffled, grasping Jess's waist to pull them together, then dropped a kiss on her nose. "How's it feeling now?"

"Oh, fine. I'd forgotten all about it," Jess whispered back. "What are you doing here?"

Melissa rolled over and guided Jess's arm around herself, holding it in place under her breasts. "Sleeping." She wiggled until they were flush against each other. "Thanks for this evening. I'm glad you came."

Jess had tensed but willed her muscles to relax so she wasn't rigid against Melissa's back. "Any time."

She closed her eyes again and tried to imagine arriving at Robbie's wedding with a new girlfriend in tow this time, but it was no use. The only person she could picture was Melissa, moaning her dress was a horrible colour and stropping.

Melissa rubbed her thumb into Jess's arm as she chuckled. "What are you laughing at?"

"Was just thinking about Robbie's wedding. You can have the best intentions, but sometimes the universe has other ideas."

Or in this case, Melissa had other ideas. Even now, when Jess was trying to put some distance between them, she kept coming along and removing it.

"That stupid cake story? You've lost the plot."

"Yeah," Jess lied, kissing her shoulder and feeling a warm jolt of arousal as their legs slipped together. "Must be the head injury again."

7

On Friday the familiar loop of her mum's handwriting appeared in the pile of post Jess collected from the work mailbox. Every year it was the same, she could recite the message from memory. The card sat in her drawer until everyone else had gone, and then she pulled it out.

"You know it's easier to read those things if you remove them from the envelope." Melissa shut the lid on her laptop and creaked back in her chair.

"I've heard that, yeah. I already know it's from Anna, though. It'll go in the bin."

It always annoyed David when Jess insisted on calling her that, so she'd started saying Mum around him. At some point it'd slipped into other conversations, but she'd given up the title after walking out on them. The occasional greetings card or email changed nothing.

"Gotcha." Melissa rolled her chair across the office and pulled up next to Jess. "You ever think about her, apart from your birthday?"

"Christmas. She sends one then. And I had an email

from her a few months ago. Sent one back answering the questions and told her I don't want to chat."

"I guess she respected it, at least."

Respect was one word for it, but she didn't have much in return. Grace moving in had provided a fresh perspective on things, and it made binning Anna's card easier this year.

"Yes, there's always that." Jess tore open the envelope and read the message. "Dear Jess, blah blah blah, thinking of you on your birthday, love Mum."

She flung her card into the wastepaper basket and huffed as she slumped back in the chair. Why Anna insisted on sending empty greetings was a mystery. It was as if she'd decided to go but liked to dip back in every so often, for the sake of her own conscience.

"You'd think she'd at least buy you a pony, what a crock," Melissa scoffed, shoving Jess on the arm. "Is it weird having a mum out there who you don't see? I mean, do you even know what she looks like?"

"Yeah, I do, she has a photo that comes up when she emails. I know her as a little circle."

Brown hair bobbed above her shoulders. Poker straight, shiny, with a harsh fringe. It was a professional headshot; something you might put on a company website or your LinkedIn profile. The smile was warm but not too friendly, and she had on a white blouse.

"How did she get your address?"

Jess turned the chair to face Melissa, grasping the handles and pulling them together so their knees touched. "It was my work one, it's on the website. Guess she got it there. She always sends my cards here, too, so I don't think she knows where I live."

"She won't turn up on your doorstep then?" Melissa

leant forward and lowered her voice. "That's good, I'd have to kill her."

Jess laughed. The notion of Melissa beating up anyone was ridiculous. "You? Now that I'd like to see."

"Hey, I'm tough." Melissa pointed to her bicep, then gave it a prod. "If anyone messes with you, besides me, they'll get a shock."

"Oh, I see, giving yourself a free pass there. And can we note that if you picked a fight, I'd end up having to finish it?"

It'd happened only once, not long after Anna left. Jess couldn't remember much from that period. It was a haze of scenes she could snatch at, but never fit in chronological order. This was clear, though. It had always stuck.

Melissa would have only been five, and they'd both gone to the same birthday party. During a game of pass the parcel a boy had snatched away her prize and Jess had knocked him over to get it back. She might have been in more trouble, if she wasn't the poor kid whose mum had walked out.

"In any case, she needs to watch out. You've already got a family who love you, so you don't need her around." Melissa folded her arms in defiance. "It's her loss."

Jess's cheeks warmed with the force of her compliment, and she laughed through a smile. "Well, that's good to know. Speaking of which, we need to leave because Grace is making us air tea. I hope you remember how to fake sip."

Melissa held out her pinkie finger and pretended to drink. "Yep, got it. I'm looking forward to this most of all your birthday celebrations. It'll be fun."

"Grace was so excited this morning. She laid out her party dress and V had to stop her from wearing it all day."

She didn't comprehend what they were celebrating but launched herself into the preparations. There were paper plates with stars, she was baking a cake, and they'd been busy making decorations since last weekend.

"That's adorable." Melissa pushed her chair back and got up, stretching and yawning. "Are you sure you want me there?"

"Why wouldn't I?"

"Because it seems to be for Grace's benefit, and I didn't know if you and V wanted to do it alone."

Jess frowned, unsure whether this was to do with Grace or if she was still worried V didn't want her butting in because of unrequited feelings. Either way, V hadn't objected to Melissa joining them. Since they'd chatted it through everyone had been getting along fine, unless Jess had missed something.

"No, we both want you there. Grace will, too. You know she loves your stories. You've found someone who doesn't mind you chatting shit at them, don't give up on that."

Melissa swiped Jess around the head and began packing her bag. "I sometimes wonder why I make such an effort for you."

"Because you love me."

"I was thinking more that you need me, and I wouldn't want to devastate you by depriving you of my company."

Jess grabbed her wallet from the drawer and made sure they switched everything off for the weekend. "The power of your ego never fails to amaze me. If you could harness that in a fight, you wouldn't need help." She cajoled Melissa out of the door. "Now hurry before I change my mind."

* * *

Less than an hour later Jess was home and changed, grabbing a beer from the fridge. She walked into the garden to find the table strung with paper chains and set with the plates Grace had chosen. They'd allowed her to wear her party dress, and she was chasing the bubbles V was blowing for her, giggling every time she popped one. Melissa was right, Jess didn't need Anna one bit.

"This looks great." She stuck a finger in her cake and licked away the icing. "Tastes good, too."

"Are you eating that already?"

She avoided V's wrath when the side gate clattered, and Melissa twirled on the patio in a long pink dress. Now all Jess had to worry about was keeping her tongue in her mouth.

"I decided since this is a tea party, I should make an effort." Melissa dumped her rucksack on a chair and kicked off her sandals, then stepped onto the grass and lifted Grace into the air. "You look beautiful. Are you going to twirl with me?"

Jess laughed as she watched them, spinning across the garden in a flurry of bubbles. When her life had become a television commercial, she didn't know, but there wasn't much to complain about right now.

"Do you want a drink? It's not quite champagne, but we stretched to sparkling grape juice."

Melissa set Grace back on the grass and followed into the kitchen. "Fancy. Shouldn't have much, though, because I don't want to read to kids in the morning reeking of grapes."

Jess pulled a bottle from the fridge and unscrewed the cap with a hiss. "You look amazing." She peered at her own outfit of denim shorts and the T-shirt Grace had bought for her birthday. "Did I miss the word formal on the invitation?"

"Don't worry, this is for Grace. I have something for you, though." Melissa held out a bright pink envelope, which sparkled with flecks of glitter. "You can open it now."

Jess set the bottle on the table and tore it open, pulling out a card and sending a square of paper blowing out of the door. Grace chased it across the patio, coming close to face planting the slabs, but retrieved it before she did any major damage to herself.

"Can I have that, monster?" Jess tried to prise it off her, but she wasn't giving it up without a fight. "Open it for me if I can't have it." Grace pulled at the edges, ripping off a corner, but got it to a point where it was readable. "You sponsored a guide dog puppy for me? Thanks, that's sweet."

"What did you expect?"

Anything was possible. Jess left the printout with Grace and pulled Melissa into a hug, lifting her off the ground and spinning her around until she slapped a shoulder and begged to stop. Jess made herself so dizzy that she had to drop her and then slumped onto a chair laughing. "You might have to pour your own drink while I'm sick."

V planted both hands on Jess's shoulders. "You won't want cake, then?"

"Like hell I won't."

V jogged into the kitchen to get the drinks and a box of matches, then Grace clambered onto Jess's lap as they sang happy birthday and blew out the candles. Grace did more spitting than blowing, but she would have put enough body fluids into the cake when it was being baked, and no one worried.

Melissa ran a finger through her buttercream and sucked it away. "I've got a suggestion for you."

"For me?" Jess almost choked on a mouthful of cake. She was trying to finish before Grace, who was already eying it.

"No, V. My only advice to you is slow down or you will be sick." Melissa shook her head, scraping Jess's plate across the table. "Jess told me you were thinking about getting a job, but I've had a better idea."

V huffed, wiping a blob of icing from Grace's chin before it dripped onto her dress. "Does it involve buying a lottery ticket? If so, I've tried it."

"No, it's more realistic than that. When I was at university I didn't want to work in a bar or a shop, so I had a little side-line tutoring English. People are always interested in core subjects and you studied maths, didn't you?"

"Yeah. Well, with statistics, but I planned to train as a maths teacher."

"Then why not explore private tutoring? I'm sure it'd look good on your teaching application, you can do it around Grace, and it pays well."

V narrowed her eyes. "How well?"

"Better than working in a supermarket. I can run through it with you later, if you like?" Melissa took V's mumbling as a sign of agreement and responded with a satisfied nod. "Great, we can talk while Jess puts Grace to bed."

"Excuse me," Jess protested, as Melissa tickled the back of her knee. "Isn't this supposed to be my party?"

"I'm staying tonight, too. Forgot to mention it. Can I get a lift to town in the morning? Stephen's doing my MOT tomorrow, so I had to drop my car at Robbie's."

"There's a good girl." V laughed and after a playful slap of Jess's shoulder, clasped both hands behind her head as she leant back. "Make sure you brush Grace's teeth after all that cake."

Jess slumped further into her chair, wondering why she'd ever thought encouraging Melissa and V to make friends was a good idea. Now she had two people barking instructions. Three, if you counted Grace.

"I was just thinking how grateful I am for you lot," she mumbled, folding her arms. "But I've reconsidered and I'm moving out."

* * *

Once Grace was in bed, they'd ended up flaked out in the garden reading or scrolling through their phones. It wasn't a banging party, but then that was best saved for tomorrow night at the hockey social. V laid herself in front of the television at ten, and Jess forced Melissa up to bed.

She'd changed in the bathroom and then pulled out a book, propping herself on a stack of pillows and squinting across the page. They'd only been in bed for ten minutes when she shuffled, twisting the covers around her leg, and smacked her book on the bedside table.

"Ugh." Melissa thrashed more for effect and then lay still, staring at the ceiling. "I forgot to bring my glasses and I'm struggling to read without them. If I don't read, I can't sleep."

"Do you want to watch television instead?"

They hadn't done this for ages, flopping out in bed watching rubbish and tearing it to strips.

"Why not? Stranger things are happening in the world." Melissa rolled and pulled the covers away, adjusting her bed shorts. "Not for long though, I'm tired."

"Alright, grandma."

Melissa tucked herself under Jess's arm and laid a hand across her stomach. "What are we watching?"

"Romance film with some bloke bumbling after a woman who's too good for him. I find it hard to relate to most of these movies, but there's nothing else on."

She didn't watch much television these days. On reflection, it'd only been on in the evenings to offer background noise because she was lonely, but now Grace did that it was no longer necessary.

Melissa laughed. "Why, I thought you were a hopeless romantic?"

"I am, but I want representation. I'd like to see someone who looks like me, having a relationship I could recognise. Is that so much to ask?"

"Mm I agree, we should write one. I'd like to see some of these." Melissa prodded the tattoo on Jess's thigh. "And a bit of this." She poked at her stomach this time and growled. "Way sexier."

"Did you growl at me?"

"Yes, it was a compliment. You're gorgeous, I'd much rather watch you in a film than some Hollywood actress." Melissa shuffled down the bed, laying sideways with her head on Jess's stomach, and wrapped a hand around her leg. "Besides which, you make a far more comfortable pillow."

"Oh great, just what every woman wants to hear. Ten out of ten for comfort, makes a good cushion, would sleep on. Cheers." Melissa only laughed, gripping Jess's wrist and moving her hand to her head. "Oh, I see, and you want me to stroke your hair now, too?"

"Yeah, I need you to help me sleep. I've got cramps, do you have any painkillers?"

"Should have said. Hang on, I'll get you a hot water bottle, too." Jess manoeuvred Melissa's head onto an actual pillow and jumped off the bed, pointing to the bedside cabinet. "Tablets are in the top drawer next to you." She stopped in the doorway, a hand lingering over the handle. "Don't go in the bottom drawer."

That would scar her for life. She ran downstairs to find V still flaked out watching the same film, half asleep and leaving a puddle of drool on the sofa. Jess crept past, stopping only to cover her with a blanket. Once she'd filled the hot water bottle and poured a glass of water, she made her way back upstairs. Melissa was pinging tablets into her hand with a smirk on her face.

"Thanks." She took the drink and threw her head back as she downed the pills. "You've got some strange cures for period pain in there. I'm wondering how the vibrator things work. Do you put them on your back?"

"You're a little shit," Jess whispered, shutting the door and lobbing the hot water bottle at her. "I told you not to open the bottom drawer."

"Relax, I didn't. Only presumed. Thanks for the confirmation though, it's cheered me right up."

Jess felt her face scorch. It had been like a heater with a faulty thermostat since Melissa came home from university, she'd never blushed so much in her life.

"Glad to be of service. Anything else I can do for you?"

"Yes, there is. Come here." Melissa hitched her legs onto the bed and climbed under the covers, gesturing to the spot behind her. Jess snuggled into her back, holding the hot water bottle to her stomach. "I want you to tell me if you're okay about that card. I know I was dismissive earlier, but I don't buy that it doesn't bother you."

"What card?"

"Don't play dumb. The one from Anna. If you didn't care you'd throw it out straight away, but you kept it all day."

Jess nuzzled into her neck. "Sometimes I wonder where she is and what she's doing, but not for long."

It was a passing interest which only occurred to her twice a year. Most of the time she forgot her mum's existence.

"You don't think it might be time to ask David what happened and why she left?"

"No, wouldn't change anything. He told me they'd agreed for him to have sole custody, and she'd moved out of the area to make it easier on everyone. Besides that, what else is there to understand?"

Melissa rolled over, the hot water bottle now warm between their stomachs, and stroked the hair from Jess's cheek. "A lot, I would have thought. Don't you want to know what caused the divorce, and why she agreed to give him sole custody?"

There still didn't seem much to know. David had always been desperate for kids and he would have had more given the chance, which was why it was always odd that he hadn't met someone else. Jess could never remember being close to her mum, but her bond with him was rock solid.

"Like I say, wouldn't change anything. I've been happy, had a great childhood, turned out pretty well."

Melissa smiled. "You turned out great."

"I'm wondering if you'd be so interested if it was Dad who walked away. Men do it all the time, don't they? I mean, if you reversed the roles, and he'd allowed Mum to have sole custody, would we even be having this conversation?"

"I guess you're right."

She was. If David had left, he'd have been another deadbeat dad, but Anna leaving them needed a detailed analysis.

Jess plumped her pillow and wiggled to get comfy. "We should try to sleep because you've got a big day tomorrow. First time reading, are you nervous?"

"Nah, piece of cake." Melissa turned over, flicked the light off, and reached to drop Jess's hand onto her head again. "Not so fast, though. I still need help sleeping."

V tugged at her dress. She'd changed it a dozen times in the last hour and was now sloping along the High Street as she continued to deliberate. Anyone would think they were attending a ball at a swanky hotel, not a hockey social in a dirty pub. There was a lot to say for wearing black, at least you never wasted much time picking an outfit.

Jess pushed through the doors of The Crown. "Stop fiddling with that, you look hot."

"Not sweaty hot?" V peered at herself, running a hand over the green satin. "The good hot?"

"Yes, the good hot."

Jess checked her watch again. It was past eight, and they'd told Melissa to be there at seven-thirty. If she'd given up and gone home, they'd be hearing about it until the end of days.

"Are you sure you don't want to go somewhere quieter for a drink?" V was still frowning, her eyes flicking between the street and the throngs of people in the bar. "We could grab Melissa and go to The Angel, instead. It is your birthday."

"Nice try. Is there a legitimate reason you don't want to stay?"

V folded her arms tight in front of herself and then her shoulders slumped forward as she let out a sigh. "It's silly."

"Can't be, if it's got you this stressed out." Jess dug her hands into her pockets, making it clear they weren't moving until she explained. "Come on, spill."

"Okay, but I'm warning you now it's childish. There's a girl on the team who hates me, and I can't shake it off."

Jess followed V's gaze to a woman in jeans and a green hockey polo, leant against the bar with a pint in hand, laughing and slopping beer everywhere. "Why are you worried about her? She looks like the hockey team threw up on her." She scrunched her face to emphasise the point. "Who comes out on a Saturday night in their kit?"

V grunted out a laugh and let her arms drop. "I guess you're right. Sorry, I'm not sure what's wrong with me at the moment."

"I understand, but don't worry. If she says anything, she'll have me and Melissa to deal with."

The group of hockey girls were filtering into the garden and Jess guided V through the crowd. They ordered drinks, then cigarette smoke clouted them as they stepped onto the patio. When Jess emerged from the smog she could see, at the far end of the lawn, a group of women converged around two picnic benches.

She stopped to scan for her new nemesis. "What's her name?"

"Lydia, why?"

"I like to know my enemy."

As they snaked a path through the tables, trying not to trip on dog leads and discarded glasses, someone turned to point at them. Jess stopped in her tracks. A chorus of happy birthday had begun, out of tune, and an entire garden's worth of people had chimed in amidst banging of hands and tinkling of glasses. It added a percussive effect that only made the song louder and more embarrassing.

"Oh my God." Jess sunk her face into her hands. "Did you do this?" She peered through her fingers at V.

"Don't look at me. I didn't even tell anyone it was your birthday tomorrow."

A few of the hockey players shifted on the bench to reveal a square chocolate cake covered in lashings of ganache. It was lit up with so many candles that you could feel the heat of them from several feet away, and the sides were slipping away as they melted.

"Happy birthday," Melissa called, her arm around Kat as both of them wore wide, delighted grins. "You're late, we almost ate it without you."

Jess fixed Melissa with a stare, her lip twitching as she tried not to smile. "I should have known you'd be to blame for this, I will kill you."

"At least blow out your candles first."

Jess inched forward, aware that fifteen hockey players were watching them and waiting to eat. She took a deep breath and blew across the cake, extinguishing them in one go. There was a cheer, and everyone returned to their conversations.

"Happy now?"

Melissa released Kat and clutched a hand to her chest. "Yes, thank you for doing that for me. I know you made a lot of effort."

"Thank you."

Jess laughed and gripped Melissa in a hug that lifted her off the floor. It was very sweet, not that she intended to be too enthusiastic in saying. They both knew part of the fun was in the wind up, and she wouldn't spoil it for her.

"See, that didn't kill you." Melissa reached into a bag on the floor for a plastic knife. "Now, who wants cake?"

There were collective mumbles of confirmation as she cut the sponge into squares, tipping it onto little pink napkins.

"Do you think she's had a personality transplant?" Jess hooked an arm around V to stop her drifting away from the group again.

V laughed, pulling out a chair. "You looked pretty shocked. Peak Melissa."

"True. Who knows what else the little bugger has planned for this weekend?"

After cake they'd allowed themselves to become embroiled in a game of Never Have I Ever, and it was clear most of the hockey team had lived very sheltered lives. The upside was that V had found her confidence, with the aid of two pints and her bodyguards.

"Has anyone done anything?" V tutted and set her redundant glass on the table as everyone got up for more drinks. "Only four people have had sex in a car? We need to play something else."

"I'm learning things about you," Melissa teased, poking Jess's leg and sipping a hideous looking bright orange mock-tail. "Which of you decided it was a good idea to have sex in a school?"

V spluttered with laughter. "Might have been my fault. We also did it in a toilet block, the leisure centre changing rooms, a tent, and in a field. When you're living with your parents, I guess you have to get creative. No big deal."

That was only the start of it. Most of Jess's anecdotes involved V. Six years since they split up and nothing all that interesting had happened since, she'd become far more sensible. V had, too, although she had her moments.

"I remember what sex is, but it's been a while," Jess mused.

V leant into her ear and whispered. "You can sort that. Do you need me to set you up with someone? Lydia? Might win her over if I can get her a shag."

"I don't want to sleep with Lydia, thank you very much."

V slumped back into the chair. "Shame. What about Kat?"

"She's got a boyfriend, don't be ridiculous." Jess shook her head in disbelief while Melissa choked with laughter and grasped her leg. "I try to go for single people. Ones with an attraction to women, too."

That was the theory, at least. Although, she knew nothing for definite about Melissa's sexuality because they didn't often discuss their love lives. There had been a guy eighteen months ago, but it hadn't lasted long. Since then, Jess hadn't been desperate for details.

"Back to Lydia." V huffed and tried to drain the last drop from her glass. "Sorry, I don't know any other single women. Well, not that are into girls."

That was handy, because this conversation was off limits tonight.

"That's me out then." Jess tried not to sound too disappointed, pulling a twenty from her pocket and waving it in V's face. "If I give you some money do you want to get us another round?"

V snatched it and collected their empties, before heading to the bar. "Thanks."

"How did it go with Kat earlier?" Jess rubbed a hand over Melissa's knee but then pulled it away, wondering if another pint was a sensible idea.

"Ask her yourself."

Kat dragged V's chair over and ran a palm along her face. "Phew, I don't think I can drink any more. Please stop me."

Melissa took the glass from her other hand and set it on the table. "Done. Tell Jess what we worked out today."

"Ah. Your non girlfriend is brilliant. She's coming to help with my next author signing, and we're looking into live streaming the event."

"Is that her official title now?" Jess leant across to Kat, resting a hand on the arm of the chair. "Don't tell her this, but she is amazing. If she finds out, she'll be insufferable."

"She already knows," Kat whispered. Then she giggled into her palm like a schoolgirl rather than a businesswoman who was in her thirties. "Hey, I need to tell you a secret. Come closer." Jess scraped her chair over so Kat could cup a hand to her ear. "Someone has a crush on V. Should we tell her? You said you wanted to cheer her up."

"Depends, who is it?"

V came back with their drinks before Kat could answer, setting them on the table.

"These two idiots think I couldn't hear them." Melissa tapped V's shoulder to get her attention, then slipped onto Jess's lap so there was a spare seat. "Would you want to know if someone had a crush on you?"

V glanced from one to the other, wide-eyed. "Excuse me?"

"You heard. Big, awkward crush. Do you want to know who?"

Trust Melissa to cut through the crap. Kat was sniggering and reached for her drink again, and Jess was trying to bury her face in Melissa's back.

V perched on the chair and put her head in her hands. "Oh shit, it's not Lydia, is it?" She looked up, scanning the garden, and then her eyes locked onto Lydia by the far gate. "Fuck, how did I not realise?"

"I take it you're not happy about this?"

"I mean, I'm relieved she doesn't hate me, but I'm not interested, and Christ she's coming over."

V hid her head behind a hand again, her lips tightening as Lydia approached. They tried to straighten out their faces, but Melissa was the only one in control. She got up and intercepted Lydia, pulling her to one side, and then came back with a satisfied smile.

"Consider it dealt with."

"I don't even want to know what you told her, so long as she understands I'm only up for being her friend."

Melissa resumed her position and reached a hand behind her shoulder, stroking the side of Jess's head. "I was sympathetic and relayed the message. You lot are useless. Poor girl seems shy."

Jess was only half listening, too enraptured by the fingertips running through her hair. She brushed away the smothering mass of blonde in her face and pressed her lips to Melissa's shoulder, closing her eyes and luxuriating in the tender touch. Her hand snuck around Melissa's stomach and she inched her thumb under her T-shirt, stroking the soft flesh there.

She heard something about Lydia being too nice, which was ironic after V had thought she hated her, but the rest was background noise. Not much else registered until a prod from Kat jolted her back to reality.

"Are we boring you?" She held up her empty glass and wiggled it. "Come on, stretch your legs by coming to the bar with me."

Jess mumbled a protest, far happier where she was, but Melissa slipped off her lap and the warmth of their embrace cooled in the late evening breeze. She stretched and yawned, complying with Kat's request.

It was busier now, as people waited for the DJ to set up his gear. They pushed through a crowd to the far side of the bar where it was quieter, and both pulled up a stool.

"I'm glad you got on with Melissa earlier, she'll be so excited to spend more time in the shop." Jess sat and tried to catch the barmaid's attention. "I hope you didn't mind me trying to set you guys up, sometimes she struggles to meet people."

"No, I'm glad. She's who I brought you in here to talk about." Kat fiddled with her pendant, leaning sideways against the bar. "Do you mind if I pry?"

Jess turned to face her and felt a pang of pre-emptive nausea at her bashful smile. "Go on, hit me with it."

"Don't say it like that, I only wondered if you needed someone to talk to. It's obvious you're besotted with Melissa, and it can be easier to chat with an outsider."

Jess's eyes prickled, and it caught her off guard. "Um. I'm not sure."

"Not sure about what?" Kat's tone softened, and she rubbed Jess's hand on the bar. "Whether you'd like to talk about it, or if you're in love with her?"

"The first bit. The second is a foregone conclusion, although I thought I'd done an okay job of hiding my feelings."

If Kat had worked it out, it was unlikely other people hadn't, and the thought turned a pang of sickness into a crashing wave. The only person she was certain didn't know was V. She'd been so preoccupied she hadn't even realised Lydia fancied her. As for everyone else, who knew.

"You don't think you should tell Melissa?"

"Nope." Jess shook her head, whipping herself with hair. "That wouldn't end well, trust me. If she didn't disown me, her mum would."

"She seems like a straightforward person. I'm struggling to see why, even if she didn't feel the same way, you couldn't work through it given how much you care for each other."

Because it'd never be the same. They wouldn't be as close anymore, and Melissa might wonder at her motivations. It was selfish, she realised now, but having Melissa or Rachel distance themselves was too hard. She knew she needed to get over it, she'd resolved to do so the previous weekend, but telling anyone was too scary.

"I can't do that." Jess wiped away a tear before it broke. "It's hard enough trying to move on now, without her knowing. I've stayed away from her before, and I've tried to see her as a friend. What if I can only get over this if I leave her behind altogether?"

The floodgates were on the verge of opening, and Jess sniffed, trying to control herself. She didn't want to end up blubbering in a crowded pub or have Melissa and V probing over her sudden change in mood.

"Presuming she isn't also in love with you." Kat wore a warm smile as she tilted her head. "In the two hours I spent chatting with her this afternoon, I must have heard your name at least twenty times. I know she's had boyfriends before, we talked about her last relationship with that Jamie guy a bit, but it was months ago. You shouldn't assume."

Jess let out a huff, trying to stop her bottom lip from trembling. "I've never heard of a Jamie. She's been seeing men, not thinking about me. It's fine, she doesn't owe me anything. I have no right to get jealous or upset."

Even so, the image of her cuddled up with someone else felt like a knife ripping through Jess's insides, and she rubbed her stomach as the nausea returned.

Kat pulled her into a tight, reassuring hug. "It's okay to feel upset about it, and if you ever need someone to talk with my shop door is always open."

"Thanks, I appreciate that." Jess rubbed her face, trying to snap out of this maudlin mood, and flagged down a bartender. "I guess we should get served and head back out in a sec, before anyone misses us."

She bought Kat a drink for the advice and pushed through the crowd again, still none the wiser about what to do but a little lighter for sharing the burden after so long.

They left V to her friends when the DJ started. Once she knew Lydia didn't hate her, embarrassed she'd ever thought otherwise, they'd seen little of her, anyway. Jess had resolved not to worry again this weekend, either. Her problems would wait for her until Monday, but she was only an hour from her birthday, and drunk. It wasn't a great time to plan how to move on with her life.

She bought chips and then slumped onto a bench, draping an arm around Melissa's shoulder as she handed her the tray. "You're cold."

Melissa shuffled over to get closer and shoved a chip in Jess's mouth. "Lucky I've got a human blanket then."

"Thanks for coming tonight. I hope it wasn't too boring."

"No, I'm glad we cheered up V. It's sweet how much you care about her. I've said it before but giving up an evening alone with me is a tremendous sacrifice."

Jess took another chip and smothered it in ketchup. "Nothing wrong with your ego." She held it out, and Melissa sucked the salt from her fingers. "But as I recall, you were the one who was so desperate to spend the evening with me you came to the pub."

"What can I say? I'm a loyal friend. Most Labradors are." She shrugged, then turned to lick Jess's shoulder.

"Um, excuse me?"

Melissa laughed, motioning towards the supermarket with her head. "Want a lift home? It's too chilly to sit here."

Jess rolled off the bench, grabbing the plastic tub containing the remaining crumbs of her cake. "Sure."

They wandered through the alley eating chips, dodging any jeering drunks as they left the pubs early, and Jess lobbed the tray in a bin before getting into the car. It was dark inside, besides the glare of the orange street lamps, and fragrant with vanilla. Everything Melissa owned always smelled the same, and it turned a common scent into something intoxicating.

Jess took a deep breath as she fastened her seatbelt, switching the stereo off when the engine started and an audiobook resumed. "How do you get everything to smell of vanilla?"

"What do you mean?"

"Your room, car, hair, clothes. It all smells like vanilla. Even when you've eaten chips covered in vinegar, nothing gets rid of it."

Melissa pulled out of the bay and crawled towards the exit, flicking on her lights. "Is that a problem?"

"No." Jess shuffled, trying to work out the source. "I like it. Now vanilla reminds me of you."

"And how does that make you feel?"

Jess paused for a few moments, running through aroused, warm, and excited, before settling on an answer. "Happy. Safe. Somewhat concerned trouble will follow. When I get into bed tonight and it smells of you, I'm likely to panic for a minute."

After talking to Kat, panic would be the least of it. She was a terrible drunk which was why she avoided alcohol most of the time. If she didn't end up sobbing into the duvet, it'd be a miracle.

Melissa laughed. "I'll tell you something weird now. When you stayed with me in Cardiff, I wouldn't wash your pillowcase until the next time you visited."

"Yeah, that's weird. Why?"

"Because I wanted you there." Melissa cleared her throat as they pulled onto the road. "When you didn't visit, I almost sent out a distress call for you to post me a fresh one."

Jess held a hand on Melissa's knee, rubbing a gentle circle with her thumb. "I'm sorry I let my concerns get in the way."

"Concerns?"

Jess let out a puff of air, trying to work out how to phrase this so Melissa understood, but didn't get the full story. "Wrong word, I guess. But, you know, sleeping in that tiny bed together. It's just, I'm gay, and you're... well, we're adults now. It's not like when we were kids and used to climb into bed together. That's all."

"No."

"It doesn't feel right. Or it's too right. Either way, you trust me, and I'd never want to abuse that."

"No."

This was going too far now. She was only getting monosyllabic answers, which was better than Melissa calling her a disgusting pervert, but still not great.

"I didn't want to risk damaging our friendship, but I should have explained so we could work something out. Could have solved it all with an air mattress, I'm sorry."

Melissa squeezed Jess's shoulder, her eyes still on the road. "Yep, that'd solve the entire thing." She returned her hand to the wheel as they pulled into the drive. "Except I'd still need you to leave your pillowcase."

"Right." Jess unclipped her seatbelt. "I can send you those. Less risky." She leant across and kissed Melissa's cheek, lingering for a beat longer than she ought, and then popped the door. "Suppose I should get to bed. Big day tomorrow."

"Yeah," Melissa whispered. "Another year older and still none the wiser."

9

Jess rolled over, slapping at her phone. "You little shit," she murmured, seeing the seven o'clock wake up scheduled with a happy birthday message. There was only one person who'd be responsible. She threw back the covers with a laugh and trudged down the stairs.

"Happy birthday," V called from the kitchen table, scraping around a yoghurt pot. "Sleep well?"

"Oh yeah, terrific. Shame it didn't last a little longer." Jess rubbed her eyes, padding across the tiles. "How come you're conscious so early? Thought you'd still be out cold."

"Are you kidding? This is a lie in. If Grace was here, I'd have been awake for at least an hour."

Jess filled the kettle and clicked it on, pulling two mugs from the cupboard and dropping in tea bags. "It's weird without her. I keep waiting for something sticky to touch my leg."

"I know. Got dressed in thirty seconds and sat on the bed wondering what to do with myself. I've spent a good ten minutes eating this yoghurt."

"You miss her like crazy though, right?"

She wasn't the only one. Jess seldom had a drink, and three pints were enough to leave her weeping into the duvet last night. A cuddle from Grace would have been a nice comfort.

"Yep." V dropped her pot onto the table and the spoon clanged over the surface. "See look, I'm even having to make a mess, so I can pretend she's here." She got up and grabbed a cloth, wiping the splatters of yoghurt, and then pulled a stack of cards from a drawer. "I've been saving your post all week. Found another card on the mat this morning, but no idea where it came from. Didn't have a stamp."

Jess took the pile and rifled through the coloured envelopes. "All this time I thought people had forgotten my birthday. I was getting worried."

"No, it was a conspiracy to stop you opening them." V snatched them away again. "And you can't have them until we get to Rachel's later. We had lunch in the week, and she made me promise."

Jess was too hungover to argue. Her mouth tasted like a sewer, and there was a salty layer of dried sweat covering her entire body. She finished their drinks, sprinkling hers with sugar, and passed a mug to V.

"You had lunch? Wow, bet you loved that."

"Mm, I did. She took us for Italian, it was delicious." V smiled as she blew over the top of her tea. "She was telling me about her sister in Bournemouth. The headmistress."

"Penny? Don't mention it in front of Melissa, she hates her aunt. It's an entire thing." Jess made a circular motion with her arms. "What did she say?"

"Penny's agreed to chat with me at the wedding, talk through other routes into teaching besides going back to university."

She was an old battle-axe, but Jess was all for it if she

could help. "That's great. They say it's who you know and not what you know. Rachel's a useful person to keep in with. I told you that life would turn around."

"Your positivity has worn off on me. I've decided I need to sort my shit out after my conversation with Melissa on Friday night. I'm making a plan."

That was nice, because Jess only wanted to vomit after her own conversation with Melissa. She still couldn't remember what she'd said in the car last night but was sure it had been a bumbling incoherent mess.

"I take it your plan doesn't involve Lydia in any way. Did you speak to her last night?"

V grimaced. "Yeah, it seems Melissa told her I was shy but would like to be her friend. I guess that's true, and it did the trick. She asked if I'd reconsider going out with her, but I'm not interested. Besides anything else, I need to sort the rest of my life before I get into another relationship."

Not to mention that Lydia wasn't at all V's cup of tea. She fancied people with more edge, and Lydia had the charisma of a blancmange.

Jess pulled out a chair and sat. "You can help me, though. I need to take charge of my love life."

"I still think it's a shame Kat has a boyfriend. She's your type. Geeky, feminine, smart..." V mused, staring at the ceiling. "We need to find you someone like her. Have you tried a dating app?"

"No, but I'm open to all suggestions."

Even taking a vow of celibacy and moving into a convent sounded appealing. It had to be an improvement on the alternative.

"Does this mean there's no chance with the girl you've been texting?"

"No, and I need to get over it." Jess huffed, banging her

mug on the table and slopping tea everywhere. "I'm taking a stand. There's no point making myself miserable forever."

"Okay, easy tiger. There's a woman for you, our job is to find her."

"Yes, but before we do, I need more sleep and a shower. Be ready to leave at noon." Jess got up and stopped in the doorway. "I'm glad you're happier."

She meant it. This wasn't the glimmer of a good mood she'd seen now and then over the past couple of weeks. V was more her determined self.

"Yeah, me too."

* * *

Jess slept for another couple of hours and woke up almost hangover free but starving, so it was a good job lunch was imminent. She took a quick shower then ushered V through the door, deciding neither of them should drive, and hoping this way they could both sweat out the alcohol in their systems.

"Happy birthday, my darling," Rachel called through a haze of steam, kicking the oven door shut as they let themselves into the kitchen. She discarded her apron on the breakfast bar and pulled each of them into a hug, then straightened out her dress. "Would you see what's wrong with my daughter while V helps me set the table?"

Jess pointed at herself. "What me?"

"Yes you. She's had a face like a wet weekend all morning and I'm damned if I can find out why. Don't take too long though, I'm getting ready to serve."

Jess shrugged and wandered out to the patio. Melissa sat on a deckchair at the end of the lawn with a book, chewing on her nail, and Jess's stomach churned with more than hunger. She thought they'd resolved their issue with her not visiting, even if the details were foggy.

"Are you okay?"

"Yeah," Melissa mumbled, turning the page.

"Sure? You don't seem it."

"Tired. Is lunch ready?"

"Think so." Jess glanced to the patio where V was setting out cutlery. "Are you coming to eat? Looks like your mum's cooked one of her feasts."

Melissa closed the book and managed a smile. "Suppose I should. Good birthday so far?"

"Uneventful. We walked here, got a sneaky ice cream. Don't tell Grace, I'll never hear the end of it."

Melissa laughed as they ambled to the table. "Of course you did."

Jess smiled to see her mood improve and pulled out a chair as Rachel served a full roast beef extravaganza. V was appreciative, reasoning she was still drunk earlier in the morning and now had a crippling hangover. As they finished their meal, she was perking up, getting through pints of water faster than anyone else sipped their wine.

Rachel stood with her hands on her hips while Paul cleared the plates. "Cards or cake first?"

Jess smiled, desperate to get her hands on the pile of envelopes after having them taken away earlier. "Cards please."

Rachel wandered to the kitchen, returning with a parcel wrapped in blue paper and the embargoed post. "Now this gift was Melissa's idea, but I've kept the receipt."

Jess tore it open to reveal three new short-sleeved shirts. She held them up and grinned across the table. "You did this?"

Melissa shrugged. "Thought you should get a jump on

those policy changes."

"I love them, thank you." Jess bundled them back into the packaging and set them aside, dragging the card pile across the table. "Allowed to open these now, am I?"

"What do you mean?"

"V's been intercepting my cards all week, so I have to open them here. Haven't read a single one yet. Well, besides the puppy you gave me on Friday."

Rachel looked at Melissa in horror. "You gave her a what?"

"I sponsored a guide dog puppy, don't panic. I know you hate animals." Melissa turned pale again. "Sorry, I'll be back in a minute." She scraped her chair back, rubbing her abdomen. "Not feeling great, I need some tablets from my room."

"Are you okay?" Jess squinted up at her as she ran a finger along the seal of her dad's card. "Do you need me to fetch you anything?"

"No, it's fine, carry on."

Jess returned to her card, relieved Melissa's mood was only because of period pains, and pulled a cheque from the middle. "Holy shit, has Dad lost his mind?"

Every year he gave her a twenty and a scratch card, but there was a cheque for two hundred quid and a note to put it towards a holiday. There were also cards from most of Paul and Rachel's extended family, her uncle in Australia, and a handful of friends.

A faint waft of vanilla hit her nostrils as she picked up the final envelope. Jess pulled out the card, sending glitter shimmering across her lap, but she frowned when she saw the front was a heart with a mushy Valentine's greeting, not a happy birthday. As she opened it, the colour drained from her face. Written in thick black marker was the message:

For the birthdays when you should have been my Valentine. It's time to take a risk.

She shut the card, the absent blood flooding her head and throbbing over her temples.

V leant over the table, trying to sneak a look. "Who sent you that?"

"Tell you later, I just need to pop to the toilet."

She pushed back her chair, not sure where she was going. It had to be from Melissa, and now she'd disappeared. By the time Jess reached the kitchen, her mouth was dry, and her stomach was in knots trying to recall what they'd said to each other the previous evening. They must have discussed more than she remembered.

She stopped on the landing, tapping Melissa's bedroom door with the pads of her fingers before pushing it open. "Are you okay?"

Melissa was reordering books and laughing to herself. "Oh yeah." She drew a deep breath and then sighed. "I just thought you'd read my card this morning and ignored it."

"You think I could have?"

"I don't know. It was a risk." Melissa wiped the tears from her face, still spluttering with laughter. "Bigger than that. There's a risk and then there's a kamikaze death mission."

Jess turned the card in her hand, sending more glitter into the carpet pile, and set it on the bed. "That serious, huh?"

"For me it is. I'm in way over my head. The plane has crashed into the sea and I'm about to drown."

She wasn't the only one. Everything was normal five minutes ago, but now Jess struggled to feel her extremities. She flexed her fingers to return the blood.

"This has taken a violent turn. How do I rescue you?"

Melissa straightened out her face, but she hadn't yet made eye contact, her gaze now fixed on her nails as she rapped them together. "By being honest."

She perched on the edge of the bed, and Jess wanted to scoop her into a hug. The black circles around her eyes showed she hadn't slept, and there was nothing much left of her nail polish.

Jess nodded, hitching her knee up as she sat. Where to start was the problem. Her brain needed a few seconds to catch up with everything. After so long trying to keep them in, it was counterintuitive to spill her feelings.

"I'm also in the sea, struggling to keep my head above water most days," she started, still not sure where she was going with this. "I don't even know how better to describe it. You did a good job."

"Thanks." Melissa took an arm and pulled it around herself. She leant her head against Jess's shoulder and removed grains of glitter from her T-shirt, flicking them onto the floor. "What do you want to do about it?"

"Not sure that's up to me, you hold all the power. I've had a massive stamp on my butt saying property of MJ for some time."

Melissa peered up with a worried expression. "Hate to tell you, but Michael Jackson is dead."

"Is he? Damn."

They fell backwards with laughter and Melissa rolled over to prop herself on an elbow, rubbing a thumb over Jess's bottom lip. "Last night I was trying to work out if you'd look at me different when you realised how much time I spend thinking about kissing you."

"How do I look at you now?"

"Like I've caught you with your hand in the sweet jar. How you ever thought I didn't know is beyond me. Do you realise how much you blush? I'm almost embarrassed for you."

With that, Jess could sense the heat rise through her chest and tried to cool it. She wasn't sure if it was embarrassment or something else, but it was no good, and Melissa poked her face as it scorched.

"Great." Jess pulled the neck of her T-shirt up over her chin, but it got stuck and wouldn't go any further. "Anything else you want to add, or are you done teasing me now?"

"It's cute." Melissa pinged the fabric away. "And yes, I'm done now." She dipped her head to dab a kiss on Jess's nose and then rubbed it with her own. "Is this okay?"

It was anything but okay. Jess's head swam more than with the three pints she'd downed last night. She drowned in the vanilla scent, the soft hair brushing her face, the breath warm on her mouth. For a second she was sure her heart stopped beating, but then it sent out a surge of adrenaline that tingled into her hands.

"If you're sure it's what you want," she whispered.

"Mhm, I'm sure."

Melissa grazed their lips together, and Jess parted hers. When they met again, the kiss was harder, and the force of it took her by surprise. She gripped and twisted the bedsheet, but by the time Melissa was on top of her she'd regained some control and could respond. A hand landed either side of her head and she reached a palm under Melissa's T-shirt as she gripped her waist, the other on the nape of her neck.

It was enthralling, the weight of her, the gentle undulation of her hips as she rocked back and forward in a deep kiss. When a hand slid down her chest and contacted a nipple she groaned, and knew they were moving too fast, but had lost any willpower to stop. They'd sunk together as if kissing each other was a well-practised art, not a first-time fumble, and she didn't want the experience to end.

Jess moved the hand from Melissa's waist along her stomach until it met a smooth cotton bra cup. As her thumb pressed a firm circle, a moan parted their lips, and she felt the nipple harden under her touch.

Melissa sat up, pulling off her top and flinging it at the floor. "Hang on." She unhooked her bra and threw it in the same direction. "I need this gone."

Jess was only half aware of the door ajar behind them, and the people still waiting downstairs. She rolled over, flipping Melissa onto her back, and knelt between her legs. The freckles, and her fingers trailing over them, were enough to push away her questions for now. She ran her palm over a breast, watching as Melissa arched into the touch.

"We need to stop," Jess muttered, trying to show willing as she swirled her tongue over each nipple. "I only left to use the toilet, and this is moving too fast."

Melissa's hips bucked into her, and as she pulled back was a momentary lapse away from tugging off her own top. They couldn't get caught doing this over lunch, though.

"I don't want to stop," Melissa whispered, as Jess lowered herself and she gripped both legs around her middle.

"Yeah, I thought you seemed to get into it."

"Suppose I could quite enjoy kissing you once you've had a bit of practise."

"Is that right?" Jess brushed away a wedge of blonde hair and indulged in another kiss, quite happy to practise at any opportunity. Then she pulled her mouth away and glanced up, hoping there would be another. "You want to do this again, then? Or have you satisfied your curiosity?"

"It warrants further investigation, yes."

Melissa took Jess's face in both hands and guided her

back down, tugging on her bottom lip and then slipping her tongue inside. She tasted sweet from the grape juice she'd drunk with lunch as they explored in a deep, slow rhythm, and Jess felt her chest contract at the intimacy.

"We need to go downstairs," she mumbled again, her lips breaking contact with Melissa's for only a second. If they didn't stop soon, she knew they'd become lost to it. "Will you come over later once I've recovered from the shock, so we can talk about this?"

"Talk? I can think of better ways to spend the afternoon."

She wasn't the only one. This had been one of the most blissful and unexpected ten minutes of Jess's life, but she would have questions. Big ones.

"You don't think we need to discuss you sending me a cryptic card, taking your top off and kissing me like this?"

"What was cryptic about it?"

"Well, I get the gist is that you'd like to kiss me, but I'm not sure what you want now."

Melissa smiled, stroking her thumbs along Jess's jaw. "Oh. I want to keep on kissing you. Does that help until we speak later?"

There was no time to respond before they were kissing again, and it took Jess rolling off to break them apart. "We have to go downstairs now, before someone comes looking for us."

Melissa reached for her bra. "Fine. You need to tell V about this if I'm coming over, because I plan to kiss you again."

Jess laughed and reached into her pocket to pull out her phone. She had a text from V asking if she'd fallen in and tapped out a reply to say she'd been looking after Melissa, which was almost the truth. The rest of the conversation could wait until later.

10

Jess struggled to keep her grin in check as they walked home. She still felt like it was a dream, or she'd slipped into an alternative reality where all your fantasies came true. Either way, it was a special birthday treat the universe had thrown her way. Telling V was the only snag.

"So, about that card." She fiddled with the handle of her carrier bag full of cards and shirts. "Do you remember me telling you I liked someone, but I had no chance with them?" Jess waited for V to nod confirmation. "It turns out she has feelings for me. So that's good, I hope."

"Go you. That's quite a turnaround from where you were this morning. It was all doom and gloom."

V needed to keep hold of that thought. It was hard to know how she'd react, given they'd already talked about Melissa pushing her out. Everyone was on good terms at the moment but if more happened it would shift the dynamic.

"Yeah, well, there are a few complications. We're already friends, for a start."

"So? You're starting a few levels up. It's not as if she'll get any nasty surprises."

If they were talking levels, she was uncertain quite where her relationship with Melissa sat. Three million must be close.

"True. I'm wondering if it'll shock you, though. I hope it won't be a problem."

V stopped, her eyes narrowing as she grasped Jess's forearm. "Why? It's not someone from hockey, is it?"

"No. God, no. It's... Melissa."

V was quiet for a moment, inclining her head as she processed, and released her grip. "The same Melissa we had lunch with?"

"Yep. Don't know any others."

"Huh." V began walking again, her forehead creasing. "I am surprised but I'm unsure why. How did I miss this?"

Jess shrugged. "If it helps, I was in the dark. I've had feelings for her since... I'm not even sure. For ages."

"She is all over you. I mean, I'd always put that down to you growing up together. You have a close relationship that's always been more than friendship, but I didn't realise it was this."

"Me either, but she kissed me today, and it was conclusive."

"That good, huh?"

"Oh, yeah."

There was no doubting the spark between them could light up the national grid. It had blindsided her on all fronts, but felt normal, as if they did it every day. There was no awkwardness or hesitation. Not on Jess's side, anyway, although judging by the ease with which Melissa relieved herself of her bra she didn't appear to be quibbling, either.

"When you went to the toilet you were kissing her, with Rachel downstairs?" V slapped Jess on the back, so hard she coughed. "Bold move, I didn't think you had it in you."

"Yep," she spluttered in reply. "And you don't have a problem if something happens between us? That's the wrong word, but you know what I mean. I want to check it won't cause a massive issue."

V laughed. "Sounds like it's too late if I did, but no. First, I don't have to worry about my room because if Melissa wants to move in it'll be with you. And second, you're not bringing home a random woman who might not get along with Grace. This suits me fine."

"Well, I'm glad she ticks all your boxes."

This was way too easy. Something would go wrong, it always did. The woman of your dreams seemed unlikely to fall into your arms with no complications.

"My opinion doesn't matter so long as you're happy, although I'm unlikely to complain you're loved up after everything you've done for us, have a brain." V nudged her with a shoulder and diverted off the path, taking an alley to a shopping complex on the estate they were passing. "If you want this to work, though, you need to buy more of her favourite biscuits because someone scoffed them when they came in drunk last night and it wasn't me."

That explained the empty wrapper wedged in Jess's jeans pocket when she got dressed this morning. They walked across the car park and into the shop, making a beeline for the biscuit section, but there weren't any hobnobs, so Jess picked up digestives instead.

"I'm sure Melissa won't mind."

V grabbed the packet and chucked it back on the shelf. "You have so much to learn. You're going to town, and I'll meet you at home."

"What? You want me to walk to town for biscuits?"

"I do. Trust me, you need to put in some effort. I hope

you've got a proper date planned and aren't inviting her over to play those stupid video games."

Now they were in uncharted territory. There hadn't been time to consider anything past the kiss, the promise of more, and making sure V knew before Melissa delivered them. Jess figured they'd talk it through when she came over later.

"Will she want that?"

V's eyes widened. "Are you joking?"

"Okay, point taken."

And with that Jess trudged off toward town, wracking her brain for a date idea that might appeal to Melissa. This was where never discussing their relationships had a major downside, because she had no clue what was romantic in her world. Well, besides driving around the countryside in a convertible stopping for beach picnics. David had already cornered the market in that activity, though. This required more originality.

Jess made it to the High Street with only twenty minutes to spare before the shops shut and waved to Kat in the bookstore window. She was putting out a fresh display, and inspiration struck.

Jess diverted, hearing the familiar ding of the bell as she stepped through the door. There were no customers, and Kat had music blaring from the stereo. She was singing away and chugging a can of cola as Jess danced over to her.

"You're in an excellent mood." Kat bumped their hips together. "Wondered if I'd made a mistake bringing up Melissa last night. I planned to check in tomorrow, but it looks like I worried too soon."

Jess opened her carrier bag and held up the Valentine's or birthday card, whichever way you viewed it. "She may have kissed me."

And the rest. There was a limit to her indiscretion,

though. Besides which, she wouldn't allow her mind to dwell on the image of Melissa's naked breasts or the satisfaction she'd felt turning her on so much. They needed to talk before anything like that happened again, otherwise Jess feared she was being set up for more misery.

"I guessed she might." Kat heaved a box of books onto her step ladder.

Jess dropped her bag and made a stilted move to help but was too late. "Why?"

"It's possible I knew more than I was letting on and I may have confirmed to her that without a nudge you were unlikely to make a move." She tore open the box and pulled out a hardback, hugging it to her chest. "But I only meddled because she'd spent the vast majority of our coffee date wondering why you hadn't kissed her yet and asking me for advice. I'm sorry if I overstepped the mark."

"Best meddling ever." Jess was unable to feel anything but overwhelming gratitude. It may have spilled into a hug if Kat wasn't already enjoying one with her book. "Want to do more?"

Kat pursed her lips. "What did you have in mind?"

"V's got it into her head I need a big romantic date gesture and I've figured out what Melissa loves more than me. The answer is books, and your shop." Jess leant against a bookcase, rubbing her hand over the top. She was going for coy but had most likely landed on creepy. "How would you feel about letting me bring her here after hours?"

She still wasn't sure what a date in a book shop might entail, but the plan was half-formed, and it was a start. Melissa's favourite pizza was a good shout, if Kat let them bring in takeaway. The rest would work itself out.

"I reckon we could come to an arrangement, so long as

clothes stay on at all times. Sure I owe her one for the help she's giving me, anyway."

Jess smiled as she inched back towards the door, running out of time. "You're an absolute legend, and fast becoming one of my favourite people."

* * *

When Jess returned from town, Melissa sat in her usual spot on the kitchen work surface cradling a mug. She never seemed comfortable using a chair. V was at the table, and they were laughing over something, but it stopped the minute she walked into the room.

"Why do I get the impression you were talking about me?" Jess glanced from one to the other as Melissa's face flushed a delicate pink.

"Because we were." V stretched her legs onto the opposite chair and blew over her tea. "Comparing notes."

"Fuck off, no you weren't."

V laughed. "No, we weren't, don't worry."

Jess dropped her bag by the draining board and pulled out the biscuits, waving them in Melissa's face. She'd made it to the supermarket with only two minutes to spare, where the cashier had glared and tapped her foot because she wanted to go home.

"For me?" Melissa set her mug down next to the hob and seized them. "You shouldn't have."

Jess lingered, noticing the eyes trained on her lips and wondering if it was appropriate to say hello with a kiss now. Before she had time to think for too long, a tug on her T-shirt dragged her closer.

"V reckoned I needed to replace them. I demolished the other packet when I got home last night in a state of misery."

She planted a hand on either side of Melissa and leant in until she could feel the warm breath on her mouth again.

Melissa smiled "Why were you miserable?"

"Because I'd decided I needed to get over you and it made me sad." Jess pouted, and Melissa kissed her bottom lip. "Now I'm happy and we have biscuits again."

"Jesus, is this what I've got to endure now?" V called. "I know you said she was a good kisser, but I didn't need a live show to prove it." She lobbed something at Jess's back, but she had become too engrossed to care. "And I hope you clean that worktop when you're finished."

Jess turned around and tried to crank her smile down a few notches. If it stayed like this, she'd get a headache. "Excuse me. I don't go sharing your secrets."

"How is that a secret?" V scraped her chair back. "I'll be in my room in the unlikely event either of you want me, but don't forget Grace is being dropped off in half an hour so make sure you've got clothes on."

She was the second person to comment that in under an hour, and the realisation clothes might come off triggered a chemical reaction in Jess's stomach. It felt like someone had emptied a bag of popping candy in there, and it wasn't only excitement. No longer was this theoretical, or even slow moving.

"She took it okay, then?" Melissa brushed away the hair from Jess's shoulder and lay a shiver inducing kiss at the base of her earlobe.

"Oh, yeah." Jess cleared her throat, finding it thick and raspy. "Seems to have cheered her up, being able to tease me. Glad I can be of service."

It was almost a shame. At least if she hated the idea, she might be more bearable. All indications pointed to her milking their relationship for entertainment value.

Jess turned again and rest her hands on Melissa's quads. "This has been the best birthday present in the history of gift giving, but I need to ask some questions."

Melissa laughed, leaning forward and bringing their foreheads together. "Thought you might. We didn't get far earlier. Well, not with that." She dipped her mouth for another kiss. "Sorry. Last time, I promise."

Jess took a firm hold of Melissa's waist and slipped her forward, hoisting her from the work surface and striding through to the living room. They fell onto the sofa, and Jess found herself placed on top again, gripped between her legs.

"This is unfortunate." She moved her hands to rest either side of Melissa's head. "We seem to have ended up in the same position as earlier."

"Doesn't seem very unfortunate," Melissa whispered. "Now what are you planning to do with me?"

There was a loud knock on the living room door. When Jess lifted her head from the soft area of skin she'd found above Melissa's collarbone, she saw V was smiling at her.

"This doesn't look like talking. Do I need to strap you into separate chairs? Don't think I won't." V breezed past them on her way to the kitchen. "I forgot my drink. When I come back, you shouldn't be touching."

"I can see why she wants to be a teacher," Melissa murmured.

Jess climbed off and straightened her T-shirt. "I don't know, the fun police might be more suitable." She slumped onto the other sofa and put her feet up on the cushion. "She's right, though. I need to know what's happening here, and I can't keep allowing your damn freckles to side-track me."

There was an uncharacteristic lack of restraint today, but doubt stalked somewhere at the back of her mind. Straight friends didn't decide they fancied you after twenty-three years. No genies had offered to grant wishes, and she had yet to find a direct dial to any angels.

V came past with her mug in hand and gave them a satisfied nod before heading back upstairs, and Melissa waited until they heard the door slam before she continued. "I need you to know, too, because I get this seems sudden to you, but it isn't for me. I've spent nine months making sure it's what I want."

"Nine months?" Jess exclaimed, the thought propelling her bolt upright. "And you didn't consider filling me in a little sooner?"

It would have saved a lot of heartache. Not to mention the guilt, which had put her one dodgy curry away from a stomach ulcer.

Melissa sat up and swung her legs around, clutching her face as they hit the floor. "I'm sorry, but I wasn't sure at first. I didn't even realise until someone else pointed it out. Do you remember the guy who started working in the pub near Nan and Pops? You met him when you came to help me move into my new house."

There was a vague recollection. He came from North Wales somewhere, and everyone had been joking with him about it. Alice, Melissa's nan, had taken it upon herself to help him settle in by introducing a few of the locals.

"What's he got to do with this?"

"We went out a few times. It was only casual, not much happened, but it still surprised me when he told me we couldn't see each other anymore. When I pushed him, he said it was because I had feelings for someone else." Melissa paused, chewing on her thumbnail. "You."

Was this the guy Kat mentioned last night? Julian or Jamie. Something like that.

"Caught you sniffing pillowcases, did he?" Jess padded across the floor and sat next to Melissa, regretting her minor outburst even if it had felt justified thirty seconds ago. "I take it this was a surprise to you?"

"You think? I've never had feelings like this for another woman before. Besides which, you're also the person I trust more than anyone else in the world."

"Yeah, that's what you are to me."

"Then you know why this is a big deal. I decided within a short space of time that I didn't have an issue with the sexuality part. I'm open to it, and with hindsight there have been other clues. You, though, are another matter." Melissa sank sideways, burying her face in Jess's shoulder. "When I realised that he was right, it was like falling in the sea and finding you're already thirty feet under before you've had a chance to react. I couldn't stop thinking about you."

Jess pulled her back into a hug, stroking the hair from her face. "Why didn't you tell me? We could have worked through it together."

Melissa was quiet for a few moments, and then she let out a lengthy sigh. "I considered it, but it scared me we'd end up in something I wasn't ready for. I didn't want to hurt you or blow our friendship to smithereens."

"But you're ready now?"

"I've been ready for a while, but telling you was tough. Didn't help that V moved in, and I faltered, wondering if I'd missed my chance and you'd moved on. Or back, I guess."

It made more sense of why she'd checked nothing was happening with V. They'd discussed it dozens of times since Christmas, though. Jess had always been adamant they were only friends. It was rare for Melissa not to trust what she said, but she tried to keep from being too hung up on the idea. She could understand the concern with moving in an ex-girlfriend.

"I guess I was trying to move on, but not with V, and it didn't work."

"Yeah, I know. Don't worry, I'm not still worrying about that. When I saw you at your dad's barbecue, I knew within thirty seconds that nothing had changed for either of us. It's also become very clear V doesn't want you, I hope you're not too disappointed."

It had been one hell of a greeting, and Jess laughed with the memory of it. How desperate she'd been not to let Rachel see her feelings pouring out when Melissa flung herself across the garden. It was enough for Jess to ignore her last comment.

"Have my feelings ever bothered you? I always worried…"

"No. I realised a long time ago, and I could see how uncomfortable it made you. I thought acting normal and showing I trusted you wouldn't overstep was the right move, but I'm sorry if it made things harder for you. It wasn't my intention; I was trying to make it easier."

It was hard to know what would have made it easier. A big awkward conversation before she'd dealt with her own feelings, or even realised them, would have been excruciating.

"Yeah, well. I could have told you too, but I guess we had the same concerns."

"It was also fine while I was a hundred miles away, or at least easier. We couldn't keep doing this forever now I'm home. I realised last night someone needed to break us out of this loop, but I still didn't know quite what to say. Hence the card."

Jess shrugged, not caring how they got here. She could

understand why Melissa didn't want to say anything, because it was a big risk if she'd got it wrong, but right now her main concern was the future.

"Is there anything else you need to tell me, or can we talk about what'll happen next?"

"No, but there are two things I have to ask, because they're on my mind." Melissa pulled her hair into a ponytail with the band around her wrist before taking Jess's hands and holding them in her lap. "Do you think it'll be a problem I've never had a relationship with another woman? I mean, I'd never even kissed one until this afternoon."

"What type of problem?"

"You know, always wondering whether I'm experimenting, or won't enjoy sex with you as much as a man, and all that crap. Because I've put a lot of thought into this, and I don't want to keep justifying myself."

Jess blinked, trying to fathom her question. "Um, no. I'm not interested in how you label yourself, or your previous experiences. I travel on gut instinct, and it's telling me you've meant every word and action today."

"Good, because I have. Kissing you left no doubts, believe me."

"Oh, I do. I was there, remember?" Jess nudged forward, pinching the fabric of Melissa's T-shirt and drawing their mouths an inch apart. But as she parted her lips, Jess diverted to her ear and whispered close against it. "Aren't you going to ask how I know I'll enjoy it?"

It seemed like a fair question because it was a risk for them both. Being gay didn't guarantee sexual compatibility with every woman on the planet.

"I suppose you think that's clever." Melissa tugged on Jess's earlobe with her teeth, then ran her tongue over it. "Let's agree we're both having a lot of fun today." She raked her fingertips up Jess's neck this time, tousling the hair at the base of her neck. "And we can have more once I've asked question two."

Jess had lost interest in whatever else Melissa needed to ask, her mind's sole focus the effect of every touch they shared. It was no surprise they were playful because every interaction was. The ease with which she found and exploited sensitive spots, though, was alarming.

"Fine, you go on while I sit here and melt." She rested her chin on Melissa's shoulder and closed her eyes.

"I'm warning you, this one is less pleasant. I'm worried how you'll cope telling Mum about us. You haven't got an impressive track record with pissing her off, and I'm not sure how accepting she'll be."

Jess grunted, knowing it was coming and trying not to let the thought of Rachel's wrath kill her buzz. "Yeah, it always terrified me she might find out. It's different if it's reciprocal, though. Isn't it? I mean, she can only object for so long if we're happy."

"Oh yeah, like she's only been digging at me over work since I turned eighteen." Melissa let her hand drop to Jess's shoulder and pushed her up, so they were facing again. "I'm not suggesting we tell anyone straightaway, least of all her, but I need to know you won't bolt. It worries me more than anything else."

"I won't. I'm all in with this, I promise. You can trust me, and I'll do anything to prove it."

That included walking on burning hot coals, or diving with sharks. They hadn't come this far to give up now.

Melissa nodded. "Good, because I want you to take a few days to consider this and make sure nothing changes. Can you do that for me?"

"If it means we can be together, then yes. I planned a date for Thursday, so how about I take until then?"

Melissa smiled and placed a light kiss on Jess's lips. "Thank you for understanding. It'll be tough staying away for four days, but that's a great idea."

Jess hadn't meant for them to be apart during that time but couldn't take it back. Besides, Melissa was right. It sounded like she'd had months to work through this, but Jess had never considered what might happen in the event they were ever together. It was worth four days apart for the reward at the end, and in the meantime, there was a date to finish planning.

11

The passage of time ground to a halt, as if whatever magic forced the weekends to speed up, was acting in reverse. Even when Melissa showed up on Wednesday evening to help V create a website for her new tutoring business, they didn't buckle, and it was excruciating. Jess responded by dedicating herself to tidying the house and within forty-eight hours every surface gleamed and was free from sticky little paw prints for the first time in months.

When Thursday evening laboured into view, she bubbled with anticipation and hoped it was mutual. This was the longest they'd gone without each other, Jess realised, in more years than she could count. Even when they were apart, they'd text every day, or speak on the phone. Four days of communicating only in a work context provided a glimpse of what might happen if they fucked this up, and it made her more determined to get things right.

She lingered after everyone went home, knowing Melissa needed to drop keys back at the office after her last appointment. They'd passed each other at lunchtime and made plans for the evening, but since then her diary had been full. Jess wanted to clear something up before their date, so they could enjoy it uninterrupted, although she'd given up and was packing away when Melissa pushed through the door.

She collapsed into her chair and put her feet on the desk. "Don't you think you should leave?"

"Nah, not in any rush. No special plans tonight."

"Huh, that's interesting. Could've sworn you mentioned a hot date."

Jess pulled the phone from her desk drawer and held up the countdown timer app. "Shit, I'd forgotten about that. Guess I should go home and make myself look irresistible, then. I hope this woman isn't a total nightmare."

"With your track record, she might be."

Melissa laughed and threw the keys into the air, fumbling as she caught them. She hadn't improved since the rugby ball incident.

"Don't you want to know my decision?" Jess swivelled to track her as she walked past to put them away. "Or have you already determined it's a foregone conclusion?"

"Yeah, pretty much. I said I wanted you to spend a few days getting used to the idea, I never expected you to change your mind." There was a rattle and a clatter from the back office, then Melissa shut the door and perched herself on Jess's knee. "Not even a wobble?"

"No, sorry to disappoint you. I considered it, as requested, but concluded I'd take a chance on Rachel hiring out a hit on me."

"Don't worry, she does her own work," Melissa whispered, her breath tickling Jess's ear. She sucked on the lobe, sending pulses of arousal in all directions. "We're on date night now, right? Because I've missed you this week. Spent most of it cursing myself for not dragging you to bed instead. Book club and dinner with Kat were poor consolations, but I can tell you I thought about it. A lot."

She wasn't the only one. After months of trying not to fantasise too much, Jess's mind had entered overdrive. There wasn't a single morning she hadn't woken covered in sweat, desperate for release. She'd gone through so many pairs of pyjamas it'd become necessary to sleep naked.

"Weird. I haven't." She traced a finger around Melissa's bare knee. "In fact, I'm not sure we should ever sleep together."

"Liar, I've seen you checking me out. I considered a yellow cone to warn people your tongue was a tripping hazard."

Jess had found far better uses for her tongue now, nipping and licking the length of Melissa's neck. She explored every inch of skin before plying it on her mouth, lost again to the fingers raking through her hair. If she hadn't made plans with Kat, she may have stayed there, but after all the effort it seemed a shame to dip out.

"I hate to stop but I have this bloody date and I can't get out of it." She huffed and fell further into the chair. "Can we pick this up later?"

Melissa climbed off Jess's lap, grabbed her car keys, and paused in the doorway. "Sure. Call me if it doesn't work out with this tramp later and I'll show you a good time."

* * *

Jess made a quick detour via the bookstore to collect keys from Kat. She'd brought a table through from the back office, plus two of the fold out chairs she used for events and was busy pulling down the blinds. It was sweet how invested she'd become in the whole thing, even bringing a tablecloth from home and laying out napkins.

Once they'd checked everything was in place, Jess jogged to the car and whizzed home. She bounded up the stairs to find a pair of black skinny jeans and one of her birthday shirts laid on the bed.

V appeared behind her, a naked Grace in her arms, wearing a satisfied smile. "Thought I'd get a jump start. Couldn't let you dress yourself, that'd be suicide."

"Aren't those work shirts, though?"

"And who picked them?"

"Point made. Thanks, I owe you one." Jess began unbuttoning her current shirt with inept, fumbling fingers. "Bit nervous, but I don't know why."

"Let's see. You're about to go on a date with the woman you desire most in the world. Then there's the fact she's your oldest friend, you'll be her first time with a girl, and her mum is likely to kill you. Yep, I'd say that'll do it."

"Thanks for the pep talk."

Jess flung her shirt at the washing basket and pulled off her trousers. The shake in her hands was now a full-on tremble and sweat dripped down her back. She braced herself on the bannister, taking a slow, calming breath.

"Hey, don't panic." V's tone grew softer. "I was only teasing. Enjoy this and be honest if you're nervous. There's no rush to do anything, wasn't that Melissa's whole point on Sunday? She wants to take this slow from what you told me."

"She does. I didn't think I did, but now I'm reconsidering."

"I get it. Big deal for anyone, and you don't let many people in. The most open I ever see you is with Grace and

Melissa, and even so I'm not sure wanting her like this is comfortable. You'll sort it, though."

"Thanks. That was a better pep talk."

V disappeared into the bathroom and there was an almighty bang, followed by a giggling noise that righted Jess's mood. She smiled, pulling on her jeans and shirt, spraying some perfume, and running a brush through her hair. Then she stood in the doorway of the bathroom and tried not to get covered in water.

"What do you think?"

V turned to straighten out the collar. "Have to admit she's got taste. Not as great as mine, but this is a nice shirt. I can see why she picked it for you, shows off your tattoos."

Melissa had an undeniable preoccupation with them, and it now seemed she made the shirt selection with more than comfort in mind.

"Yeah, reckon she'll fancy me?"

"Hang on." V undid the top three buttons and then hefted Jess's breasts. "Yep. I've seen her looking at these, too. Might as well flaunt them."

"Has she?"

"Oh, please. You need to get used to the fact she is after way more than your intellect and sparkling conversation. I'm not saying there isn't a deep, boundless love in there too, but that girl is also having an affair with your tits and tattoos, for which I cannot blame her."

There wasn't time to linger on that thought because the front door crashed open. Jess peered over the bannister and Melissa smiled in the pink dress she'd worn the previous weekend, spinning around a few times so the skirt flared out.

"Thought you liked this outfit." She ran up the stairs and

planted a kiss on Jess's lips. "I intercepted the other woman outside and told her she could go. Hope that's okay."

"You look gorgeous. Fuck me, have you even brushed your hair?" Jess smoothed back the loose strands falling across Melissa's eyes with no concern for what she'd just said. "This must be a special occasion because you didn't even do that for your graduation."

"Haven't scrubbed up so bad yourself. The shirt is a particular win."

She ran a hand over the collar and trailed it into Jess's cleavage, as V appeared in the doorway. The satisfied smirk was unmistakable, and Jess smiled back, wondering how long this fascination had gone unnoticed.

They both waved Grace goodbye, then Jess grabbed Kat's keys and Melissa shoved her out of the door with excitement. "Where are we going?"

Jess laced their fingers together and gave a brief squeeze. "It's a surprise, I already told you that. Please don't badger me like lunchtime, I've come this far and don't want to crack."

"Hate to tell you, but nothing in town is a surprise. If you've made a fuss over a date in the pub, we need a discussion about expectation setting."

"Pipe down for ten minutes and you'll find out."

Melissa grumbled and huffed, but did as instructed, which made a change. As they reached the High Street Jess almost walked into The Crown for a joke but decided against it. There was a pizza delivery arriving in five minutes, and she didn't want to be late. For a start, all the nerves had given her an appetite.

When they ended up in front of the bookstore Melissa's expression turned quizzical as she studied a poster in the window. "What are we doing here? I'm attending an event tomorrow night, but there's nothing on today."

Jess held the door open for her. "Nothing public."

The blinds shut out most of the natural light, but there was a lamp on at the back and an unlit candle on the table, and Kat had also left a note that there was a surprise in the fridge. It was perfect, and as she shut the door, Jess felt a shot of satisfaction at how her plan had come together.

Melissa inched further into the room. "Did you do this?"

"With some help from a friend, yeah. What do you think?"

Before she could reply there was a knock from the guy who ran the Italian a few doors away. They didn't do delivery, only takeaway, but he had taken little persuading. She unlocked the door again and thanked him, setting the box down on the table and lighting the candle with a match.

"You got my favourite pizza, too? I'm not sure I can convey how cute you are right now. I can't even think of anything witty or disparaging to say."

"Hallelujah, I've done the unthinkable and shut you up." Jess pulled out a chair for Melissa to sit. "That's a relief, because I was fretting."

"Why? We could have done anything tonight."

"Fine, I'll take this pizza away, then."

Jess slid the box across the table, and Melissa snatched it back. "No, I didn't say I was unhappy." She lifted the lid and tore off a slice, grinning as she licked away a string of cheese. "My point was only that I don't want you to worry. I'm satisfied so long as we're spending time together, you don't need to impress me."

"What can I say? I'm a hopeless romantic. Our first date seemed worth the effort."

The second, third and fourth would happen with less

planning, but this was special. V was right on two counts. Already knowing each other meant there were no nasty surprises, but there might be some pleasant ones. There was also no rush and they could enjoy themselves. Once dinner was out of the way, that meant delving into whatever Kat had left in the fridge.

Jess wandered out to the tiny kitchen tacked on the back and crouched to open it. There was a chocolate gateau on the top shelf, with a post-it note warning against stains. She laughed and pulled out the box, carrying it through and setting it on the table.

"Tonight gets better and better." Melissa rubbed her hands together and dragged the cake closer, removing the packaging. "Spoon," she demanded, holding out her hand.

"Not so fast." Jess scraped her chair across until they were almost facing, their knees bunched up together, and dipped her finger into the smooth mousse. "You need to be patient." She licked it away and returned for more, holding her finger out this time.

Melissa smiled and then laved it clean, a hand grasping Jess's thigh. "I see your game." She ran her index and middle fingers across the top of the cake and then smeared them down Jess's chin, leaning forward to suck away the chocolate. "And it's one I'm happy to play, since we've found a way for you to relax."

"You're still on that, are you? I thought you'd accepted my shoulders are now gliding." Jess nudged them up and down to prove her point. "See, no crunching."

"For clarity, it isn't a onetime thing, and it wasn't only about your shoulders. I love when you're happy and smiling. Glimpsed it last Friday at your party, you were radiating some content vibes." Melissa wiped her fingers on a napkin and leant forward, stroking a hand across Jess's cheek. Then she lay a kiss on her lips which was so delicate it sent a tingle all the way down her spine. "I want more of that." She pinched a blob of gateau and jammed it into Jess's mouth. "And I want more of this."

Melissa began nibbling the chocolate crumbs and mousse smattered across Jess's lips. Jess pulled her closer, maintaining the kiss while running a trail of dessert from the base of her throat to the edge of her cleavage.

Then she hooked both hands around Melissa's back and ran a slow course with her tongue. "You're dirty, come here."

She felt the heart hammering hard against her mouth as she sucked a tender square of skin. It was a shame Kat had vetoed the removal of any clothes.

"I didn't realise I was, but I'm thinking that might be true." Melissa grasped the back of Jess's neck, guiding her head up so they were facing. "I'm a very innocent girl, you may need to go easy on me."

"Are you, though?"

Jess's smirk met with a far more concerned expression.

"Yes, I'm being serious," Melissa whispered. "I know I come across confident, and with some things I am, but my experiences are... limited. Robbie jokes about me being boring, but it's true. I spent university reading books, not eating chocolate off people in bookstores."

Jess laughed, kissing her nose. "If it helps, I've never done this either. Well, the shop part."

"And the other bit?"

Not for a long time, but with previous girlfriends. It was coming back, though, like an engine purring back into life following months on the ramps. Even her earlier anxieties were falling away, replaced with a confidence she hadn't felt in a long while.

"Well, yeah, but it doesn't matter. First time for everything. I thought you didn't want me worrying that you haven't been with a woman before. Or did I misunderstand?"

"This isn't about your gender. I'm telling you because we've never discussed this stuff. I've not been with many people; it's not how I've spent my time. Two boyfriends, run of the mill sexual encounters, and no casual hook-ups. You catch my drift?"

Even so, Jess wasn't desperate for further details. Her aversion to imagining Melissa with anyone else had only strengthened over the past week.

"Yeah, I understand. We won't do anything you're not comfortable with, though. It's not like I'll get out the sex penguin. Not for a while, at least."

Melissa narrowed her eyes as she leant forward. "Don't even joke, because I've seen your bedside drawer. It's a little intimidating."

"Thought you didn't look?" Jess laughed, but then her tone became more earnest. "Don't think about that. I promise when you're ready to do this it'll be you and me, and nothing will happen that you don't want." She cupped Melissa's cheeks, smiling as she kissed away a blob of mousse. "I love you."

"Yeah, I love you too."

12

After spending Friday night at an author signing, on Saturday they had the treat of twenty sweaty rugby players crammed into David's cottage for Robbie's stag do. Jess spent the afternoon baking brownies, with Grace's expert help, then Melissa picked her up so they could eat together before the party. They arrived at nine-thirty, and as the car pulled up on the verge, one of the neighbours was out watering his plants. He tutted and peered over the wall until Jess got out and offered him a square of brownie.

"It's weird, because I don't remember inviting my sister," Robbie called, as they reached the patio. "And yet, here she is."

He strode towards them, his shirt already beer-stained, almost inaudible over the rock music blaring out of David's stereo. The speakers pointed out of the living room window, but at least looked unharmed from a cursory glance.

"Yeah well, if you're using my dad's house you can lump it." Jess thrust the box of brownies at his stomach. "I invited her. In fact, I begged her."

Melissa was in the skirt and halter neck she'd worn for

dinner and looked so far out of place she might as well have worn a ball gown. Robbie's other guests sprawled out on the lawn, chugging from cans of lager, and the only thing louder than the music was the sound of back slaps and raucous laughter.

Stephen appeared, smoothing his T-shirt to reveal his abs. "Hey, Jess. You look nice."

"Hi Stephen, you look drunk already. Make sure your empties go in the recycling bin."

"I love it when you boss me around. How do I get more of that?"

"Given she's taken, I'd suggest you don't." Melissa's tone was thick with vitriol as she looked him up and down. "Besides the fact she's never shown the slightest bit of interest in you."

"What's up, jealous I fancy your mate and not you?"

"Gross. I just think you should have more respect than to make comments like that when she's gay, has always been gay, and has a girlfriend who wouldn't appreciate it."

"I can't give her a compliment?" Stephen gestured at Jess as if everyone needed a look to prove his point. "She's a very attractive woman."

Melissa crossed her arms but remained calm. "Not when it's unsolicited and unwanted, no."

"And you speak for her now, do you?"

"Yep."

Stephen turned to Jess again. "Who is this woman? Are we sure she's good enough for you? And why didn't you bring her instead of this buzz kill? I bet she's far more fun."

"I'm certain she's good enough for me, but thanks for the concern." Jess took hold of Melissa's hand and guided her towards the kitchen, hoping to have a far more interesting conversation once they were in private. "Girlfriend, huh?"

She checked there was no one inside before pulling Melissa closer, and they kissed for about as long as Jess dared before someone walked into the room. She didn't care much who saw them but becoming the entertainment for a bunch of lads held no appeal.

"That's what I am, isn't it?" Melissa hooked her hands behind Jess's neck and kissed her chin. "Or are you having second thoughts now Stephen's here?"

"No, but you've never called me that before. I like it. I also liked you standing up for me. It was hot. I'd show you how hot, if we weren't at risk of interruption and didn't need to tidy."

"Bugger that, come with me."

Melissa marched out of the kitchen and down the drive and Jess jogged behind, crossing the road and jumping over a stile into the field. It was darker still under the cover of the oak trees, and Melissa crunched over leaves and twigs until they were both squinting to see. She stopped in a clearing, fumbling for Jess's hand, but it was already busy creeping around her waist.

Jess drew her close again. "I'm sure you're only doing this to get out of cleaning."

Melissa's breath was warm in the chill night air, and raspy with exertion or excitement. Either way, it was enticing, and Jess grazed their mouths together.

"Yeah, I am. Is that a problem?"

Jess allowed her hand to wander up the back of Melissa's skirt, hoping that answered the question. Then she lifted her back towards a tree, kissing harder. Fingers curled into her hips, another hand caressing the tattoo on her thigh, and she placed her own palm between Melissa's head and the wood.

"If you want to stop at any point we will," Jess whispered against her ear.

All she got by response was a moan as Melissa's hand travelled up the inside of her T-shirt, and it took her by surprise. She was wondering if the brakes needed a tap for her own benefit, before she became aroused and wasn't able to do anything to relieve herself.

"I can't see them, but these are spectacular." Melissa took a handful, her thumb pressing a deep circle. "I need more of them. Soon."

"They'd like that, but right now you're turning me on way too much. Could you ease it back a touch?"

"Fine, but give me a second," Melissa whispered, one palm flat in the base of Jess's back and the other rubbing a firm line up and down over her nipple.

Jess thrummed with arousal, her hand creeping under Melissa's skirt again and tickling up the back of her leg. It was travelling higher, but then a twig snapped behind them.

"Did you hear that?"

There was a giggling noise, and Jess backed away. "Who's there?"

The light of a phone torch shone on them, Robbie and Stephen sniggering beyond the glare. They sat on an over-turned log about fifteen feet away in a haze of smoke.

"Alright, ladies? Want some?" Stephen took a drag of his spliff and then held it up, but then withdrew his hand. "Although, come to think of it you were having enough fun."

Melissa tried to straighten her dress and marched forward, swiping the phone away. "If you tell anyone about this, I'll make sure your fiancé knows you were smoking weed. Got it?"

Robbie spluttered with laughter, but then regained his

composure. "Calm down. I wouldn't say anything. Don't tell her."

"You can carry on now," Stephen teased, clutching his chest. "You know, to mend my broken heart."

Robbie clouted him over the back of the head. "Hey, that's my sister. Not cool." But then he grinned. "And look who she was out here trying to shag on the sly."

"Shut up, Robbie," Jess snapped. "We weren't shagging, just…" She didn't know where she was going with this.

He laughed. "You were what? Having a friendly chat with a lot of heavy breathing?"

"No, well, we were kissing, but that's it. Not that it's any of your business."

"Never said it was. You interrupted us, remember?"

He got up and shoved her on the shoulder as he walked away. Stephen trailed after him, still emitting puffs of laughter, and took the phone from Melissa as he passed. It plunged them back into darkness, and Jess groaned.

"We should talk to him about this. I know we weren't going to, but Robbie's a sympathetic guy, he'll be supportive." She grasped for Melissa's hand.

"Easy to say when he likes you."

"Yeah, well. An actual conversation would help with that."

Melissa slumped against her chest. "I know," she murmured. "But I was enjoying having you to myself, without my family giving their opinions. I get it was me worrying about you not wanting to tell Mum, but I'm not thrilled at the prospect either."

"It'll be fine with Robbie, he's the least of our problems. Come on, let's sort this out with him before Stephen makes a public broadcast."

* * *

They found Robbie opening a fresh beer in the kitchen. Jess ran through to the living room to turn down the stereo a few notches so they could hold a conversation without shouting, and she was about to launch into a fuller explanation of their relationship when he beat her to it.

"So, what is this thing with you and my sister?"

"Are you about to give me the talk?"

Jess was more amused than worried. If they couldn't even tell him, there was no chance with David or Rachel. Robbie had no reason to complain or object and might even prove a useful ally.

"Why, reckon it's more than a bit of fun? As hard as it is to believe you could have fun with her."

Jess took Melissa's hand, surprised she didn't have a retort for that jibe. "It's more than a bit of fun."

"Then we're having the talk." He wrapped an arm across Jess's shoulder. "I don't care who you are. If you hurt her, you'll have me to answer to." Then he walked around to the other side and stooped to peer at Melissa. "Same goes for you."

"We'll both bear that in mind."

Melissa rolled her eyes and excused herself to the toilet, while Jess pulled a beer from a bucket on the side. She hadn't intended to drink but might need alcohol for this conversation.

Robbie leant against the Aga to steady himself. "Are you telling Mum and Dad?"

"Not yet. How do you think they'll take it?"

"Well." He inclined his head, considering the question. "When I told Mum about Sam, she went ballistic. I don't like your chances."

"Yeah, but that's because she caught you two having sex on her new sofa."

"True. Don't make the same mistake."

There was no chance of that. Anywhere in their house was off limits for now. Unplanned kissing in the bedroom aside, there was no way they were doing anything like that until Rachel and Paul knew about their relationship.

"I have no intention. You know what she's like with Melissa."

"I do, but if they want her with anyone, I bet it'd be you."

"How do you figure that? You don't think Rachel's been planning a wedding like yours, to a man, for the past twenty-three years?"

If she'd thought David's barbecue packed, Robbie's wedding would be on another level. They must have invited every distant family member and close friend on both sides, and there were even more for the reception.

"Nah, she wouldn't care whether Melissa married a man or a woman I don't reckon. So long as she's happy."

"Yeah, right," Jess scoffed. "Like she only wants her to find a job she enjoys? And only wanted her to go to a school that didn't give her crippling panic attacks? I love your mum, but where Melissa's concerned, she has very set expectations."

"I guess," Robbie mused, peeling back the label on his bottle. "It's not only her, though. Sam's always said Mum doesn't think she's good enough for me."

She didn't. That was no secret.

"Point proven. You realise Melissa thinks you've always got it easy with Rachel?"

"Are you kidding?" Robbie choked on his drink and Jess thumped his back. He was a tank, and it was easy to overcompensate. "We've had so many arguments it's untrue. This wedding for a start. We wanted to go to Vegas."

"I didn't know that."

"She vetoed it. Part of me wishes we'd buggered off and done it, anyway."

"She would have killed you."

"I know, but she means well."

Robbie set his bottle on the work surface and squinted at the pictures on the wall. He kept a light-hearted resignation with Rachel, which his sister never seemed to achieve.

"Hey, do you want to come for dinner at my place in a few weeks?" Jess found herself struck by the idea. If Melissa knew Robbie had also struggled, it might help.

"Oh, very cosy. I'm not sure my sister has the social skills for holding fancy dinner parties. Or the table manners. Have you run this by her?"

"No, why?"

"Because we're not what you'd call close. She's only ever happy when you're around. The rest of the time I don't think she can stand the sight of us."

Jess gave a dismissive wave. "That's not true."

She wouldn't have come home otherwise. It's not like she had to move in with her parents or spend time with any of them. No one was forcing her to be here.

"How would you know? You only see her when you're there."

"Yeah, well, she finds things difficult with Rachel, but if she didn't care, her opinion wouldn't matter." Jess pointed her drink at him and tried to sound authoritative. "I know she can appear difficult, and believe me sometimes she is, but you don't see her the way I do."

"That's lucky."

Jess narrowed her eyes, finding the comment unnecessary when she was trying to help. "You know what I mean. Come to dinner and see what your sister's like when she hasn't got your mum breathing down her neck."

"Nope, sorry." Robbie shrugged. "I love Melissa, but we don't hang out, and it's fine."

"Even for more chocolate brownies?"

"Why are you so bothered by this?"

Because she wanted to bring about some harmony. It was the first step in any of this working, of that she was sure. If they were all arguing to begin with it wasn't a solid foundation. Besides which, she needed them if David was buggering off to Devon, as seemed likely.

Jess surveyed the kitchen as Robbie made his escape. There were empty bottles and cans lined up on the worktop, and lager trickled into sticky pools on the tiles. She grabbed the recycling box from by the door, chucking cans into it but running out of space at an alarming rate.

The cottage was David's pride and joy. He'd fallen in love with it four years ago when they'd gone out for a rental appraisal, deciding it would be his forever home. You didn't treat your forever home like this, and Jess stuffed a can into the bag with such force that she split the plastic.

"Woah, easy." Melissa dumped it in the sink before everything spilled. "Are you okay?"

"Yeah," Jess murmured, ripping off an extra bag to wrap the rubbish and then dumping the roll on top of the counter. It fell off and hit the floor, along with her mood.

"No, you're not."

Melissa tugged Jess's shirt to pull her closer and she slumped forward into a hug, pressing her face into a shoulder. After avoiding the topic for two weeks, it was on her mind again.

"I'm worried Dad might move," she whispered. "And I

know it shouldn't be a problem, I'm a grown woman, but I don't want him to. He's the only family I've got, and I need him here to support me with this."

"Have you asked him?"

"Bit difficult, he's on a ship in the Mediterranean. Not sure it's a conversation I want to have on the phone."

She didn't want to have it anywhere. The number of difficult discussions kept racking up. The only consolation was that she had a hug, until Stephen came into the kitchen, and then she didn't even have that anymore. He only wanted a fresh beer and refrained from comment, which was lucky because Jess wasn't in the mood. She wasn't a violent person, but events could drive her to lash out at him.

"You'll see David next weekend, and you need to talk with him about this. For now, though, we'll make sure Robbie knows on pain of death that this place needs returning to its original state. Then I'm taking you home, making you tea, and we'll watch one of those awful films in bed. How's that?"

Jess gave a weak nod, surprised by the force of her own reaction. She wanted to cry again, for the second time in as many weeks, and wasn't prone to that either. Melissa gave Robbie the serve of his life, then scooped Jess into the car with the promise of a cuddle. It wasn't what she'd intended them to do tonight, but right now she couldn't imagine anything better.

13

Jess dumped her bag on the hotel room floor, surveying their suite. It was what she'd hoped for, besides the minor matter of the double bed. It didn't seem to bother Melissa that Jess was sharing it with V, but she felt uncomfortable with the idea. Not because anything would happen but sleeping with your ex-girlfriend with your new one a few doors down seemed an odd predicament.

They were six days on from Robbie's stag party and hadn't shared a bed again, despite having reached the point where brushing past each other in the kitchen at work was a dangerous game. Never had making tea been so charged with sexual tension. It had to happen at some point, but Melissa had made no push to change the room arrangements, and that worried Jess. On top of David's return in the morning, she had a lot on her mind.

"Are we heading to the bar?" V jumped on the bed and ran her hands over the duvet, luxuriating in the high thread count. "You promised me fun this weekend, and I'm waiting for you to deliver."

"Sorry, no can do. I promised Melissa I'd spend some

time with her grandparents. It's the only thing getting her through this wedding."

"That sounds dull, what will I do in the meantime?"

Jess was already halfway out the door, slipping a room card into her pocket. "The pool is still open. You should make use of the facilities. Milk them for all they're worth and then meet me in the bar at nine?"

"It's a done deal."

Jess made her way to the terrace where Melissa sat on a rattan sofa opposite her grandmother, Alice. Her pops was nowhere in sight, which meant he'd found somewhere for a pint of stout in front of sport on the television. There was a pot of tea on the table, and Alice leapt up when she saw Jess, almost spilling it over the patio.

"I thought you'd disowned us," she cried, drawing Jess into a suffocating hug and then kissing both of her cheeks. "Tell me why you haven't visited."

It was a command more than a question, and Jess was stumbling for answers. "Been busy," was all she managed. "But I'd love to come over soon."

"Then make it happen, cariad. Bring my granddaughter, I've missed you both. The house isn't the same without her, although the moping was getting a bit much. I'm delighted you've sorted yourselves out."

"Moping, was she? That's interesting to know."

Jess fell into the sofa and nudged close to Melissa, dropping a soft kiss on her lips. Everyone else was off engaged in other activities, so they were safe. She'd double checked the itinerary Rachel emailed to be sure.

"I wasn't moping," Melissa protested.

"Well either way," Alice continued, with a gentle shake of her head. "I'm pleased you're together now. It's all that matters, although the poor lad whose heart you broke may not feel the same way."

"So dramatic. We only went out a few times, and you were more interested in it than I was. Now I understand why."

Jess watched Melissa spar with her grandmother, her face lighting up with pleasure. They were still going on about the bartender, but she'd zoned out, interested only in how happy the reunion made them both.

"What's this news you've got then? Out with it now Jess is here." Alice leant forward, clasping her hands together.

"I've got a job offer. Need to turn it down, but it's a step in the right direction. Even calls for a celebratory cup of tea."

"That's amazing, well done." Jess pulled her into a tight hug and dropped a kiss on her temple. "I didn't think you'd applied for much, so even better."

"I haven't, I didn't. Kat's only got one full-time member of staff, the rest she does herself, but she's going back to university in September. Offered it to me without even needing to interview."

"Because she knows you'd be perfect, so why are you turning it down?"

This was ideal for her. She loved the store, and it meant working with books all day. Even if she didn't want to do the job forever, it was a start in the right direction.

"Because it's crap pay with no career progression. Mum would go loco."

"So? If you can get by and this is the job you want, take it. You can always supplement with other work, like monetising your blog, or tutoring again. Don't give up on this because your mum wouldn't approve."

Rachel had said any job would do at this stage, and Jess

was taking her at her word. This may not be right for Rachel, but it was right for Melissa, and that mattered most.

"I'd love it. Kat's great, and she's got so many ideas. We were talking about how we could promote the shop online, which plays into my idea of learning more about digital marketing."

Alice balled her fist and shook it. "Jess has got the right idea, cariad. You didn't come back here rather than staying with us to be miserable."

Jess went to continue persuading her but had tripped on Alice's last comment. "Hang on, I didn't know staying in Wales was an option, you didn't tell me you'd considered it."

"I didn't consider it." Melissa rubbed the side of her finger under Jess's chin, her eyes sparkling as she smiled. "There's no way I was living so far away from you, even if it meant arguing with Mum every day for the rest of my life."

"You came back here for me?"

"Yeah, that was part of it. The offer to go back to Wales was open-ended, so I figured I'd reassess if things didn't pan out. I knew I'd kick myself if I didn't give it a chance. Is that a problem?"

"I guess not."

Melissa had clocked the shocked expression and leant over to kiss Jess's cheek. "I don't regret it, if you're worried. I also missed Dad, and if Robbie has kids at some point, I want to be near them."

"So long as I'm never holding you back."

"That's so far from the truth I don't even know where to begin. If I told you I wanted to be an astronaut, you'd be calling up NASA trying to get me in."

It was true, she'd get no argument. Alice observed them with a warm smile, and as she wandered inside to get menus, insisting on buying dinner, Jess had a moment of bravery.

She hitched her knee up on the sofa and took Melissa's hand when she was sure they were alone. "I've had the best time these past two weeks. I'm so glad you came back, but can I ask you something?"

"Anything."

"Why don't you want to share a room? I know it was me who decided to stay with V, but that was before we were together. We wouldn't need to do anything, I understand if you still need time, but I want to go to sleep with you, and wake up with you, like last Saturday."

She felt empowered by the directness, even if she'd rambled a little, but now Melissa needed to deliver a bearable answer.

"I always wanted you to stay with me this weekend, but you made a promise to V and I respect that." Melissa pulled a room card from her pocket and tucked it into Jess's. "If you've changed your mind, this is no longer a spare. It's yours."

Jess smiled and leant in to kiss her. "And I'm yours whenever you want me."

* * *

After dinner and more catching up with Alice, including setting a date to visit, Jess found V. She was on a stool, already at the end of a pint, and laughing with Stephen.

"I've been hearing what you got up to last weekend." V leant an arm on the bar as she regarded Jess with a smile, raising her eyebrows a touch. "Very enlightening."

"I bet. Can I have a quick word? In private."

Jess directed the last bit at Stephen, and he sloped off

but didn't stray far, which meant only one thing. Not that it was a problem. V said she wanted some fun, without a relationship, and she'd get that with him.

"What's up?" Her eyes trailed Stephen across the room until he sat on a sofa to watch television.

"Nothing bad, I only wanted to check it isn't a problem if I change rooms. It looks like that might suit you, anyway."

"I never understood why you were sharing with me. You know my opinion."

Hard not to when she kept voicing it. Jess pulled up a stool and ordered a beer, grabbing a handful of nuts from a bowl near her mat.

"Don't worry, I'm confronting the problem head on."

"Good. You need to take control, not wait for her while she waits for you. You'll end up where you were two weeks ago, with no one making the first move. Melissa's a big girl, if she doesn't want something she'll say."

"I know, I know. Willing to admit I was taking slow and respectful too far."

"And do you understand why?"

Jess rolled her eyes, flinging a nut into her mouth and catching it on her tongue. She'd heard this a few times, too, and wasn't sure she bought into the idea.

"Something about fear or rejection, blah blah blah."

"No, don't dismiss this. You can tell me your mum leaving hasn't affected you until you're blue in the face, but I've never believed you. This isn't about Melissa. You know she's going nowhere." V circled her finger and then jabbed it at Jess's chest. "Somewhere inside you're still worried that once you have sex, you're only one step away from having to tell Rachel about this. You're terrified of losing her."

"Thank you for that psychoanalysis. You must tell me what I owe for the session."

V signalled the bartender again, draining her glass. "Another pint, and then I'm sending you to bed. Might head there myself." She shot Stephen a brief smile, and he held up his room card. "Start your lecture. Come on, I know you're dying to."

Jess took a sip of her drink and as she laughed the bubbles popped in her nose. "Why would I lecture you?"

"Because I plan to have frivolous sex with a virtual stranger, and I know part of your fear of rejection is taking care of people. You'll be desperate to tell me how it's a terrible idea, and he isn't good enough for me, and so on. Am I wrong?"

"You are. Stephen has more than met his match with you, and you're a grown woman who can make her own mistakes." Jess put a hand to her mouth. "Oops, did I say that last bit out loud? Sorry."

Even two weeks ago she didn't have enough confidence for this, and Jess had no intention of changing her mind. Stephen wasn't a terrible guy. Enjoying casual sex wasn't a hanging offence, so long as both parties knew where they stood, and V knew the score.

"How disappointing, I was looking forward to a bit of disapproval. Oh, well."

Jess shrugged. "I'm a judgement free zone, so long as you're happy. But make sure he knows if he puts one foot wrong, I'm coming after him with a pitchfork."

V leant in to whisper. "That's more like it. Thanks."

* * *

Once she'd finished her drink, Jess went via the suite to collect her bag, and wished good luck to the bed. She grabbed her dress from its hook in the wardrobe, smoothing out the creases, and walked the three doors down to Melissa's room. For a second she considered knocking but remembered the key card in her pocket. The handle flashed green as she swiped it, and she peered in to see if Melissa was back yet.

The sun had almost set and there was a lamp on by the bed, filling the bedroom with warm light. A breeze drifted in from the open balcony door, and the shower was running, sending a haze of steam into the bedroom. Jess hung her dress and set her bag on the dresser, then leant against the bathroom doorframe as she joined in with Melissa's song. Their voices reached a crescendo, each competing in strained tones to be the loudest, until she turned off the shower.

Melissa grasped from behind the curtain. "Can you grab my towel?"

Jess took a fluffy white bath sheet from the rail and passed it to her, then returned to her position. "Do you mind if I take one?"

"Of course not. Do you want a drink on the balcony? It's a beautiful night, and you can see the stars. Countryside perks."

"Very romantic. Give me five minutes and I'll join you."

When Jess had showered and changed into her pyjamas, she emerged from the bathroom and realised clothes were a misstep. Melissa laid on her front facing the end of the bed, her legs swinging in the air as she read a book. She wore nothing, besides her glasses, and Jess was so startled she almost tripped on the discarded towel.

"Are you sitting on the balcony like that? Aren't you worried about being caught for indecent exposure?"

"No, there are people on the next balcony, so I changed my mind."

"Can I tell you something?" Jess regained her composure, not waiting for Melissa to respond since it was more of a rhetorical question. "I find your body confidence very sexy. Out of this world sexy. For someone who went to pains pointing out their sexual inexperience, you never seem to mind putting a lot of yourself on display."

Melissa's eyes remained trained on the page, but she grunted out a soft laugh. "I'm not like this with everyone, but I have no issue with you seeing my body. Do you mind me looking at yours?"

Jess inclined her head, considering the question for a moment. "No. I already know how comfortable you think it is."

"Oh dear, is that coming back to bite me? If I recall I also said you were gorgeous. When I was in agony, comfortable was a positive thing. Either way, I love your body."

"You should pay attention to it, then. Rather than reading."

"Convince me there's something more interesting on offer."

Jess laughed but felt equal to the challenge. She knelt on the bed, taking a soft grasp on a dangling ankle, and traced the pads of her fingers as far as Melissa's knee. Then she replaced them with kisses, moving down one leg before switching to the other. They were smooth from the shower, and Jess covered every inch.

"Do I have your attention yet?" She rested a hand on each side of Melissa's back as she leant over, still kneeling between her legs, and lowered herself to whisper. "Or should I keep going?"

Melissa now used a finger to follow the lines of print. "You may continue."

Jess nipped her ear, then resumed. She paid focussed

attention to Melissa's back this time, tracing the freckles with her tongue and laying kisses as she travelled. How long she'd been at the task she didn't know or care. When she reached the subtle curve at the base of Melissa's back, she ran her tongue over the dimples there before moving her fingertips in a gentle caress over each buttock.

"You okay there?" Jess teased, smiling to see the goose bumps rise, and Melissa's hips twitch.

Melissa kept up the pretence of reading a while longer, even when a gentle jet of air blew across the backs of her legs, but there were signs it was affecting her. She kept flicking at the hair on her neck, her breathing had quickened, and the page hadn't turned in a long while. Jess enjoyed every moment, wondering how far she could push it before she buckled.

"Do you need access to the front now?" Melissa's eyes remained on the book. "I can turn over if it's helpful."

"Doing me a favour, are you? Thanks."

"Mhm. All for your benefit."

She rolled, and the action revealed a flush of pink extending from her chest to her face. Jess took a moment to absorb the image, a bolt of arousal starting in her stomach and earthing in her legs. Then she began again, placing butterfly kisses from each knee to hip bone.

When she lingered to breathe warm air where Melissa was already wet, she squirmed, but it was the gentle flick of tongue against nipple that undid her. Melissa's hands fell limp behind her head and the book and glasses dropped to the floor as she writhed and moaned, arching her back to push the flesh into Jess's waiting mouth. She devoured each breast, no longer careful and considered, and thrummed with arousal at the response.

Jess only paused to tug off her shirt, desperate to feel

Melissa's skin against her own. She slipped out of her shorts, pushing them aside, then lowered herself back into position. Their hips rocked together as she nipped and sucked any piece of sensitive flesh she could find, from Melissa's neck, down her chest, and over her breasts again.

Melissa laced their fingers together and pushed between them, trying to guide Jess's hand. "Please, touch me. I'm in actual pain here. I can't take any more."

"You can," Jess whispered, holding the hand above her head, and then sliding down to kiss her stomach. "Patience."

"I've been patient for weeks, now you're being cruel."

"Think how good it'll feel." Jess sucked on the inside of a thigh, then parted Melissa's lips and ran her tongue in one slow circle of her clit to give her the idea.

"Oh, fuck," Melissa yelled, loud enough that the people on the next balcony might hear. "It already feels good."

"It'll be better."

Jess was struggling too. Everything pulsed, and it was edging towards discomfort. She'd also waited a long time, though, and intended to savour the experience. Every taste burst through her mouth and the scent was more intoxicating than ever. She was in heaven and didn't want to leave.

She made her way back up, Melissa's hips once again bucking, and kissed her deep on the mouth. Their bodies pressed together until there wasn't a slither of broken contact, the slip of their thighs providing some relief.

Melissa clawed at Jess's back. "I'll do whatever you want, but I need you to touch me now."

Jess relented, knowing what she wanted next because her mind came here often. She rolled them over so Melissa was on top, then grasped the backs of her knees and guided her into a kneeling position.

"Come up here," she whispered, shuffling so her own

head was on the pillows. "Hold the headboard if you need." Melissa nodded, even if she didn't look sure. She crawled up Jess's body, stopping to kneel over her chest. "Come the rest of the way and take the weight on your knees."

Melissa did as instructed but then tensed for a moment, suspended over Jess's head, before relaxing enough that their lips met. "God, that feels good. Jesus."

She took control for the first time, Jess's hands stroking gentle caresses wherever they could reach while Melissa lowered herself and pulled away. Fingers worked over nipples and trailed up the back of legs with a gentle touch. It was hard, but Jess wanted her to feel empowered and in charge of her pleasure.

While she did, Jess's tongue explored every sensitive spot and returned to those which generated the most enthusiastic noises. Every time Melissa moaned it sent desire coursing through her body until it was hard to tell who was more aroused.

It was only when she felt the speed of Melissa's writhing pick up and she bent further forward that Jess's tongue slipped deep inside. She gasped as her hips writhed and bucked, and Jess couldn't hold back any longer. She wrapped both hands around the tops of Melissa's legs to hold her tight in place, pulling her deeper until she felt her muscles tense.

As she rode out her orgasm, Jess was almost there with her, so turned on by the experience that she had to stop from touching herself. It wouldn't take much, but she wanted to feel Melissa there.

"Are you okay?"

Melissa lifted herself off and flopped onto the bed beside her. "I think you almost killed me." She swiped Jess's cheek with a shaking hand. "Tell me why we've waited to do that?"

"So long as it was worth the wait, that's all I care about."

"I'm not sure I can live up to that." Melissa's expression showed the concern was genuine.

"There's nothing to live up to, go with whatever you feel."

Melissa pushed Jess onto her back and knelt between her legs. She sucked hard on a nipple, then peered up for a second with a devilish grin. "Tell me if I'm not doing what you need."

There were no complaints, apart from the position. Jess rolled until they were face to face on their sides. She hitched up her leg, Melissa's left arm trapped underneath her, holding her while she traced firm circles around her clit with the other. Melissa's mouth explored her neck and chest until Jess felt her orgasm build and captured it with her own.

She pressed their tongues together and ground her hips forward to increase the pressure until her muscles clenched, and warmth shot out to every extremity. She swatted the hand away, unable to bear any more, but held Melissa's body tight and kissed her again. It was lazy and languid now, and as her heart rate steadied her eyes became heavy.

"Mm, I'm tired now," Jess mumbled.

"You need a rest before we go again?" Melissa whispered, stroking the damp hair from Jess's forehead.

"Yeah, give me five minutes." She smiled, her eyes still closed, and listened to the rustle of the duvet as Melissa pulled it back. The lamp clicked off, and they both slid underneath. "I was serious. Don't dare go to sleep because I'll wake you."

"Okay, if you say so."

14

Jess folded her arms as she squinted down the long drive that wound through the grounds. The ceremony began in less than half an hour and David hadn't arrived yet. She'd try calling, but he hadn't figured out how to use the Bluetooth system in his car despite several frustrating attempts to get him acquainted with it.

She looked down at her watch again and then perched herself on the wall to wait. It felt like far longer than four weeks that he'd been away. Although she feared for him if Rachel noticed him coming in late, she was also eager to see her dad again. It was the longest they'd ever gone without each other, and though they'd been arguing she'd still missed him. There was always an ease she could never replicate with anyone else. With the looming threat of Rachel's disapproval, the security was comforting.

Ten minutes passed, and the phone vibrated in her hand with two messages from Melissa. The first warned Rachel was on the prowl. The second said only that she loved her, and Jess smiled.

David's Jag careered up the road with fifteen minutes to

spare and he leapt out, hoisting his trousers up as he strode towards her. He'd lost weight and his face glowed with a warm tan, but there were also bags under his eyes.

"You look knackered," Jess called.

"Early start, traffic and bloody hell it's hotter here than in the Med." David recoiled, the midday sun beating down on them. "How late am I?"

"You're not yet, but only if we shift. The ceremony is on the other side of the building."

"Lead the way then." He pulled a tie from his pocket and looped it around his neck as they marched to reception. "How is Rachel doing? Has she gone full throttle mother of the groom yet?"

"I don't know, I've been keeping out of her way."

Out of everyone's way, in fact. It was getting hard to remember what normal levels of contact with Melissa looked like. They'd always been tactile with each other, but at some point, people might notice a shift.

"Wise. Is Robbie nervous? I remember my wedding day. The only time I've sweated more is the night you were born."

"Charming." Jess pushed through the last set of double doors to the hallway next to the ceremony room. "Don't worry about Robbie, he's found one or two ways to stay relaxed."

"Do I want to know?"

"No."

There were a few guests still lingering, fanning themselves with leaflets and adjusting outfits. Jess stopped to straighten David's tie and flatten his collar and then stood back to regard him again.

"There you go, almost presentable, but you might need to think about a new wardrobe if you plan to keep seeing this woman." Jess frowned as David tightened his belt. "Did she have an agreeable time? I presume she came back with you and no one went overboard?"

David laughed, offering her his arm. "We had a lovely time, thank you very much. It turns out your old man hasn't lost his charm."

They stepped into a high-ceilinged room with two gold chandeliers and an enormous bay window at the front. In the window was an old desk with a vase of lilies in the centre, and on either side of a red-carpeted aisle were rows and rows of guests. Robbie was already at the front with Rachel fiddling with his bow tie in a monstrous hat and elegant cream suit. She'd saved them both a seat near the front with the family.

"Hello, David." V shuffled two seats across so they could join the end of the row. "You look very dapper."

"And you, that's a striking dress."

David gave V a genuine smile as she ran a hand over the piercing blue satin.

"Thanks. Jess helped me pick it."

"You asked my daughter for fashion advice? Then that dress is a lucky accident."

Was this how they'd get along with each other? Jess looked down at her own outfit, feeling pleased with the selection. V had picked out a yellow dress with a whacking great slit up the leg to show off her tattoo, and while she thought it was too racy, she had to admit it looked great. She was about to tell them as much when a quiet fell over the room.

Jess felt a nervous twist of her stomach. She knew Melissa wasn't looking forward to having to walk down the aisle. Reading books for kids was one thing, but an entire room full of adults all watching her was different. The regis-

trar asked everyone to stand, and then all they could hear
was the click of the photographer's camera as the bridesmaids entered.

Melissa's cheeks were bright red and her eyes glued to
the floor as she walked into the room. Jess clutched her own
face in sympathy, a wave of relief flooding as she reached the
front. Tiredness hadn't helped the situation, but she didn't
regret that one bit. There were three bridesmaids, and then
Sam entered wearing a full white gown sparkling with
beads and jewels.

David tapped Jess's shoulder and pointed to Robbie,
who was almost in full floods of tears. "Poor lad," he whispered. "He's realised there's no escape."

"Dad!" She scorned, trying to keep the volume down,
but V had heard it all because her shoulders were heaving
and she had a hand over her mouth. "Be quiet until the ceremony's over."

David's tolerance for sentimental weddings hadn't
increased with his new romance. As they all clapped the
happy couple back down the aisle after signing the register,
he leant over again and this time didn't hush himself. "Well,
that's it then. Until the next time."

"What do you mean?"

"Nothing, sweetheart. I wish them every happiness, and
I hope it lasts. You and I are a little more pragmatic."

"Are we?"

Despite being prone to caution, she liked to think she
could have love and a lasting relationship.

"You know what I'm saying. A big wedding with all the
trimmings isn't a guarantee. You'd be better off down the
registry office and saving your money, spending it on experiences you can share for a lifetime, not one day."

"Oh." She thought he was going somewhere else with that. "Then yeah, I guess I agree."

"Do you think you'll ever get married?"

"I don't know. I suppose I'm with you, I'm not sure you need to. So long as you're with the right person, what's the point in a piece of paper?"

David bobbed his head, sticking his hands into his trouser pockets as they shuffled out of their seats and waited for the crowd to move. "I'm not even sure there's a right person. You need to work at any relationship, it's who you do that with," he mused. "People expect that an attraction to another person means it should work, with no further cultivation required."

"You're in a very philosophical mood today."

He pursed his lips, then smiled and waved to Rachel. "Blame the wedding, it got me thinking. What about children? I am right to presume your attachment to Grace is a cry for help in that department?"

Jess hooked her arm back through his and laughed. "I'm not sure I'd call it that, but I guess. Well, okay, no. I'm sure. I want kids. Please don't tell me you're turning into Rachel, though?"

"No, wouldn't suit the hat. Only wondered, is all. Need to find you a woman first. Tricky given your current living predicament."

"Sorry to disappoint you, but I've found one. And before you say another word, it's not V." She'd slipped away from them as they reached the terrace and latched on to Stephen again, and Jess waved.

"Well, hallelujah. When do I get to meet her?"

"When I get to meet yours."

"Touché. Next weekend? I'd like you to meet her on your

own first, but afterwards you could invite your new lady friend for dinner."

Jess laughed at his terminology. Melissa would get a kick out of it later, too. Whether she'd appreciate telling people as soon as next weekend, though, was another matter.

"I'll check, but yes in theory."

"Good. I'm heading to Devon tomorrow, for the week, but I'll be back Saturday so let's do the evening. I'll text you with details."

"You're leaving again already?"

"Yes, there's something I said I'd help her with at home."

Jess felt a stab of disappointment. He'd only been back an hour, and now he was calling it home. None of this was a surprise, but it still made her want to vomit.

"Are you moving there?"

"No, of course not."

Jess let out a sigh of relief, clutching her stomach to quell the churning. "Good. You don't understand how worried I've been."

"About me moving? Silly girl, as if I'd ever leave you by choice. You have been okay while I was on holiday? Seems like it, if you've snared a girlfriend after all this time."

He made it sound like she'd resorted to laying traps. It'd been a long wait, but she'd never been that desperate.

"Of course. Everything's fine at work, too. Melissa's been great, although we may need to let go of her earlier than planned because she's got a permanent job. Don't tell Rachel, she's doing it on Friday."

"I'm pleased, and I presume you're happy to remain managing the place?"

"What, why? I thought it was only to cover your holiday?"

"It was, and now it can cover my retirement."

Jess stared at him, open-mouthed. She never expected to see the day David retired. Besides which, he was only forty-eight. If he could afford it, though, good on him.

"I want the job, yes. Wow. Sorry, I wasn't expecting that today."

"It was always coming at some point, and you've shown you can handle it."

Jess couldn't smile enough with the relief of it. "It's good to have you home, old man. Come on, let's eat."

V disappeared after dinner, as if by magic, and Jess spent twenty minutes searching for her before giving up and going back to the room for a cheeky nap. It cleared the dull headache caused by drinking in the afternoon, and by the time the reception began at seven she was ready to go again. She slipped back into her dress, cleaned her teeth, and spritzed some perfume, before heading to the bar.

Melissa hadn't been so lucky and spent most of the intervening two hours bored to death by distant relatives. So it seemed, anyway, from the stream of moaning text messages. She was hiding behind the cake when Jess found her, shoeless and huddled on the floor.

"Hard day, champ?" Jess gave her a hand as she stood. "Do you know what I'm enjoying? The juice stain here." She prodded a deep red patch on the front of Melissa's dress. "And the butter mark here." This time she pointed at a streak of grease somewhere around her lap. "And then whatever the hell this is." She laughed, swirling a finger around a nondescript mark on the strap.

"Making sure I can never wear it again. And yes, after a spectacular evening I have had a hellish day. I got stuck chatting to Aunt Penny for a full thirty minutes. She wanted to talk with V, but I couldn't find her. Do you know where she is?"

"Not a clue, sorry, but would a cuddle help?"

Before Jess could so much as blink, Melissa threw her arms around her and let out a long groan. "I missed you today. Undercover is fun until it's not fun."

"We should change that, then. Dad wants me to meet his girlfriend next weekend. Will you come to dinner so we can tell him? If it goes well, your mum's next."

"Sure you're ready?"

No, but it had to happen. The longer they hid it from people, the worse it'd be. Rachel would see it as a lie and use it as another reason to object.

"Yeah, let's do it."

They went in search of V after that, finding her chatting to Rachel on the patio with a glass of champagne. It was a surprise. Jess expected she'd done a bunk with Stephen.

Rachel escorted her off to where Penny stood with her sons and Melissa held Jess back, hiding behind a bush so they couldn't drag her into the conversation. She didn't want to return for round two.

Instead, they talked to Paul and David for a while, catching up on his holiday while the evening guests filtered in and the DJ set up his gear. By eight-thirty the place overflowed with people, and music was thumping out of the hall they'd eaten in earlier. Melissa stuck a finger in each ear, more than done for the day and not wanting to endure any more. As David insisted on a dance before he left, Paul pulled her in too amidst an angry torrent of protest.

David attempted to twirl Jess and failed. "We haven't danced together in years."

"Try never." Her arm twisted at an awkward angle and she winced. "There's a reason."

"What's that?" David mouthed, squinting as if it'd help him hear over the music.

Jess shouted it this time, and he nodded. When the track switched to a soppy love song and they could hear again, she leant over to his ear. "Are you sure you should drive to Devon tomorrow? You look exhausted. Can't it wait a day or two?"

"Don't fuss, I'll have a lie in and wait until the afternoon."

She accepted his response, even if she was still worried, and they danced a while longer. Jess tried not to laugh as Paul trod all over Melissa's toes, and it was a relief when David dipped out, so she could cut in to rescue her from a meltdown.

He led Paul out, the two of them chatting again now they'd had what they wanted, and Jess guided Melissa off the dancefloor in search of somewhere quieter to sit. She'd had enough with the entire day and was no longer hiding it.

"Can we go to bed yet?" She came close to rolling her eyes as they sank onto a stone wall on the terrace. "The only thing getting me through is the thought of you continuing my sexual education later."

Jess laughed. "Is that what we're calling it now?" She grazed her hand over Melissa's back and leant in close. "I'll tell you what, why don't you go upstairs. I'll cover with your mum."

"Then you'll join me?"

"Yes. Not sure how long I'll be, though. I still need to catch up with V and make sure Rachel doesn't go on the warpath because you've done a bunk."

"You are my hero. Do you know that?"

"Thought I was your teacher a minute ago."

Jess kissed her cheek and went in search of V, hoping she wasn't also giving a sex education lesson.

* * *

Stephen had backed V against a wall with his hand in a place Jess wanted to wipe from memory, and they were best left to it. The only person remaining on the list was Rachel, who was holding court with Sam's parents sipping champagne. Jess joined in the conversation and explained Melissa wasn't feeling well but freed herself by nine-thirty with no complaint. When she made it to the room, she couldn't find the key card and had to knock.

Melissa inched open the door. "Oh lovely, it's the woman I ordered. Quick, come inside before my girlfriend sees you."

"Very funny." Jess stuck out her foot to catch the door before it slammed in her face and found Melissa bouncing across the carpet wrapped in a towel. "What are you doing?"

"Bath. I need to wash away the wedding. Care to join me?"

She dropped the towel on the tiles and stood in the doorway, and Jess was halfway across the room with a hand on her zip before she'd even finished speaking.

"Hell yes." Jess wriggled out of her dress and flung it across the room, and her bra followed. "Let me in then."

As the fabric fell away, Melissa replaced it with her mouth, and Jess had to guide her backwards as she pulled down her underwear. She hit the sink and then stepped back, dipping a toe into the water before submerging herself.

Melissa pouted and crossed her arms. "Hang on, what has happened here? I was busy."

"You invited me for a bath, so get in."

Jess flicked water at her and slid backwards to create a space in front, sending a torrent over the back and a river flowing towards the bedroom carpet. Melissa narrowed her eyes but got in, leaning against Jess and creating a wave that tickled between her legs.

"I still don't understand why we couldn't have a little more fun first. You spent ages kissing me last night, when is it my turn?"

Jess laughed, snaking her hands around Melissa's waist and dabbing her shoulder. "Your turn?"

"Yes." Melissa trailed her fingertips down Jess's leg and over her knee. "I loved you taking charge last night. It was sexy." She turned her head, looking Jess deep in the eye and lowering her voice. "Very sexy. For the record, I'm happy for you to do what you did last night whenever the mood takes you. Doesn't mean I don't want to try it myself sometimes, though."

"It was alright, then?" Jess laughed again, then nipped a line of kisses up Melissa's neck, stopping to tug on her ear lobe. "You were right to assume sex with me would be satis-factory?"

She also felt sure Melissa would enjoy tonight, if her response to the hands now cupping her breasts was any indication. Her back arched into the touch, and her breath hitched when the caress became firmer. As Jess ran her tongue in one motion around the top of her ear, Melissa grasped her calf.

"This bath is over."

"Are you being impatient again? We only just got in."

"Yes."

Melissa squirmed, and Jess raked her fingers between her legs. This was an advantageous position, and she wasn't ready to give it up yet. She ran her hands up Melissa's sides and over her stomach, pressing her breasts forward and enjoying the pressure. There had been a gentle pulse between her legs since she thought about last night, and it was increasing in intensity.

"If we get out, will you agree to get back into this position?" she whispered. "I want to be behind you. Promise it'll be worth it."

Melissa twisted her head, lacing her fingers through Jess's hair. She pulled herself up on the bath handles and water cascaded over the curve of her back. "Right now, I'd do anything you asked me."

When she'd stepped out and patted herself with the towel, Jess stood and followed suit. As she emerged into the bedroom, Melissa was throwing open the balcony door and stood to admire the view. It was a clear night, and the sky graduated to an inky blue as it met the horizon.

Jess crept in next to her, running her fingertips in a light trail over each buttock. "You're right, you can see more stars out here. Sure you don't want to just sit outside?"

Melissa turned her head and smiled. "No way."

She climbed onto the bed and Jess knelt behind, pulling Melissa back to sit on her lap. Reaching around, she slid both hands over the soft tender flesh of her inner thighs making slow caresses, and as Melissa arched Jess pulled her legs wider, wrapping them against her own.

"Is this comfortable for you?" She curled both sets of fingers around Melissa's hips and drew her further back. "Or do you want to move?"

Melissa twisted to seek Jess's mouth. "I wasn't looking for comfortable, ask a more relevant question."

"Let me rephrase that. You enjoyed sitting last night, will this work too?"

"We should carry on and find out."

Melissa's lips were still parted, and Jess gave her what she wanted now, kissing for a few seconds before sucking on her tongue and palming her breasts. The moan against Jess's mouth sent a shiver down her spine and she rubbed the heel of her hand between Melissa's legs as she rocked into it.

Melissa grunted each time, trying to push herself harder against the hand, until Jess relented and slid a finger over her clit. She pressed her lips to an ear, wanting to hear how much Melissa was enjoying this even though she already had the evidence.

"How are you feeling about this position now?" she whispered, her nose rubbing against damp strands of hair.

"I want more."

Her voice carried an unexpected determination which made Jess's chest contract. She took Melissa's wrist and pushed her forward onto all fours, hoping she'd get the idea. The low guttural sound as two fingers entered signalled that she did. Melissa arched her back again, gripping tight on the duvet.

Jess remained purposeful and controlled as she pulled her into each thrust. "Better?"

"You're teasing again. I want you to go harder."

Jess laughed, undeterred. She continued, keeping a slow rhythm, the motion of Melissa's breasts and her deep growl building a fire which she was trying to keep from engulfing her. Hard wasn't her aim, and Melissa was about to find out why. She rotated her wrist, so her fingers pointed down, and teased over a rough patch in small circles, returning each time she entered. She smiled at the gasped response and felt her hand become wetter each time.

"Still want me to go harder?"

Melissa's voice was thick and catching. "Fuck it, do what you like."

Jess shuffled for stability and, when she was sure she wouldn't topple, reached with her free hand to run her fingers over Melissa's clit. The action caused her to sink onto her forearms, twisting the bed sheets as she moaned, and Jess knew she was close.

Struggling to hold out, Jess added a third finger and entered her as deep as she could muster given her arms were aching and her legs trembled. Whatever Melissa said next became muffled by the bed and came out closer to a cry which sent arousal coursing through Jess's body. She'd never tire of hearing that sound or seeing how much Melissa wanted her.

Jess pushed deep again, hoping to elicit the same response, but this time as Melissa became tight around her fingers, she could only hold her. She felt the pulses as she rode out her orgasm, the sounds once again strangled. When she relaxed, Jess withdrew her fingers, and Melissa shivered. She collapsed face down on the bed, and Jess lowered herself on top.

"Don't try to tell me you wanted more than that," she whispered close to an ear, and Melissa let out a gentle laugh.

"No, that was pretty good. Nine out of ten. Tired now, though."

Jess kissed her neck for a while and then rolled off. She closed her eyes and smiled when Melissa stroked a hand along her side. "Thought you were going to sleep?"

"I hadn't forgotten about you."

A moan passed Jess's lips as two fingers slipped inside and a thumb splayed into her clit. She reached to grasp Melissa's buttocks, rocking into her thrusts as her stomach muscles clenched and the fire travelled down her legs. It didn't take much for it to overcome her, and as the orgasm took hold Melissa remained inside for what felt like an eternity, before withdrawing and flopping on top of her.

Jess smiled with her eyes still closed. She trailed her fingertips over Melissa's back, both hands shaking, and luxuriated in the weight of her body. "We should put our pyjamas on and watch the stars on the balcony."

"That's what you want to do, right now? Aren't you exhausted?"

"Yep, but I want to enjoy this moment before we go home tomorrow."

15

They woke balled together and Jess was grateful there was no early start. The previous day Melissa's alarm buzzed at eight and she'd left, but now they could have a lazy morning. Or at least they would have been able to, if she wasn't moaning because she was hungry.

"I want to stay here but I know there's a free breakfast waiting for me," Melissa grumbled. She engaged in a genuine struggle as she held Jess's arms tight around herself and gripped both hands over her stomach.

Jess laughed, nuzzling into her neck. She spooned behind, lost in a blanket of soft blonde hair. "I'm hungry, too, so let's eat then come back to bed. Three hours until check out."

"But I'm so comfy, and you're so naked."

They'd spent half an hour on the balcony before heading back to bed and soon made their pyjamas redundant again. The second time, though, they'd been happy to kiss and hold each other a while, rather than rushing.

"You need clothes for breakfast, but I promise we'll take

them off again when we get back. Is that a fair compromise?"

Melissa rolled over and cuddled in tight. "I wish we didn't have to go home today. The wedding part was a nightmare, but there have been compensations." She sighed, propping herself on an elbow and trailing her fingertips over the small of Jess's back. "What do you think will happen once Grace is screaming in the next room?"

"You could give her a run for her money on the screaming front. You'll need to keep it down, and I'm buying a lock for the bedroom door."

"I can stay, though?"

"Of course. You're welcome in my bed any time. But right now, we're eating."

Jess shoved Melissa backwards and then climbed over her, even though the easier route was to get out on the other side. It had the desired effect of mumbled protestations and attempts to drag her back down into the duvet until Melissa huffed and kicked the remaining sheets away.

They dressed and made their way to the dining hall where V was eating on her own at a circular table by the window. Melissa joined her while Jess got them both food from the buffet, loading two plates with bacon, sausage, eggs and beans.

"I have never loved you more than I do right now." Melissa's eyes widened as she grabbed for a sausage before Jess could put her plate on the table.

"Good to know." Jess scanned the dining hall for wedding party guests, before leaning to kiss her. "Last night was a waste of time, then? I only needed to bring you a fried breakfast?"

"Mm, no, but last night gave me the appetite for it."

"Oh, yuck." V recoiled, pushing her plate away. "I'm glad you had lots of sex this weekend but some of us are trying to eat."

Jess set her food down and sat between them, in a playful mood and undeterred. "We aren't the only ones, are we? What happened with Stephen the stud?" She took Melissa's hand under the table and picked up a fork to stab a rasher of bacon. "He didn't want to join you for breakfast?"

"I didn't invite him. He was angling for us to go out, though, when Grace is next with her dad."

"He only wants to see you when Grace isn't around? Doesn't that strike you as a problem?"

V cradled her tea mug, staring down the lawn. "I haven't said I'll go, yet. We had fun, he's sweet, but I'm still not sure I want to get mixed up in anything. I'll consider it."

Jess grunted and ripped off a chunk of bacon, irked by the idea Stephen was only interested if Grace was out of the way. "Will you? Sounds like he's being a moron."

"Hey." Melissa gripped tighter on her hand, giving it a sharp tug. "That's not fair. It's up to V who she wants to spend time with, you don't get a say in this."

"I know I don't, but anyone who doesn't want a relationship with Grace as well isn't worth bothering with."

"They only met this weekend, and besides anything else it's not your call. I get you're protective, but you're overstepping."

Jess knew she was but struggled to stop. "Fine," she murmured. "I'm sorry."

V laughed, setting her mug on the table and shaking Jess's knee. "She's got you on a tight leash already." Then she narrowed her eyes and nodded. "Good work."

"When was she not?" Melissa shrugged, then leant to

kiss Jess's cheek. "Don't pout. It's sweet that you care but this isn't your business. If you need something else to focus your attention on, try me."

Jess attempted to scowl, but it didn't work. "If I wasn't do damn happy, I'd argue."

"You should be. Life's good, enjoy it."

She did have a point. Four weeks ago, V was miserable, David was the bane of their lives, and Melissa was so far out of reach Jess was in a pit of misery. Life hadn't quite ascended to the apex of perfection but it was close.

* * *

After another two hours in bed, they packed up to leave. Melissa moaned like hell when Rachel loaded her car with leftover decorations, hoping to spend the afternoon as she had the morning. She relented, though, and let Jess drive off without her in tow. They both knew they couldn't spend every single night together without it looking suspicious.

On the way home, Jess stopped via a shop to buy a bolt for the bedroom door. It may have been overkill but given how often Grace liked to hop into bed with her at five o'clock in the morning, the effort seemed justified. When her little helper arrived, Jess took a box of screwdrivers from the kitchen drawer and carried her upstairs.

"Hand me the little one, monster," she requested, kneeling next to the door. Grace was using two of the screwdrivers to play drums on the bedframe, and Jess prised one from her hand. "This is so you don't walk in on anything. No offence, but I'm not sure Mummy wants me to scar you by demonstrating how grown-ups like to bounce on the bed." It didn't take long to screw the bolt on, and she slid it open and closed a few times to make sure it lined up right. "Perfect."

The doorbell rang and Jess swung Grace into the air, whooshing her down the stairs still holding a screwdriver.

Rachel was in the entrance hall with a box of cake and a handful of balloons. "Hello, darling. Hope you don't mind me calling in, we had a few bits left over. Thought Grace might enjoy them." She stepped into the living room and left the balloons by the sofa. "Seems a shame to waste everything."

Jess set Grace on the carpet and she tugged and jumped at them, stabbing with her screwdriver. "That's sweet, thank you." Jess took away the tool, fearing what would happen if one popped, while V knelt to play. "Will you stay for a tea?"

"Wouldn't say no. I haven't visited for a while, how are you getting on with the house? You should say if something needs doing, I hope you haven't been repairing things again."

Jess held up the screwdriver. "Oh. No. I put a lock on my door to stop Grace waking me up early. I hope that's okay."

Rachel slid the cake onto the kitchen table and began filling the kettle while Jess lagged behind. She was noting all the smears on the wall and the slight dent where Grace had whacked a toy train into the kitchen doorframe. Sometimes she forgot Rachel was her landlady, given she never bothered with any formal inspections.

"Of course. Do you still want to buy it from me at some point? I presume you haven't stopped saving."

"Yes. I'm putting money away for a deposit, although a little less now I'm covering extra bills. Getting there."

She was wondering now whether this house would be big enough, though. It was already bursting at the seams.

They might need something older which she could renovate.

"Hang on." V crawled across the living room floor and tugged the bottom of Jess's shorts. "You didn't tell me you were putting less in savings because of us."

Jess shrugged. "Not much. It's a bit of a hike on the utilities where we're using more water and electricity. No problem."

"I beg to differ, if it's stopping you saving your house deposit."

"It's not. I am, but slower. It's not the end of the world."

When you were taking years to save for something, a few extra months was nothing. Besides, them having a place to live was worth a few quid, but V was still frowning.

"You said it wouldn't be a financial burden at all, though, and that's not the entire truth. I could live with you missing out on a few pints."

"You're making way too big a deal of this. I'm choosing to live as I did before you moved in and put forty quid less into savings each month. Relax."

Rachel had progressed to adding milk to their tea, and after handing V a mug pulled out a chair at the kitchen table. "You know I still think you should take your father up on his offer to lend you the extra so you can get on the ladder sooner." She held a hand up as she sat. "And before you say anything, listen. He wants to help, it's a parent's prerogative. Nothing would give him greater pleasure, I assure you. It's why he's worked so hard."

"I know that, but he's already given me a job, and I wanted to do this for myself. I'm sure you can relate."

"You could pay him back, if it bothers you. At least consider it again. It's not like he's got anything else to spend it on, besides cruises and this romance, which is a concern."

Jess began to argue over the deposit but stopped at Rachel's final comment. It'd been niggling after seeing David yesterday. He looked exhausted, and his desperation to rush off there again was troubling.

"Why?" Jess returned the screwdriver to its drawer and took her tea mug, then sat on the chair opposite and leant forward on her elbows.

Rachel scrunched her face. "Something feels off. He's lost a little weight, which I can only assume is for her benefit. Then I'm almost certain he paid for their entire holiday. I'm worried he's losing himself and she may be taking advantage. It would explain why he hasn't let any of us meet her yet."

"I made a crack about it to Melissa the other week, and at the time I wasn't serious but now I'm starting to wonder. Did he tell you he's retiring?"

Rachel's expression went from one of confusion and concern to abject shock, which was close to what Jess had felt when he told her. At the time she was more interested in her own affairs to consider it but was now reprocessing.

"No. We didn't have time to talk yesterday before he rushed to Devon again. That's another thing I can't understand, how on earth he met someone who lives so far away." Rachel set her mug down and also leant forward, lowering her voice. "I hope it wasn't some internet dating site, and she's prayed on him. You read about these things."

"He's crap with computers, but anything's possible. I'm meeting her on Saturday, so I guess we'll find out."

Although quite how she'd uncover whether this woman was a gold digger who prayed on middle-aged men was unclear.

"That's progress, at least. I will reserve judgement until then." Rachel rubbed the back of Jess's hand and raised her eyebrows as she smiled. "Did you meet your new girlfriend online? Don't think that slipped past me."

Sweat burst across Jess's back and she cleared her throat, breaking eye contact. "He told you about that, did he? Good old Dad and his big mouth."

"I'm happy for you, darling. A little disappointed but pleased if you've found someone, and it's working out well enough that you want her to meet your dad."

"Disappointed?"

"Oh well, you know. I had hoped you two might get back together, despite your protestations." Rachel gestured to V as she played with Grace beyond them. "I always thought you made a good match, and Grace adores you. The three of you make a lovely family unit, but if it's not meant to be..." She shrugged, letting out a brief sigh.

"It's not meant to be, sorry. We are kind of like a family, I guess. An unorthodox one where I'm in love with someone else and V is free to date whoever she chooses."

Jess raised her voice for the last part by way of apology for earlier and V laughed. Melissa had made it clear she needed to repent for sticking her nose into V's business.

"And how does this new girlfriend fit into your family dynamic?"

"She gets on with Grace, and accepts our situation, so it hasn't been an issue yet." Jess smiled as she took a sip of her tea. "Although sometimes it feels like she's here to spend time with Grace rather than me."

"Good that she likes children. It bodes well for the future, if you catch my drift."

"Oh yes, I catch your drift. You're not subtle. Dad was making similar hints yesterday, but it's way too soon for anything like that. Stick to your own kids for now."

She realised the implication and coloured. Rachel had

already spent a lot of time pressuring Robbie, and Melissa was next. Whether she'd be pushing as hard when she knew they were together, was less clear.

"Don't worry, I am. In jest, of course. I wouldn't want either of them jumping into something before they're ready. Children are an enormous commitment, believe me." Her eyes widened, and she gripped the mug. "They're more of a worry at twenty-seven and twenty-three than they ever were as babies. Jobs, money, relationships. You want them to make good choices."

Jess fidgeted with a loose thread in her shorts. "Both seem to have turned out alright."

Rachel nodded, stroking her chin. "I suspect my daughter may have found herself a boyfriend at long last. She's been in an excellent mood. Not that she'll tell me anything about it, she never does. Has she mentioned anything to you?"

Jess shuffled with discomfort, because they hadn't intended to outright lie. "Nice try, as if I'd gossip about her."

"Damn, I didn't think you would. She's offered to cook for us tonight, which is when I know something's amiss. Suppose I should milk these precious moments for all they're worth before her romance turns sour, and she hates me again."

"Melissa doesn't hate you."

"No, I know darling, I was only teasing. Things are improving, we're getting on a little better. Now if she can sort out this job situation..."

Jess went to jump in but knew Melissa wouldn't want her spilling the details of her job offer. She planned to talk through it with Kat and check the specifics when they met on Tuesday, then tell Rachel over dinner on Friday. It was Melissa's news, and Jess clamped her mouth shut, knowing two over shares in one day was asking for trouble. They had a whole weekend of revelations to look forward to, but for now she intended to do as suggested and enjoy a week of harmony. Starting with ending this conversation before she said something incriminating.

16

Jess glanced at the clock on the office wall. It was half six on Friday evening and she was still working. More to the point, Melissa was still working. Or at least, she was in the office, after everyone else had defected to the pub.

"You can meet me at the restaurant if you want." Jess typed out the last few words on an email to a landlord about their leaky boiler. "I won't be too long."

Melissa looked up from the computer screen. "Oh. I thought we could spend some time together before we meet Mum for dinner. Alone."

"Where do you think we'll do that in the next hour?"

There was silence for a few moments, punctuated only by the sound of Jess's fingers rattling over the keyboard. She hit send and then checked the appointments for Monday, to make sure no one had put in an early viewing or something stupid. David would be back, and she presumed he'd come to work wanting a debrief.

"There's always one place we can be alone and make as much noise as we like." The chair creaked as Melissa pushed it back. "I know you said we had to be careful in here and keep it professional, but it is the end of the working week."

She wandered across the office, rubbing both hands into Jess's shoulders and causing her to flinch. Even with the lock on her door, they were never alone, and Jess had the bite marks to prove how hard it'd been to keep noise at a respectful level.

Jess shut the computer down and tugged her shirt collar, pointing to the bruises. "Ouch and forget it."

"I promise to stay away from your war wounds." Melissa dropped her lips to Jess's neck, kissing a slow line to her ear lobe. "You haven't ever thought about doing it over one of these desks?"

Jess swallowed hard, trying to keep her arousal in check. She'd thought about it many, many times, but that didn't mean she was going to buckle. If they did this once, it'd happen again, and then it was only a matter of time before someone caught them out.

"Of course I've thought about it, it's torture having to sit in here with you every day. On many levels. But why don't we book into a hotel for the weekend? Could go to the coast."

Melissa had still been nipping and sucking on Jess's neck but paused. "What, now?"

"Sure, why not?"

"Because we're supposed to be meeting your dad's girl-friend tomorrow night, for a start."

Jess grunted. She'd overlooked that and couldn't post-pone. They were driving from Devon, it'd be rude, and she wanted to meet this woman. It had become even more important after the conversation with Rachel on Sunday.

"Alright, a hotel here. Tonight. It'll be like last weekend."

"Why waste money on a hotel when we're alone now?"

Melissa persisted, and Jess could feel her resolve ebb away with every kiss. It'd be better when David was back and they could tell everyone. At least, that was the story she was telling herself to justify what she was about to do.

The chair rolled back and Melissa spun it around before pulling the glasses from her pocket and setting them on her nose. She peered over the top, leaning forward to suck on Jess's bottom lip.

"Good God, woman, are you trying to kill me with those?"

Jess was no longer able to resist the temptation to guide Melissa sideways onto her lap, although she hadn't tried very hard. She undid the top two buttons of Melissa's blouse and pulled it down to lay kisses on her collarbone.

"Does it turn you on every time I wear these?"

Melissa undid another button, and then the rest until the blouse fell open. Jess stroked a hand across her bare stomach, then up over the lace of her bra.

"Turn me on?" She teased a finger under the cup and swirled a nipple. "I don't know what you're talking about."

Jess placed one arm under Melissa's knees and the other supported her back, then she grunted as she hoisted them both out of the chair. Melissa hitched her skirt up as she came to rest on the edge of the desk and wrapped her legs around Jess's middle, hooking a finger through her belt loop to pull them closer.

"You promise me this is a one-off?" Jess was already palming and sucking her breasts through the fabric, not all that interested in the reply.

Melissa nodded, her legs tightening so there no escape. "Yep, and I'm all for a slow build-up but I've been thinking about this for hours and right now I want you to—"

Jess didn't wait for her to finish. She reached an arm around her waist, eliciting a gasp as she sucked hard on her neck and slid a hand between their bodies. She moved the fabric aside and slipped a finger inside, then another, curling and twisting with each thrust.

Melissa was already wet, and the thought she'd been sat there imagining this was exhilarating. Jess took a rough grasp of her waist as she pushed deeper, biting and sucking on Melissa's lips as she clawed to pull them closer.

"More," Melissa whispered against her mouth, the desperation in her voice sending thrills of pleasure tingling down Jess's neck and into her chest. She added a third finger, angling her palm to apply pressure, and gripped tighter at the top of her buttock to stop her moving backwards.

Hands ran down Jess's chest and teased her breasts, a thumb rubbing into her nipple, but as she increased the speed Melissa had to reach back and brace herself on the desk, varying the angle and allowing Jess to sink deeper. When she could feel Melissa starting to tense, her entire hand slick, Jess rotated her hand to splay her thumb.

"Oh fuck," Melissa cried, as she rolled into it, gripping tighter still with her legs.

Jess's arm tired under the strain of holding her close and stopping her inching across a pile of paperwork. It was hot, despite the new fan which blew behind her, and sweat was dripping down her back. She leant over, both of them now almost flat, and a pot of pens clattered over the desks as she climaxed.

Jess was still, but they remained in the same position. "Like that?"

"Yeah, like that," came the panted reply. "Good job. Positive scores on your performance evaluation."

"Thanks, but we can't do that again. I mean it."

"I love it when you get all stern." Melissa sat up and seized Jess's waist again. "But you're still inside me and we're not done yet."

"Yes, we are. This doesn't always need to be a reciprocal thing."

Even as she was saying it, she knew they hadn't finished. Melissa still pulsed around her fingers, and she was fighting to remain there.

Melissa raked her hand over Jess's wet underwear. "It doesn't need to be, but right now I'd say it should." She slid her palm inside the fabric and Jess pushed against it. "See, I know you want me."

"I always want you. If we had sex every time that I thought about it, we'd never do anything else."

Melissa ran a finger either side of Jess's clit, up and down in a slow gentle motion with her mouth pressed against an ear. "Tell me what you think about."

"What do you mean?"

She jerked her hips up, pushing Jess's fingers further inside while she touched her. "You said you thought about it. Tell me what happens."

"Do you need detail, or can I tell you it involves the full contents of my bedside drawer?"

She hadn't mentioned it after the bookstore but things had moved on since then. They'd spent almost every evening together since Robbie's wedding and her confidence was increasing.

Teeth tugged on Jess's ear as the pressure built and she was desperate for Melissa to move faster. It was payback for last Saturday, and she knew it.

"You know I want detail."

It was enough trying to stay upright without having to

think of any other ways to generate pleasure. Jess gripped the top of Melissa's buttock to keep them together, rocking between her legs and tugging a piece of soft skin between her teeth, but as the rhythm slowed, she fumbled for an answer.

"Strap on," she blurted.

"Specifics."

The speed picked up and as her quads trembled, she couldn't concentrate. "Either you're on all fours, or I'm on top of you."

Melissa kissed the pulse point in her neck, then ran a line down to her collarbone as she changed direction, running circles around her clit. "What else?"

"I wish I had it now."

"Something different, what am I doing to you?"

"Uh…" Jess fumbled for an answer but gave up, panting against a shoulder and digging her nails into Melissa's side. "Your mouth… on me," was all she got out.

It wasn't an eloquent response, but it was all she had right now. As the orgasm took hold she gasped for air and had to withdraw her fingers to grip the desk. Melissa tightened her legs around again to hold her up and stroked the hair from her neck.

"Need your report, too?" Jess still clung onto the desk while the shaking subsided.

"Think I got my answer."

They remained intertwined as Jess lay kisses along Melissa's shoulder and up her neck until she reached her mouth. Even when the door rattled, they didn't notice that they were no longer alone.

"What the hell is going on here?" David's voice echoed in the hallway with the door now wide open.

Jess's eyes shot up over Melissa's shoulder, and she could

see a woman hung back by the stairs. "Oh shit," she murmured, tapping Melissa's leg and feeling her unwind them. She seemed to have been too busy trying to button her blouse up to think about that. "Turn around a minute. Please. Don't look."

"You think I want to?" David retreated into the hall and pulled the door closed. He began chattering to the woman, but it was difficult to make out what they were saying. All Jess could hear was the ringing in her ears as her face pounded with embarrassment.

"Sorry," Melissa whispered.

Jess tried to smile at her. "It's not your fault, I didn't take much persuading."

Melissa climbed off the desk and adjusted her skirt, then reached to button up Jess's trousers. She'd forgotten all about those, and her face scorched again with the realisation.

"Oh Christ, this is not how I wanted him to find out." Jess clutched her face. It was one thing being caught out by David, in the office of all places when he'd asked her to take over as manager, but now she'd also made a terrible first impression on his new girlfriend. He'd never forgive her for that.

"It's okay." Melissa pulled the hands away from Jess's face. "One day we'll all laugh about this, I promise."

Would they? That seemed unlikely. Wasn't she at all worried what Rachel would think, too? David would tell her about this when they compared notes, and it was going to result in a whole heap of fury.

Jess squeezed Melissa's fingers and then released them, taking a deep breath for courage. "You can come in," she called, still wishing they wouldn't.

"Are you decent?" David's voice had a tinge of amusement now, but perhaps that was only to spare his girlfriend some awkwardness. Fingers crossed she had a sense of humour.

"Yeah, we're decent."

Melissa gave her hair a last-minute tidy, tucking it back behind her ears, and then sat on the chair and crossed her legs. She leant forward, chewing on her thumbnail. Jess reached out and pressed her shoulder, and she clasped the hand that wasn't in her mouth to hold it there.

David pushed past the door with a hand dug into the pockets of his chinos. He jiggled some loose change, looking almost as nervous as they were, then perched himself on the edge of the filing cabinet.

"So, hard at work then?"

Jess was trying to keep it casual, but her foot was tapping on the floor and giving her away. "We were, yeah, but we closed an hour ago."

"What was this, a new initiative you've brought in with the staff to celebrate the end of the week? I think buying them a round of drinks in the pub is more traditional."

"No, don't be ridiculous. We were just—"

"I can see what you were just, let's not recap it. Not sure you should do it in the office, though, what if a client had come in? I can think of one in particular who might not have wanted to stumble across this."

"No, I know. We haven't done anything like this before. We've been careful at work and this was a one-off."

"Well, the office thing was a one-off," Melissa chipped in, her thumb still hovering by her mouth. She looked up, and Jess realised what she'd implied.

"Oh God, yeah, that's what I meant. This isn't. We're together, it's not anything..." Jess was tripping over her words, far more concerned that Melissa might think she was ashamed of their relationship and wanting to reassure her than anything else. She met Melissa's gaze. "I mean that I love you. Sorry."

When she turned back to David, he had his arms folded and regarded them with a quizzical expression, but at least didn't look angry. "Blimey, how long have I been away? I only saw you both a week ago."

"We were together then, too. I was going to tell you, but the wedding was already stressful for everyone."

A female silhouette moved in the frosted glass and David jumped as if he'd forgotten she was there. "Now, listen, Jess." He scratched at the back of his neck. "This isn't the time for introductions. Perhaps we should stick to dinner tomorrow. Let's talk then."

"Why?" Jess laughed. It wouldn't be any less uncomfortable, they might as well meet each other now. "Don't be silly, let her in."

"No, I don't think that's wise. I'll leave you to it. Lock up that is." He clarified the last point, and then his demeanour shifted. "You've got a house you can use for this, even if you have chosen to make life difficult by filling it with people."

Jess would have fought back over that, but she chose not to with her dad's girlfriend in earshot. Instead, she stepped across the office and pulled the door open before he could protest further. The woman turned, her dark shoulder-length hair moving as one piece and then settling as if it was never out of place for long. Jess studied her face, the wrinkles in the corners of her eyes that were new, the silver locket around her neck that she reached to clasp.

"What the fucking hell are you doing here?" It came out with more vehemence than she'd expected, and she flinched with the strength of her own response. "Is this a joke?"

"No, it's not a joke. I'm sorry, I didn't want to see you under these circumstances, I know it must be a shock."

"Too right, it's a shock." Jess stepped back into the office, swinging the door so that it slammed shut. "What in the depths of all hell is that woman doing here?" She addressed her dad this time, and he fidgeted with his face again. "Come on, I want you to explain."

Melissa frowned at the door. "What's wrong? Who have you seen?"

Jess's mind was connecting the dots, her eyes darting around the room. Was this who he'd spent the last five weeks with, or was it a coincidence she was here?

"Melissa, it might be a good idea if you gave us a few minutes." David smiled, and she went to stand but Jess was fuming and having none of it. Who did he think he was sending her away?

"You don't need to do that. Dad doesn't want you to witness a scene but I want you here. Not that he's paying any consideration to my feelings."

"Okay, I'm sorry. Calm down, sweetheart."

David reached out to Jess's shoulder, and she batted it away. For a few moments, the anger was raw and all-consuming, but then it settled as a ball of knots in the pit of her stomach.

"You know what, we should leave. You're right, we shouldn't have been in here." She turned to Melissa, who was back to biting her thumbnail again. "We're meeting Rachel for dinner, so we should go and wait."

"I'm worried about you because I don't understand what's going on." Melissa strode across the office with a sudden determination, taking hold of Jess's hand. "But if you want to leave, we will. You can tell me outside if it's easier, okay?"

David rubbed a hand across his forehead. "Don't leave like this, let us explain first. Please. Then you can judge me as much as you like."

He didn't need to worry about that, she was already way ahead of him. If he'd let that woman back into his life—their lives—after the eighteen years of misery she'd caused, he needed professional help.

"I can't think of any explanation that will help. You're a bloody idiot and I can't watch you fall to pieces over this a second time."

The message seemed to get through to Melissa and as the door inched open again, her features fell. She looked to Jess, as if for the first time, and then gripped her hand tighter.

"Take a shot at me rather than David." Anna removed an immaculate camel coloured trench-coat and hooked it over a peg, then slid her hands into her pockets. "I'm the one you're angry with."

"Despite what you think, I couldn't care less about you. I'm worried about Dad." Jess jabbed a finger at David. "Because he's weak where you're concerned, and I don't trust for one second that you're not going to break his heart again."

Anna nodded and then turned her attention to Melissa, who was watching it all unfold with a hand still welded to Jess's. "Gosh, I can tell you're Rachel's daughter. You're the spitting image of her."

"If you're trying to win her over, that's not the way to do it," Jess snapped.

"Still, I expect she's thrilled about this. You two make a lovely couple, don't they, David?"

Even he looked a bit perplexed. "Yes, they do."

"Enough of this bullshit." Jess now felt tired of it more than angry. She let go of Melissa's hand, her knuckles white from how tight they'd been gripping, then grabbed their jackets. "I'm hungry, and I just want a peaceful evening with my girlfriend celebrating her new job. Is that too much to ask?"

"Will you please come to dinner as planned tomorrow night?" David rubbed a hand over his tired features. "There are things we need to discuss."

Melissa stroked her thumb over Jess's forearm. "Maybe you should hear them out, for your own sanity. I'll still come with you."

Jess balled her fist, trying to fight the urge to tell them all where to go, but she knew Melissa was right. They couldn't leave this, but the knot in her stomach was growing. She swallowed down the sick in her throat and nodded with resignation.

"Fine. We'll come over tomorrow, but don't expect me to play happy families. I'm doing this for you, Dad, not for her."

"I appreciate that, sweetheart."

He nodded, choosing not to say any more, and Jess pushed past Anna. She wasn't even going to bother trying to communicate with her so-called mother.

When they reached the restaurant, Jess slowed, but her breathing didn't. She peered through the window to find Rachel already at a table tapping away on her laptop. Her breath fogged the glass, and she stepped away, clasping her hands above her head.

Melissa wrapped her arms right around Jess's middle.

"I'm so sorry, I didn't clock who it was until we were already half out the door. Are you okay?"

Jess tensed, worried that Rachel might see. It took a moment to remember a hug was normal.

"Yeah." She relaxed into the embrace, taking a deep breath. "Well, no. I'm not sure. He lied."

"That's what you're focussing on? You've just seen your mum for the first time in eighteen years."

"She's not my mum, though. That's not how I view her. It's Dad I'm worried about, even though he's been a duplicitous old git. He said he'd moved on, I thought he was happy. How can he go back to that woman?" Jess stepped away and kicked a can against the wall. It clattered and rolled across a drain, and she reached to pick it up, lobbing it into the bin. "Why do people fucking litter? It's disgusting."

"Dinner with Mum might be a bad idea. Do you want me to cancel?" Melissa soothed.

"No. We're telling Rachel about your new job, end of story. He's not ruining it."

She was adamant about that. If he thought bringing Anna back into their lives would change anything, he was wrong.

"Okay. Take a second to calm down, and we'll go inside. Should we explain, though?"

Jess considered for a second, then nodded. "If it comes up, but I don't want to ruin the celebration. I pray to God she's supportive because I'm not in the mood for any negativity."

"She may not be but let me deal with it tonight. This anger isn't for her any more than the can."

Melissa pushed the door open and Jess followed her in, putting on a smile for Rachel as she stood and pulled each of them into a hug. She closed her laptop and slotted it into a bag on the floor while they took their seats.

"This was a lovely idea. With the wedding over and Paul off playing golf I was at a bit of a loose end this weekend." Rachel took a sip of her wine and then picked up a menu. "Besides which, I thought someone had kidnapped my daughter. You've not been home."

Melissa shuffled her chair forward and poured water from a jug on the table, pushing it in front of Jess. "I've been hanging out at Jess's house with Grace and V. I told you I've helped her get set up as a tutor."

"So long as you're not outstaying your welcome." Rachel turned to Jess, peering over her menu. "Let me know if you're having trouble ejecting her."

"No, she's proven to have her uses." Jess's smile was genuine this time, and some of her tension eased with the normality of their exchange. "Besides, Grace has become attached to her. Seems a shame to force out a playmate who's on her level."

Melissa let the comment slide, smirking as she ran her finger down the food options. "There was a reason I suggested dinner tonight, besides giving you two an opportunity to tease me. We're celebrating my new job."

"That's wonderful news, well done." Rachel raised her wine glass. "What is it? Did you find something in digital marketing as you suggested?"

"In a manner of speaking. It's working at the book shop in town, but part of the role involves helping run events and managing the online sales."

"Retail? Is that how you want to spend your life?"

Jess saw Rachel frown as she was about to speak again and cut in to stop her. "Kat, the owner, has got tonnes of ideas. She thinks Melissa will be brilliant, and I agree." She clinked her water glass against Rachel's, turning to face Melissa. "I'm proud of you. It'll lead to good things."

"Thanks, but I'm worried about you. Right now, there are more important things on my mind. Can we talk this through please?"

Jess set her glass on the table and ran the side of her finger down the condensation. "If we must."

"We must. You were furious five minutes ago, and now you're acting like everything's normal. Let Mum help you."

So now Rachel was Melissa's best friend? That was a tough turnaround to accept, even if they were getting along better. If it stopped them getting into any more conversation about the job, though, it was worthwhile. Jess shuffled, drumming the pads of her fingers on the table.

"Fine. Rachel, did you know who Dad's new girlfriend was?"

Rachel's eyebrows knitted together as she leant back in her seat with the wine glass hung in her hand. "No, I'm not meeting her until tomorrow. He's invited me for drinks in the evening, I presume for introductions."

"Well brace yourself, because it's Anna. They came into the office together and didn't realise we were there." Jess blushed to recall the bits of the story she wouldn't divulge to Rachel and sat on her right hand, realising she hadn't yet washed it. "He thought we were all going to have a cosy reunion tomorrow evening."

"Anna who?" Rachel's frown deepened and Jess gave her a few moments to consider it, her eyes widening as it dawned. "Your mum?"

"The very same. She waltzed in and started chatting like it was no big deal."

"Then I'm sorry, but for once I have to agree with my

daughter. You did the right thing telling me and mark my words I'll get to the bottom of it. Has he lost his mind?"

It was a relief Rachel was also in the dark. Having her keep it a secret, too, would have been a double blow.

"Yeah, well. I hope he knows what he's doing. Tomorrow night will be fun."

"Oh, believe me," Rachel grumbled, glaring over her wineglass. "It'll be anything but enjoyable once I get my hands on him."

17

There was an unfamiliar silver Mazda on the drive when they arrived at David's house the following evening and no prizes for guessing the owner. Jess had wondered, after their exchange in the office, whether Anna might have taken the hint and buggered off home. No such luck.

"Do you reckon she's staying here?"

"Guess so." Melissa unclipped her seat belt, but then her hand hovered over the door handle. "Will you be alright seeing Anna?"

"Doesn't seem like I have a choice. Is this life now? If I want to see my dad, I have to see her?"

Jess shoved the door open and stretched her shoulders, trying to release the day's tension. They'd taken Grace to the bookshop for Melissa's reading in the morning, then caught the end of V's hockey match. Both were welcome distractions, but now her stomach was in turmoil again.

"Is it my turn to be your support animal?"

Jess smiled, stroking the hair from Melissa's shoulder. "I said you have a Labrador like quality."

"What's that, soft, blonde, and adorable?"

"I was going for moulting, needy, and always licking my face, but okay."

Jess was almost disappointed when Melissa let that one slide because it was easing her anxiety, but as they reached the gate, it became clear why. There was a spaniel in the garden, with big floppy ears and a brown coat. He looked like a younger version of Melissa's grandparents' dog, and she gripped Jess's hand.

"Can we get a dog?"

Jess crouched to stroke his ears as he darted towards them. "Where the hell would a dog live?"

"At your house, and I would visit every single day. I'd walk him, and feed him, and bath him..."

"Oh yeah, that'd help V's problems. I can imagine what she'd say if I brought a dog home."

She'd love it, and so would Grace, but that admission would lead down a slippery slope. When all three ganged up, there was no escape.

"I will wear you down on this. You realise one day you'll be living in a house full of animals?"

"Is that so? Are you one of them?"

Melissa smiled, but her cheeks had also coloured. "Thought I would be."

"What, when we've told your mum, and I'm not living with a toddler who'd expect you to read her stories at five o'clock every morning?"

"I love story time."

The novelty would wear off, though. Four people and a menagerie of animals crammed into a two-bedroom house sounded like a nightmare.

"It's cute, but if you could stop encouraging her so I can get some sleep that'd be great."

A clanging noise disturbed them and Anna appeared in

the doorway, dressed in a pair of loose jeans and a patterned blouse. "David's on his way down, he was taking a nap. Do you still want dinner? I wasn't sure, so I've got pasta on the hob."

"I don't." Jess stuck her hands in her pockets. It may have been the original intention, but she didn't have much appetite now.

Melissa rest her forehead on the top of Jess's arm. "I do. Is that okay? I thought we were eating here and I'm hungry."

"Of course it is, don't look so worried."

Anna retreated, dog in tow, and they followed her into the kitchen. Melissa sat at the table, trying to catch his attention, and Jess pulled glasses from the cupboard.

"I can do that," Anna offered. "What would you like?"

Jess stepped back with her hands suspended in front of herself. She'd always been free to eat and drink what she wanted in her dad's house and didn't need Anna's help. "I'll do it."

"Okay. Sorry."

Melissa bent to stroke the dog again. "What's his name?"

"Um, it's Harry." Anna smiled, appearing glad of the diversion as she reached for a box on the work surface and tipped biscuits into her hand. "I've got some treats here."

David stumbled into the kitchen with his hair ruffled from sleep and stopped to pat Harry. "Hi, Melissa. Good to see you clothed today."

He wandered, still bleary-eyed, to the kettle and filled it while Anna busied herself around him. She pulled out plates with the efficiency of someone who already knew the place well, and the thought irked Jess. How many times had she stayed here in secret?

"Yeah, sorry about that." Melissa made Harry sit for his treats, then asked him to give paw. "We got carried away."

"We saw. I presume you're the girlfriend Jess mentioned at the wedding?"

"I hope so, unless she's got a spare lying about."

David set out two mugs and dropped in tea bags. "And how's your mum taken it? I dare say that was a fun conversation."

"We wanted to tell you today and then her after. Scuppered."

"Yes, well. I'm sorry about yesterday. We only swung by so I could grab some paperwork. If I'd imagined for a second that you'd still be in the office..."

Jess shrugged with resignation, joining Melissa and handing her a glass. "Can't change it now."

"No, but I need to explain. I'd intended to chat with you before Anna came into the equation, so it was less of a shock."

Did she need every detail of how they'd got back together? All the times Anna had been here, and they'd met up in secret? It wouldn't change anything, and it would still have been a shock regardless of how he broached the introduction.

Anna set plates of pasta down on the table and Jess pushed her chair back, waiting for them to finish. David made conversation with Melissa about how she'd got on working in the agency and she was polite, if a little uncomfortable. She looked to Jess for reassurance with a hand always on her knee and Jess's clasped over the top. Any concern she might have had about what her dad thought of their relationship evaporated yesterday. He couldn't judge.

David pushed back half a plate of untouched pasta. "Pudding? I've got some fresh fruit coming off the garden."

Jess glanced at Anna, already sick of the sight of her.

"Why don't you get on with it, so we can go home and enjoy the rest of our evening."

'Enjoy' was a strong term because she'd had a foul mood brewing all day, but at least they wouldn't be here. If they hurried, she might even get home before Grace's bedtime. They didn't need to hang around for Rachel.

"Alright." He twisted his hands in his lap and looked to Anna. "I've not been quite honest these past few months."

"What does not quite honest mean? You either lied, or you didn't."

"Your mother and I aren't in a relationship. We've been spending time together, but as friends. Everyone assumed it was more, and it seemed easier not to correct them."

"Then why are we having this conversation?" Jess let out a sigh of relief and went to stand, but Melissa tugged her back onto the chair. "Why didn't you say last night? Be friends with whoever you like, so long as you're not getting remarried or something stupid."

It wasn't ideal, and he'd still lied, but it was a million times better than she'd expected to hear. David could pack Anna back off to Devon and they could forget last night ever happened.

"Because the reason we've been in touch with one another is relevant, sweetheart. She emailed, but you weren't open to talking. Not that anyone is blaming you for that."

"Good, because I still don't want a long reunion chat, so spit it out. What does she want?"

There was silence for a few moments, while Anna and David exchanged glances. It was as if they couldn't decide who needed to continue this.

"Alright, I'll come to the point." Anna set her palms flat on the table and leant forward. "I have a son and I wanted to tell him about you. I didn't want to do so without also making you or David aware."

Jess felt the hand tighten around hers, and Melissa's lips press against the top of her arm. "What's his name?"

She didn't have a clue why this was the first question that sprung to mind, but it popped out while her brain was still connecting dots and processing. He needed a name.

"Jason."

"How old is he?"

"Eleven. He's been asking a lot of questions over the past year, since his father had another child. I thought now was the right time."

"Eleven years ago would have been the right time." Jess slid forward on the chair, a wave of scorching blood coursing from her feet to her head. She turned to David. "When did you find out about this?"

He shuffled before answering. "January."

Jess loosened her grip, realising she was at risk of crushing Melissa's hand. "How the fuck? That's months ago, why are you only saying now?"

"Because I wasn't sure whether it was wise."

"Not your call." She jabbed a finger at him, then folded her arms tight and sat back. "I'm twenty-four years old, you don't get to decide who I live with, who I love, or whether I find out I have a bloody brother who might come knocking on my door one day."

She didn't expect any better from Anna but David was another matter. He'd had multiple chances to clarify what was happening, rather than allowing them all to assume.

"I can see it was the wrong decision, but this was an enormous surprise. It never occurred to me your mother would have any more children, or that I'd ever hear from her again."

"You seemed to get over it, given you've spent the past five weeks together and enjoyed a cosy holiday. Unless that was a lie, too."

"We went, for a week. Then I was in Devon."

Jess was upright again, banging a palm on the table. "How does that even work? She comes back after eighteen years and you take her on a cruise to celebrate? If I murder someone will you buy me a car?"

He rubbed a hand across his brow. "It's not that simple. We parted on poor terms and we've been taking the time to work through what happened. It's been good for both of us, and I meant it when I said I'd moved on. I can see why you'd think this is the opposite, but it's not."

"Well, bully for you. I'm glad you feel better and made peace. Should I expect extended family Christmases from now on? Will there be two extra stockings above the fireplace?"

"Don't be silly."

Jess's eyes widened, and she lurched forward. "I'm silly? This whole situation is ridiculous. She left, end of story. You told me that yourself enough times. I can't imagine what's changed your mind, or why you've brought her back here, and I'm not interested. She can fuck off home to Devon." Jess pushed the chair back and strode out of the kitchen, pressing the heels of her hands into her eyes and laughing. Melissa clung around Jess's middle, holding her tight. "I'm not even sure what I'm crying about. I couldn't tell you."

"Wasn't asking."

Tears rolled down Jess's face and soaked into the shoulder of Melissa's T-shirt. "How do we make her leave?"

Melissa released her grip and wiped the tears away with her thumbs. "I know it's painful, but do you think you should ask why she left? I promise I'll hold your hand."

Jess slumped forward, pulling her into another hug. That was the last thing she wanted. Erasing the past twenty-four hours was the only thing likely to make her feel any better, but she knew it wasn't possible.

"Do I have to?"

"No. If you want to leave, we'll go." Melissa placed a hand in the centre of Jess's chest. "But you're furious and I don't think it's all for David. This will be hard but I'm also sure you're curious."

"Mm. Curious about how you kill someone and make it look like an accident."

"Yeah, there are the jokes. You're uncomfortable, and I understand why, but this is your chance to find out what happened. You also have a brother and even if you hate Anna for the rest of your life, you won't hold it against him. It's not who you are."

Jess shrugged. "No. If he wants to know more about me, I wouldn't deny him."

"Right. There's a kid out there wondering what his big sister is like, and I'm certain she'll be doing the same."

It was true. Underneath all the anger was a glimmer of interest, hope and positivity. The trouble was digging it out.

Jess huffed, squinting through the kitchen window at Anna shaking her head, with David's hand on her shoulder. "If we go back in there, could you be less reasonable and punch her?"

Melissa laughed, cupping Jess's cheek and kissing her. "One wrong move and I'll claw her eyes out. That make you feel any better?"

"A little."

Jess wiped her eyes on her T-shirt and took Melissa's hand, leading her back into the kitchen. She still didn't want to stay and face this but imagining her brother assuming she'd rejected him was almost harder to bear than anything else.

"I want to answer your questions." Anna's eyes glistened, and she fixed them on the floor as Jess and Melissa took their seats again. "There is no other agenda. I understand I can't expect anything from you after all these years."

"Too right you can't. You left. Decision made."

Anna nodded. "I made that decision, yes."

"Why?"

Jess felt a compulsion to close her eyes. Somehow it made the answer more bearable. She held tight onto Melissa's hand and heard the scrape of her chair moving closer until their legs were touching.

"Because I was unhappy in the marriage. I was seventeen when we got together, nineteen when you were born." She paused for a moment of consideration, letting out a gentle sigh. "Before I knew it, I had a husband and was living a life I hadn't taken a breath to consider was right for me."

"Oh lovely." Jess's voice was almost a whisper as she willed back the tears pressing hard on her eyelids. "Well, I'm glad we cleared that up. You didn't want me."

"That's not true. I wasn't ready. You and David were in your own world. When he pushed for more children, it broke us. I knew the marriage needed to end, and how could I take you away from him?"

"You didn't need to leave though, did you? We still could have seen each other."

Anna shuffled in her chair, crossing her legs. "I kept in contact, always, but our attempts at shared custody didn't go well. You never wanted to come with me, and it left me hanging around here only to wrench you from your dad or Rachel every weekend. No one was happy, and it was like being in limbo, halfway between two lives. It was better if I left so everyone could move on."

"It's my fault? You're saying I didn't want you around and forced you out."

"No, of course not." Anna leant forward, her palms on the table again as she considered her words. "None of this is your fault. Leaving you was the hardest thing I've ever done, but I want you to know why it happened. I'm sorry, for what it's worth."

Jess kicked a stray biscuit across the tile and sent Harry scrambling after it, his tail beating a furious rhythm on a cupboard door. "Not much."

"I would love to be a part of your life, but I have no expectations. Jason wants to meet you, too, and I've warned him that may not be possible. There is no pressure."

Jess nodded, the anger and hurt settling into exhaustion. Her limbs were heavy and even that simple action took more effort than usual. She couldn't even consider meeting him in person, but Melissa was right earlier.

"I can't do that, not yet. He could email me or something, though. I'd be okay with chatting and getting to know him that way. What did you tell him?"

Anna drew a deep breath. "I was honest, to a degree. I'm prepared to be more so when he's older. For now, he knows I have a grown-up daughter, but I didn't explain the circumstances of how or why I left."

"A lot for a kid to process. I wouldn't tell him."

"I appreciate that."

"It's not for you," Jess snapped. "I won't outright lie if he asks me a direct question, but I won't bring it up, either, because none of this is his fault." She yawned and rest her head on Melissa's shoulder. "I want to go home now."

David followed them into the garden, leaving Anna in

the kitchen, and dug his hands into the pockets of his trousers. "There is something else we need to talk about, but it sounds like you've had enough for one night. Can I pop over tomorrow evening?"

Jess came close to rolling her eyes, wondering what the hell else David would hit her with this weekend. He might have an illegitimate daughter or have accepted a job with the secret service.

"Do we need to? I'm still pissed with you for lying about this, I could use some space for a few days."

David nodded and leant against his Jag. "Afraid so, sorry. Eight okay? I presume Grace will be in bed by then?"

"Yeah." Jess pressed the car remote and popped open the door, squinting up the drive at her dad. "You're not bringing Anna, are you?"

"No, she's heading home tomorrow."

"Good."

18

Ten minutes later they pulled up at home and let themselves in through the side gate. V sat at the patio table with a glass of wine, reading a book with Grace cuddled on her lap in her pyjamas. The thumb fell out of her mouth when she saw them, and she tore the book from V's hand.

"Well, that's charming." V smiled as she set Grace on the patio and watched her run into Melissa's legs. "I will consider myself redundant."

Melissa hoisted Grace into the air and kissed her cheek. "How about we take this inside while mummy talks to auntie Jess?"

"That good, huh?" V cringed, taking a sip of her wine. "Are you okay?"

Jess mumbled, pulling out a chair. She wasn't sure what to make of anything they'd discussed, or how to answer V's question. Melissa had reminded her there was no rush to decide if she wanted contact with Anna, but her gut was telling her she didn't. Whether that would change over time, she couldn't say. She was only tired.

"I have an eleven-year-old half-brother who lives in

Devon with Anna and their pet dog, Harry. It paints an idyllic scene, doesn't it?"

V raised a hand to her mouth as she almost choked on her wine. "What?"

"Yep. She didn't want to stick around for me, but she's got another kid. Dad's known for months."

"Does Rachel?"

That was a good question. It seemed unlikely she'd keep something like this secret, although a few days ago Jess would have said the same thing about her dad.

"No idea. I hope not, but I intend to ask her."

V jogged into the kitchen, returning with a cold beer. "I'm sorry." She twisted the cap off and chucked it at the table with a clang. "Did you ask Anna why she left?"

"Yeah. Too young, wasn't happy, I was closer to Dad." Jess gave a dismissive wave, then propped her head in her hand. "That's the gist, anyway. The thing is, it was tough to hear, but what's bugging me is Dad lied. Regardless of his motivations, he's kept an entire person secret from me. This isn't as if he killed my goldfish and replaced it, I have family I never knew existed. When you don't have many relatives, that's a massive deal."

No matter what was happening in their lives, they always shared the important stuff, regardless of whether it would cause an argument. The business with V was proof of that, but David had deceived everyone for the best part of six months.

"It's huge, but this stuff with your mum will be as big when it sinks in."

"Yeah." Jess ripped the label from her beer bottle, watching the flakes of paper twirl to the patio. "She said she wasn't ready for marriage and kids, and I want to understand, but it's tough. You weren't ready for Grace, it was awful timing, but you didn't leave her."

V took a sip of wine and inclined her head. "No, and I never would, but I'm trying to imagine in different circumstances..." She trailed off, rapping her nails on the arm of the chair. "Parenthood is terrifying sometimes, and I have days where I don't think I'm a good mum. People expect motherhood should be this natural, effortless thing that all women ace, and it's not."

"You think I'm being too hard on her?" Jess mumbled.

"No, I'm not saying anything like that." V smiled and shook her head. "Only musing, I guess. Sorry. Whatever the reason she left, you can rationalise it to death and try to see her point of view, but it doesn't change the impact it's had on you." She leant forward, gripping Jess's knee. "It's okay if you're angry and hurt, regardless of the circumstances."

"Yeah, I guess."

"You know I speak sense. Always do." V was defiant as she sat back, folding her arms. "It's not your job to make her feel better. What about your brother, though?"

"I'll respond if Jason gets in touch. When I first agreed it was more for his benefit, but now I'd like to find out more. We shouldn't miss out on knowing each other because of decisions our parents have made."

It was odd, dropping his name into conversation. It made him less abstract. Jess considered what he'd look like while removing the last of her label but didn't get far. It was probable he'd be more like his dad, whoever that was. It hadn't occurred she should ask, but given Anna had spent so long with David, it seemed unlikely they were still together.

"Can't you contact him and make the first move, if it's what you want? Why do you have to wait?"

Jess sat back. She hadn't even considered that. "I guess because he's only eleven. I don't want to force this on him."

"How are you forcing him? You have Anna's email address, so you can drop a message and ask. If he or they decide now isn't the right time, they can say. You're allowed to tell them what you want, don't forget that."

Melissa reappeared with a sleepy Grace in her arms, back to sucking a thumb. She let out a whimper as she grasped and leant forward.

"Oh, you want me now," V teased, turning to tickle her chin.

They each took a turn to kiss Grace goodnight, and she waved as V carried her off to bed. All the while Jess considered what it would mean to contact Jason, but it wasn't comfortable. Not least because it would mean emailing Anna. If he wanted to meet her, as Anna said, he'd be in touch.

Melissa took the now bare bottle from Jess's hand and set it on the table, slipping onto her lap. "Hello," she whispered, leaning in for a kiss. "Are you okay?"

"Yeah. Have you come to cheer me up?"

"In a manner of speaking. I wanted to see if I can make you some food because you haven't eaten today."

Jess smiled. Food was still the furthest thing from her mind, but she wrapped Melissa in a tight hug, grateful for the thought. "You want to cook for me? Is that safe?"

She slapped Jess's shoulder. "Yes, it's safe. When you walk to the chippy it is, anyway."

"I guess. I'd rather sit here and kiss you all night, but I doubt you'll let me do that."

It was another one of those very welcome distractions, and by far the most pleasurable, but Jess's stomach rumbled and betrayed her.

"No, I won't." Melissa prodded it and then cupped Jess's cheeks, kissing her one last time before jumping off her lap. "Will that do until later?"

Jess huffed and hauled herself from the chair. "I suppose."

They called up to V, so she knew where they were going, then began a slow trudge to the fish and chip shop.

"Do you want me to call Nan and cancel next weekend?" Melissa squeezed Jess's hand, the other wrapped around the top of her arm. "We can visit Wales another time if you're not up to it."

Jess's shoulders slumped forward. She'd forgotten about the trip, with everything that'd happened over the past twenty-four hours. It was the ideal place to be, though, with the family who weren't a smouldering train wreck. A few days on the beach, getting some fresh air, and escaping the drama would do them both good. Decisions about brothers and long-lost mothers could wait.

"No, let's go," she decided, also knowing Melissa was looking forward to seeing her grandparents. "It'll be a fun break."

* * *

After Melissa had monitored Jess's fish and chip intake, making sure she'd eaten enough, V decided it was time to bring out the big guns of ice cream and films. She drew the curtains across and plonked herself down on the sofa, and Melissa wrapped under Jess's arm on the other with a pint of chocolate.

"I haven't had a scoop for ages," Jess protested, as Melissa spooned in more ice cream.

She smirked, digging out a tiny chunk and holding it to

Jess's mouth. "Sorry."

"You're supposed to be making me feel better, or are you out of sympathy already?"

"I have lots of sympathy, but I'm not good at sharing ice cream. It's unnatural." Melissa shivered, holding up another. "Suppose I could try harder. For you."

When they'd finished, she set the tub on the floor and lay on her side, wrapping Jess's arm over herself as they spooned. When you couldn't concentrate, kissing freckles was at least a pleasurable way to pass the time. Jess had been at it for several minutes when there was a tap on the window.

"Did you hear that?" V crept across the room and peeked through the curtain. "Oh, it's David and Rachel." She clutched her chest, then paused the film and let them in while Melissa hurried to straighten out her hair.

"Hello, darling," Rachel almost whispered. "Your father told me what happened this evening. Can we have a private word?"

"I'll help Melissa tidy." V gestured at the kitchen and then pushed her out with the empty ice cream tubs.

Jess shifted over so Rachel could sit, and she perched on the cushion. David loitered, digging his hands into his pockets and resting against the arm of the other sofa. He looked like a school kid dragged in front of the head-mistress. God knows what Rachel had said to him.

"I know David told you he'd come tomorrow but we've had a chat and decided it's best getting everything out in the open tonight. If that turns out to be a mistake, I apologise."

The worried look on David's face showed he was less sure, but he nodded all the same. "I should have told you everything earlier, but you were already so upset. None of this has gone the way I'd planned."

"No, well, I'm sure we can all agree you haven't handled it well." Rachel was in business mode now, crossing her legs and smoothing a hand over her skirt. "Let's tackle this head on so everyone can move forward. You were wrong to withhold this information from Jess, and I'm sure she'll forgive you with a simple apology and explanation, so off you go."

Jess almost laughed at Rachel's last comment. She was the only person able to put David in his place. He shuffled, rubbing his stubble and then wiping his hands down the front of his trousers.

"Okay. When Anna first contacted me, I shared your anger. It was a tremendous shock, and all I wanted was for her to away." He squinted, as if trying to recall. "But we chatted, and it resulted in us having some discussions about the way our marriage ended. They were difficult, and I've had to accept some responsibility." He scratched the back of his neck this time, letting out a huff. "I tried to protect you from everything with Anna, and I worried knowing she had another child after leaving would be too upsetting. I didn't want you to go through that, but I understand now it was the wrong call." He gestured to the kitchen. "You're an adult, you have a right to know, and to make your own decisions. I'm sorry."

Was he even apologising for the things he'd said about V? That was a turnaround. It didn't negate the anger, but his admission helped.

"Thanks, I appreciate you saying that."

David looked to Rachel. "Hold that thought, because there's more." He wrung his hands, his gaze now somewhere out the window. "In the throes of this, I had some health news. Don't panic, but I found out I have testicular cancer."

"Don't panic?" Jess's mouth gaped open, and she slumped back against the sofa cushion as if someone had punched her in the gut. "This seems like something to panic about. Are you okay?"

He nodded. "It's stage one and hasn't spread. I've had an operation, and then when I went to Devon it was for a single round of chemotherapy to stop it returning."

"You'll be okay?"

"They seem confident. I need to go for regular tests, and the chemo wasn't much fun, but I'm lucky. Caught it early."

"Why didn't you say? We could have helped."

The implication was that Anna had been the one to support him through this, and the thought created a lump in Jess's throat. How could he want her instead of his family?

"I didn't want to worry anyone. My medical insurers let me pick a hospital, and by that point Anna and I were on better terms..."

Rachel wrapped an arm across Jess's back. "Are you okay, darling?"

This was the day that kept giving. She shrugged, unsure how she felt. The anger dissipated, replaced by worry and more hurt. Feeling upset that he'd lied again seemed selfish when the main thing was his health, but it remained.

"I guess. Struggling to understand why you couldn't tell any of us about this." She lay her head on Rachel's shoulder. "I take it you didn't know?"

"No, not about the cancer, your brother or Anna. I won't say I wasn't a little hurt that he didn't come to me, but it's done now."

"Yeah. Do you need anything?" Jess managed some approximation of a smile.

"No thank you, sweetheart. If you can carry on what you've been doing in the agency, I'd appreciate it, but otherwise I'm okay."

Jess nodded. She could do that. If he wanted to take his usual matter-of-fact approach, it was his choice.

"Did it cause the weight loss?"

Their conversation about a woman from the internet taking advantage of him seemed ridiculous now. It also looked like the better option, and Jess wondered if they could do a trade.

"Yes. The operation was straightforward, I only stayed in hospital for a night. The chemo knocked me about, though. How people do more than one round, I can't imagine."

"Then I'm glad you had someone with you."

She meant it, even if that person had to be Anna.

"Thanks. I know it's hard to understand how we've reached this place, but something like this gives you a kick up the bum."

They chatted a while longer and the more detail David went into, the closer Jess nudged towards Rachel. The realisation dawned that this could have been worse, and still might be if it returned. She'd never even conceived of losing her dad and as Melissa joined them Jess was desperate to hug her, but knew she couldn't. All she could do was sit with her discomfort and focus on what David told her so she knew what would happen next.

When he stood to leave, an hour or more later, Jess still found herself clung to Rachel. The tight grip of her hand had left them both with white knuckles. "Are you going too?"

Rachel pulled Jess into a hug, dropping a kiss on her head. "Yes, my darling, but I'm here whenever you need me." She straightened her skirt as she stood and ushered David towards the door. "And I'll see you next weekend."

"Next weekend?"

"Yes, Alice rang Paul in the week and invited us. I

presumed she would have mentioned it."

"No, but that'll be nice," Jess lied, a twist of apprehension disrupting the mixture of chips and ice cream. There was no room to consider telling Rachel now, not with everything else that had happened, and spending a weekend with her was a minefield. There was no way out, though.

Jess hugged her dad, almost afraid to squeeze too hard. It was odd, they never did physical affection, but this felt like the time to start. Melissa followed them through, frowning as she waved to her mum. When they were out of sight, she closed the door and tugged Jess into a firmer embrace.

The longer they stood there, the more Jess struggled to breathe. Tingles shot through her fingers, and her feet were blocks of ice. She tried to take deep breaths, but the harder she concentrated, the more her lungs burned. She looked up and swooned, the television in her line of vision blurring around the edges.

"You've had a lot to cope with today. Relax, focus on the here and now." Melissa's thumbs stroked across her cheeks as she whispered. "Look at me for a second, follow my breathing."

Jess watched Melissa's chest rise and fall as instructed. She placed a hand in the centre and closed her eyes until they were in sync. Every inhalation gave her a comforting hit of vanilla.

"Today needs to do one," Jess murmured, when she was capable of coherent speech again. "Not even ten litres of ice cream can help, it's a lost cause."

Melissa grunted out a laugh. "Oh dear. Not sure what else we've got to offer. Suppose I'll have to put you to bed and hope tomorrow is better."

Jess peeked out of one eye. "If a cuddle doesn't work, I'm screwed."

19

They drove to Wales straight from work on Friday evening, with a car full of everything required for a restful weekend. That is to say, anything able to reduce the time Melissa had to spend with her mum. Body boards, because Rachel never went in the sea, running gear, because she didn't jog, and the Xbox so Melissa could play with Paul. She agreed it was a good chance for some family bonding, but still needed a means of escape.

It was eight by the time they arrived, and Rachel's Mercedes was already in the drive. Alice waved from the front window and then appeared in the door, Lucky the spaniel darting past her legs.

"Hello, girl," Melissa cooed, crouching to pet her and almost falling back onto the block paving. "I missed you so much."

"She missed you, too," Alice called. "Grab your bags and I'll show you to your room. Everyone else is already in the pub."

It wouldn't be the same if she didn't make it feel like a bed-and-breakfast. Jess pulled their cases from the boot, leaving the rest of the paraphernalia in the car, and followed them up the stairs.

Alice gave them Melissa's usual room and Jess wandered to the window, squinting against the orange light straining over the trees at the bottom of the garden. She'd worried what Rachel would think of them sharing a bed, but Melissa had assured her it was a practical necessity. Otherwise someone would need to sleep on the sofa.

"How are you, cariad?" Alice pulled Jess into a robust hug. "We were so sorry to hear your dad's news."

"Thanks."

She'd soon learned it was the correct response, because people seldom wanted details. All they needed to know was the prognosis was good, and he didn't want a fuss. Several more chats during the week had confirmed that fact, and Jess was trying to share his positivity.

"Do you need to get changed?" Alice released her stranglehold and ushered Lucky onto the landing. "I'm famished."

She locked up, and they wandered along the lane, Melissa swinging Lucky's lead and throwing a tennis ball for her to retrieve. Their local was a thatched pub at the other end of the sleepy village, surrounded by rolling countryside that shimmered in the evening light. When it came into sight, Melissa clipped the lead on and tucked the ball in her pocket.

Alice held the garden gate open and the sound of chatter and clinking glasses floated across the still summer air. Jess smelt vinegar and stout, finding it familiar and comforting. They used to come here whenever she visited for the weekend, but it had been almost a year since the weather had been good enough to sit outside without a thermal coat.

"Hello, darlings," Rachel called, waving from a picnic

table on the far side. "We ordered when Alice said you'd arrived, so it shouldn't be long."

Jess kissed her cheek as Melissa tied Lucky to the bench, and she shuffled to make space. Paul continued discussing sport with his dad over a pint, and Alice swatted them over so she could sit.

She clasped her hands together and rest her elbows on the table. "I'm so glad you all came, this is a treat."

Jess smiled, for what felt like the first time in a week, but she also was uneasy. This weekend was about forgetting her problems, not adding more, and she still worried Rachel or Paul might rumble them.

A server picked his way across the garden with plates of food and everyone moved their empty glasses. He set bundles of cutlery on the table, and passed the first fish and chip dinner to Alice, then the other to Rachel.

He went to move away but then stopped in his tracks, smiling at Melissa. "Hang on, I want to ask how you are, but I need to fetch the rest of your food."

"Is that boy a friend of yours?" Rachel reached for the salt pot as he jogged off toward the bar.

Melissa let out a nervous burst of laughter, rubbing a hand across her brow. "No, not quite. We went out for a little while."

"Well, this is a learning experience. Will I be meeting any more of your ex-boyfriends over the course of the weekend?"

"He wasn't my boyfriend, it never got that far."

Jess squirmed as Jamie returned, balancing all four remaining plates on a large tray. She'd been so caught up in her own problems, he hadn't been a consideration, but now the thought he might be about to out their relationship was giving her palpitations. It'd turned mild discomfort and apprehension into a lava surge from an erupting volcano, and the only thing she could do was keep her head down.

Jamie passed food around the table. "So, how's life? It's been a few months."

"Yeah, good." Melissa smiled, stuffing a chip into her mouth and pointing at her cheeks. "I tell you what, why don't I come in and chat once we've eaten? I'd love to catch up, but I'm hungry."

He smiled back and checked no one needed anything, then retreated into the pub. Jess dabbed her T-shirt against the bottom of her back, mopping up the trickling sweat. They'd got away with it for now, or so she thought.

"Speaking of boyfriends, I wondered if you were seeing someone." Rachel leant backwards so she could prod Melissa with her fork. "Jess wouldn't tell me anything, she's far too loyal."

Alice had been talking with Paul until Melissa kicked her under the table. She chuckled for a second and then drew Rachel into a conversation about work, which was a sure-fire distraction. They chattered for the rest of dinner, but Jess was struggling to find an appetite and only picked at it, leaving half her chips for Paul to pilfer.

She tapped Melissa's shoulder. "Come with me for a round of drinks?"

Now everyone had finished, she wanted to make sure Jamie kept his mouth shut. As they stepped inside the pub, squinting to adjust to the dim light, she spotted him clearing trays by the kitchen door.

Melissa ignored him and headed for the bar. "What do you want to drink?"

Jess didn't follow, only inched towards Jamie. "Do you think we should...?" She gestured in his direction. "First. In case he says something in front of your mum."

"I doubt he'll talk to her at all, that's why I said I'd chat to him later."

She ordered the drinks but Jess couldn't settle. The risk seemed too great, and she was in danger of dehydrating from all the sweating.

"Could we check?" she pleaded, trying not to sound like a whiny child but struggling. "I can't relax."

Melissa huffed, but somehow managed a sympathetic smile. "Would it be so bad if we told them? Mum's already asking about boyfriends, and it's only a matter of time before she mentions your mystery girlfriend. Isn't it weird she hasn't been around at all while this has been going on?"

Jess blanched and her fingers tingled. "It's too soon. I can't argue with Rachel on top of Anna and Dad, it's overwhelming." Her hands shook now, and she held them both out. "Can I have a few days, please?"

Melissa nodded, taking Jess's hands and pressing them to her mouth. "Yes. Be honest, though. Are you wavering on this? Please don't lie. I want to help, I'm not accusing."

She was. Not on the relationship, but last weekend had broken her resolve to tell Rachel. Jess's foot tapped on the hardwood and tears prickled her eyes.

"Only because I'm scared. I want to tell her, and I want to be with you, but it's tougher than I thought."

"Okay." Melissa tugged Jess closer, cupping a cheek as she dropped a soft kiss on her lips. "I understand. We need to sort this out without giving you a nervous breakdown."

* * *

When she woke the next morning, Jess felt a shot of panic to find Melissa wasn't in the bed, until she realised it was almost noon. She hadn't slept in this late for years and the experience had generated a dull headache. Rubbing her temples, she got up and dressed, padding down the stairs into the kitchen.

"Ah, you're alive." Alice sat at the table with a newspaper and a pot of tea. "Can I get you some breakfast?"

"Wouldn't say no to toast, if it's no trouble."

Alice sucked her teeth and shook her head. "I don't know, might be tricky." She stood, pulling some bread out of a bag on the side and dropping it into the toaster.

"Where is everyone?"

"They've gone to the beach already. Melissa wanted to wait for you but I told her I'd hang back, give her some time with her parents. It's a relief to see them getting on better, I worried after the wedding. Wasn't sure how Rachel would react to this job."

Jess had too, but the effort on both sides seemed genuine, despite Melissa's initial protestations. They'd all enjoyed the pub, after sorting out the Jamie issue, and ended up playing board games in the living room until late.

"Rachel and Melissa are too much alike, that's the problem."

Alice laughed, leaning back against the counter and folding her arms. "Best not say that to them. The same as I'm unwise to point out how much you remind me of your father."

Jess's face dropped. It would have been a compliment in the past, but right now it only reminded her she was a hypocrite. All the time she'd spent over the past week upset with him for withholding information, and she was doing the same. It's not like it was even for Rachel's benefit, or Melissa's before that.

For the best part of a week she'd found herself suspended between abject terror at the thought of losing her dad, crippling fear of disrupting her relationship with Rachel, and hurt at all the lies. Which one took precedent varied hour by hour.

David wanted them to carry on like nothing had happened, at least in respect of his cancer, but it was difficult. He'd had months to take it in but lumbered Jess with a lot of information in short order. She couldn't shake the deception, as relieved as she was that he was okay, or reconcile the knowledge that she'd have done the same thing.

"Truth hurts, I guess."

"Now why do you say it like that? You're both caring, generous people. You could show a little more of it to yourselves, but the fact remains."

Jess shrugged. "I've protected myself more than enough. Justifying that I'm doing it for another person's benefit is the line I'd take, too. I do it with V, but I hadn't realised until the other day. I'm smothering her, under the guise of help."

Alice plated the toast and set it in front of Jess, along with her home-made jams. "It is help, but if you're worried, check in and make sure it's what she wants."

They'd already had a lengthy discussion in the week about V contributing to the bills once she was earning. Jess had also apologised a third time for interfering with Stephen.

"V pointed it out weeks ago, and I didn't listen. She said I need to take care of people, and she was right. I'm terrified of letting anyone down."

"Well, you're not the only one who suffers from that."

Jess covered her mouth as she munched through a bite of toast. "Melissa with Rachel? Yeah, I know."

"Not only with her mum, with you." Alice leant back in her chair, cradling a mug of tea. "She was so worried about not being everything you need. Drove me to distraction, all the deliberation. You two are both thinkers, which is great, but it is possible to create problems where they don't exist."

"Is that what I'm doing with Rachel? You think she'll be okay with this?"

"I hope so, but even if she isn't, so what? She'd come around in time and it has to be better than this fretting."

Jess huffed, sending toast crumbs scattering across the table. She wanted to believe that, and she knew it was unfair on Melissa to make her keep secrets from her mum. It was an odd juxtaposition. She'd wanted them to get on better, so this became easier, but she also didn't want it to destroy their progress.

"I have to trust her and say something, don't I?"

"You don't have to do anything, cariad, but it'll come out. My advice is to be brave and take control."

With that Alice balled her fist and gritted her teeth, and Jess tried to do the same. Shame hers was far less convincing.

* * *

The beach was three miles from the house, and Alice spent the ten-minute car journey nattering about all the people she'd caught up with at Robbie's wedding. When they pulled up in the car park, Jess peered over the cliff. Below, hundreds of people lay on towels or kicked balls. There were several groups of body boarders and surfers, but she knew where Melissa would be swimming. She liked the rock pools at the far end, so they'd be somewhere nearby.

They walked down the steps and across the scorching sand, with handfuls of cold cans and crisps from the shop by the toilet block. Rachel reclined on a blanket, dozing with a straw hat over her face, and she jumped when Jess sat next to her.

"Oh, hello darling." Rachel propped herself on both elbows and wriggled her toes in the sand. "Are you feeling better for a good sleep?"

Jess lined her cans in the shade, then banged her hands together as she got comfortable. "A little. Had a good chat with Alice."

"I'm pleased, and now I'd like one with you. I've given more thought to your living situation. How far adrift are you with your deposit?"

"About three thousand, give or take. That's without legal costs. Depends what I buy, but that's based on the figure Dad's mortgage guy recommended."

Rachel nodded, squinting down the beach and waving to Melissa as she dragged Alice into the water. "Would you consider accepting a loan from us, if not David? I've discussed it with Paul and we'd like to help."

"That's so generous, but I can't let you do that."

"Why not? We loaned Robbie a good deal more. There are very few people able to buy with no help at all, in our area at least. You've saved the lion share and proved you can do it. This would only be a top up, so you don't have to wait."

Jess wrapped an arm around Rachel's shoulder. "I don't mind waiting."

"No, I know you don't. There are three of you crammed into that tiny house, though. Four, if you count the time Melissa spends sleeping on your sofa."

Jess balked at her last comment, although it turned to relief as she realised Rachel's assumption. "We manage, though, and it isn't forever."

Rachel shook Jess's knee. "But why struggle at all? It can't be easy having your girlfriend over with a full house.

People want to help because they love you. I won't force you to take my money, but at least consider."

"Thank you, I will. It means a lot you've even offered."

Melissa ran towards them in shorts and her pink bikini, a body board under her arm. She shook like a dog, Lucky scampering along behind, and dropped to her knees.

"Are you coming in?" She looked at Rachel and then laughed as she narrowed her eyes. "Relax, I didn't mean you."

"Yeah, I'm coming in a sec, but you need to sort the dog out first. She's crapping in the sand."

Rachel chuckled as Melissa tramped off with a poop bag. "I haven't seen her this happy in a long while, and I'm understanding why she couldn't tear herself away. Another of Alice's fried breakfasts and I'll move into the spare room."

"I'm glad you're getting on better. You know she only wants you to be proud of her."

Rachel sighed, rolling onto her stomach. "And I am, but sometimes she infuriates me because I know she can do more with her life. At some point I suppose I have to let her get on with it, she's her own person."

Jess watched Melissa chasing Lucky, searching for dog poo. "She's an amazing person. I don't know what I would have done without her this week, she's been so supportive."

"That doesn't surprise me at all. With friendships, I can't fault her."

Jess tugged off her T-shirt and slung it onto the blanket, then threw her trainers and socks on top. She chased Melissa down the beach, catching her in time to throw her over a shoulder and stride into the sea, before dumping her into a wave. She knew they needed to tell Rachel, but it could wait until they'd had some fun.

20

Melissa lowered herself face down on the bed, wincing as her chest hit the duvet. She'd worn sun cream, or so she claimed, but still burned to a crisp. Jess shook the bottle of aloe vera and squeezed a blob onto her hand, massaging it into the angry skin.

"We'll put some more on in a while," she soothed, stroking the hair off Melissa's shoulders.

Melissa grumbled, her feet motoring up and down, slapping against the bed frame. "It hurts."

"I know. Make sure you drink plenty of water tonight."

"Oh what, instead of sipping champagne?"

Jess laughed. "Yeah, you need to cut back on the booze. I could use a drink, though. How would you feel if we told your parents about us tonight?"

Melissa was silent for a few moments, her legs still. "Are you sure? I wasn't trying to pressure you last night."

"I know you weren't, but I've considered it this afternoon and I need to trust my bond with Rachel is strong enough to survive this."

Jess wiped the excess aloe on her legs and rest back on

her heels while Melissa pushed herself up to kneel. "Do you think it might be easier if I tell her I'm seeing a woman?" She took hold of Jess's hands. "Less of a shock."

"Won't she put two and two together? It might be simpler to go with a straightforward approach, but she's your mum."

"Let's tell her, then." Melissa leant forward, tilting Jess's chin and dropping a gentle kiss on her lips. "And pray."

They changed for dinner and went downstairs to the kitchen. The rest of the family already sat at the table, sharing drinks while the smell of lamb and rosemary wafted from a roasting tin on the counter.

Melissa fanned herself and pulled out a chair. "What is it with this family and serving roast dinner in the height of summer? Have none of your heard of salad?"

"Do me a favour, you hate salad." Jess sat next to her, setting the tube of aloe beside her placemat for later. "What you mean is, why aren't we allowed to eat ice cream for dinner?"

"You never let me skip vegetables at your house, either. It's irritating."

"And you irritate me in return, so I guess we're even."

Rachel smiled over the wineglass she was raising to her mouth. "That's not quite the word you used earlier. What was it you called my daughter?"

"What?" Melissa gawped at her mum. "Do I need to hit her?"

"Let's see. Annoying was it?" Rachel laughed, and as Melissa was turning to launch an assault, she put her other hand out to stop it. "Amazing. She said you were amazing. I'm told you've been a tower of support. I'm proud of you."

Jess might have given a little fist pump at that, if it wasn't so obvious. She couldn't remember the last time Rachel said something so complementary. Not when Melissa could hear, anyway.

Melissa smiled as she pulled at a thread in her dress, the power of her mum's words causing her to blush even through the sunburn. "Thanks."

"It's always reassured me you girls have each other. Never take your friendship for granted."

Melissa peeked at Jess and prodded her leg. The word friendship needed challenging, and she took a deep breath to steel herself, but Alice interrupted. She set a bowl of potatoes on the table, then grasped Jess's shoulder for a second before resuming serving the food.

Jess recomposed herself, taking a scoop of vegetables and finding it made the exchange less intense. "We don't take our friendship for granted, or at least I hope we don't. I wouldn't classify it as that, though."

"No darling, me either." Rachel cut her off, staring across the table with her wineglass hung limp in her hand. "You're more like family. This business with David and Anna has made me think. I hope you realise that's what you are to us."

"I know that now, but for a long time I worried we didn't have the same permanence I get with Dad. It's only now I've realised my mum going has had an impact, more so than I'd admitted. If she left, and we're blood relatives, I guess I couldn't see why anyone else wouldn't."

It was a hard admission to make, but it was true. V would be unbearable to know she was right. Again.

"Dare I hope this means you'll take up our offer?"

Jess let out a nervous laugh, scratching behind her ear. "That's not what I meant." She set the spoon down and wrung her hands in her lap. "There is something I need to tell you, though."

Rachel raised her eyebrows, waiting for a response, and

Jess grabbed the seat to still her hands. "When I said Melissa isn't just my friend, it's because for the past couple of years I've been in love with her. I didn't tell anyone because I was afraid it'd horrify you, and you might not want me around anymore."

Melissa put her hand over Jess's and moved it to her lap, the other holding a green bean. She took a bite, then kissed the top of Jess's arm, before returning to her meal. "Well done."

Rachel frowned. "And how do you feel about her?"

They had to wait for Melissa to finish her mouthful before she leant back in the chair, crossing her legs towards them. "I'm in love with her, too."

Rachel was quiet for a moment, her gaze fixed on their hands. "But you're not... are you?" She looked to Melissa, but then seemed to change her mind and shook her head. "Well, I don't suppose that matters. Gosh." She tapped Paul's arm. "Did you know about this?"

"No, love."

Rachel speared a potato, chewing it like a lollipop. It was about the least refined thing Jess had ever seen her do. She was still staring at them, and her face scrolled through a range of emotions before settling back into a frown.

"So, are you telling me you want to be in a romantic relationship?"

Melissa shook her head, taking another bean from her plate. "No, I'm telling you we're already in one."

"And how long has this been going on?"

"We got together on Jess's birthday." Melissa shrugged, lacing her fingers through Jess's and stroking a thumb into her palm. "Feels like longer because it's normal now. I can't imagine how we carried on for so long pretending this was only a friendship. Will it be a problem?"

"No, darling. So long as you don't think when you split, I'll take sides. You will still see each other, you know that, don't you?"

Melissa's face twitched. Jess knew which word she'd found objectionable and squeezed her hand. She could see how hard Melissa was trying not to blow up, her lips tightening and her chest flushing.

"Yes, Mother. We know it will be very difficult if we break up, but we're not intending to. This is a long-term thing for both of us. Thanks for assuming it's inevitable, but I don't share your pessimism."

"I'm only being practical. You're twenty-three, relationships don't always last at that age. I'm sure it feels fun and exciting right now, but it'll get harder once the novelty wears off. You won't be able to walk away from this."

"I don't want to walk away from it, I love her. Even if we no longer want to be in a relationship, that will remain true."

Jess cleared her throat and took a sip of water. "Neither of us has rushed into this, we both know how painful it would be if it didn't work. But it was also problematic not acting on our feelings. I'm sure it won't always be easy, because no relationship is, but this makes us both happy. We work."

She didn't know what she'd expected, but this wasn't it. Rachel was calm, returning to her food and pausing every so often to survey them again. It was a relief she wasn't ranting and raving, but Jess's palms were still sweating as she picked up a fork and tried to eat. Paul gave his support, not seeming to care much either way so long as it was what they wanted, but Rachel was unreadable.

She picked up her wineglass again once they'd finished

eating, and the frown deepened. "So, what do we call you now?"

Melissa grunted out a laugh. "Melissa's still fine."

Rachel's eyes narrowed. "You know what I mean. I'm trying to understand this. You can't drop a bombshell and not expect me to have questions." She huffed, swirling the contents of her glass. "It is a little confronting finding you know so little about your own daughter."

Melissa stiffened again, and Jess jumped in to save an argument. "She's still the same person."

"I am, and I don't want to label myself right now. If you're asking whether I'd be with a man or a woman, if we split, I don't know." Melissa shrugged, scraping her leftovers onto Jess's plate and taking them to the sink. "I can't imagine being with anyone but Jess, so it's hard to say. I guess we'd have to wait and see. Does that answer your question?"

"Yes, it does." Rachel leant back and thanked Paul as he took her plate away. "Please don't bite my head off when I ask the next one, but do you still want the same things? You were always dead set that you'd have a family."

"And nothing's changed. Who I have one with, yes, but the fundamentals are the same." Melissa softened, wrapping an arm around Rachel's shoulder and kissing her head. "You can relax, I know all you're interested in is where your grandkids are coming from."

Rachel laughed and Jess's limbs went limp, as if all the tension she'd carried around for months had drained out. She could go to sleep right there and had to rub her face to keep herself awake. The pretence was so ingrained now that she couldn't remember what it felt like to relax. It had taken a lot of energy to maintain.

"Now that's over, how about we head to the arcades?"

Alice suggested, both hands gripping Jess's shoulders. "You can't come down without a play on the two penny slots."

For someone who hated loud noises and crowded places, Melissa loved the arcades. For about ten minutes, anyway, until they overwhelmed her, and she had to leave.

"Is that it?" Jess struggled to believe there wasn't more. "We're carrying on as normal now?"

Alice gave her a gentle shake. "What did you think would happen?"

She stared at Rachel's vacant face as she considered the question. "I have no idea. You're not angry?"

Rachel laughed again. "No. A little disappointed you didn't feel you could tell me. It's been a bad week for that. I can't say it won't take some getting used to, but I'd never be angry to hear how much you care for one another. Am I really such an ogre?"

There was only one correct answer to that question. Rachel was formidable on occasion, but not an ogre, and Jess shook her head.

"Good." Alice grabbed her keys from a pot on the sideboard. "Let's leave these boys to the pub, once they've done the washing up, and enjoy a night out."

Even if it hadn't still been daylight, the fluorescent facades would have lit the pleasure beach like a lurid disco, and Melissa had a daft grin plastered across her face as she took a twenty out of the cash machine.

"Don't let me spend more than this." She held the note in Jess's face. "I mean it. Last time we were here together I spent a fortune. You were no help at all."

Jess laughed, remembering when that was. "If I recall,

the last time we were here was in September after lugging all your junk, and I was so desperate not to go home that I kept handing you more coins. It was me who almost bankrupted themselves."

She'd eked it out until gone ten before submitting to driving home and spent the whole of Monday in an exhaustion fuelled grump.

"You get to take me home with you this time." Melissa wrapped her arms around Jess's torso, the cash flapping in the breeze. "And I can have you back in my bed now everyone knows, without pretending you're only sleeping with me because there's nowhere else." She stood on tiptoes to rub her nose along Jess's. "It occurred to me earlier that I could have arranged for you to stay with my grandparents at any point, and I never did."

"I didn't need to feel horrible guilt for enjoying it so much, then? All those nights I laid there awake with you gripped onto me to keep from falling out of the bed, and it was only a ruse." Jess dipped her head, bringing their lips together, and lowered her voice. "What would you have done if I'd kissed you?"

"Back then? Freaked out." Melissa scrunched her nose. "Well, I don't know. Might have enjoyed it." She reached lower, tucking a hand in Jess's back pocket.

Jess kissed the top of her head, smiling at the vanilla now mixed with a faint whiff of coconut sun cream and aloe. Then there was a snapping noise as someone ripped the twenty pound note from Melissa's hand, and Jess loosened her grip, ready for a fight.

"Should be more careful," Alice chided, waving it between them. "Someone will steal this off you."

Melissa snatched it back and tucked it in Jess's pocket. Alice and Rachel had returned with ice cream cones, passing them around and licking drips from their hands, and her eyes lit up as she took one.

"Does this mean you might come home?" Rachel mused as they wandered along the strip, her voice competing with the loud music and jingles pouring out of the arcades. "I'm relieved you weren't only staying out to avoid me. At least I now know what Jess's house has that ours doesn't."

"What's that, hobnobs?" Melissa smirked, removing her hand from Jess's pocket to swipe hair out of her face before it became matted with ice cream.

"If that's what you want to call it. I wondered when Jess spent time with her girlfriend, now I know the answer is every night."

Jess took Melissa's hand, trying to adjust to this newfound freedom. "Are you okay with me staying at your house?"

"I don't know why it would become a problem now."

"Well, because it's different if we're sharing a bed. Together. As a couple."

Rachel stuck out a hand to halt the conversation. "Yes, I get the picture, and I've had enough trouble erasing the image of Robbie and Sam so please don't continue."

They soon reached the end of the strip and turned to look out over the sea. It really was beautiful here, if you didn't think about what was behind you. So many times they'd walked it together, and Jess held Melissa tight as they all sat on a wall to admire the view.

Rachel dangled her legs, the sandals almost slipping from her feet. "You must reconsider your stance on this house business. I've just forwarded on a property that might work. At least look."

Jess smiled, reaching into her pocket to pull out her

phone with an arm still wrapped around Melissa's waist. "Is this what I can look forward to now?"

"What, the dreaded mother-in-law?" Rachel gave Alice's shoulder a gentle nudge. "No, darling. It's nothing new, but I'll admit I'm even more invested if it's for the two of you."

"Steady, you're not my mother-in-law yet."

Jess scrolled to her emails, seeing the forwarded property details. They'd sent Rachel an advance draft, no doubt because she bought so many to renovate and sell or rent out. It was the email from Anna with the subject 'Jason' that caused Jess's heart to skip a beat, though. She locked the phone and slid it back into her pocket.

"Any good?"

Jess mumbled, distracted as she tried to imagine what the email said. She didn't want to open it here, with everyone watching. "Oh, yeah. Looks good, I'll arrange a viewing. Thanks."

21

Every day Jess felt a bubbling apprehension when she opened her work emails. She sensed a reply from Jason was coming and gripped the phone in her pocket, trying to resist the urge to check them again. He'd been sending a message every evening for four days now, and another was imminent. For now, though, they had a house viewing to concentrate on, and she tried to push it out of her mind.

Melissa stopped the car outside a three-bed house a few roads over from the end of the High Street. It wasn't quite an old cottage with wonky walls, but Jess's budget wouldn't stretch that far. It did have a garage, big garden, and open-plan kitchen and living room. All it needed was a lick of paint and new carpets.

Jess dangled the keys in front of Melissa's face. It turned out she knew the agent dealing with it and, since the house was empty, they'd agreed to let her have them for an hour.

"Don't you want your dad's opinion on this?" Melissa took Jess's hand, and they wandered up a stone path flanked with flower borders.

"No, I want yours."

Jess opened the front door and a waft of musty air hit
them. The current owner lived in Australia and when his
last tenants moved, he deliberated for a while before
deciding to sell and stay abroad. It would smell better after
an airing.

"Can you afford something this big?"

They stepped into the entrance hall. At the end was a
door to the kitchen, and on their left another into the living
room. An archway joined them, so you could walk straight
between the two spaces.

"With the pay rise I got as manager and the dividends
I'm receiving now. It turns out I wouldn't even need to
borrow money from dad or your parents. Couldn't get
anything newer or in better condition, but with a little work
I can add value. Rachel says it's all cosmetic."

She'd volunteered Paul and Robbie to help decorate,
and herself to make cups of tea while she took on the role of
foreman. David had also offered but Jess felt uneasy asking
him to do manual work when he'd been unwell. It might be
silly, he said he was up to it, but she wouldn't take the risk.

"I like the kitchen." Melissa ran her fingers along the
granite effect worktop. It sat over cheap but serviceable
oak effect units, and they'd save money not having to
replace anything expensive. "Looks good to sit on." She
tapped a spot by the sink. "This would be mine." Then she
opened and closed the window a few times. "These seem
okay, you'll save a packet not needing new double
glazing."

Jess nodded and took Melissa's hand to lead her upstairs
into the master bedroom. "What about this? Our bed on
that wall." She pointed to her right before leaning on the
windowsill and looking down the garden. "Thoughts?"

Melissa laughed, wrapping an arm around Jess's waist

and tickling her side. "Our bed? Heavy hint, there. What are you alluding to?"

"Well, since you brought it up, I thought I could persuade you to move in with me."

"How did you plan to do that?"

"I've got about twenty packs of hobnobs and a drawer full of sex toys. What more would it take?"

She hadn't considered needing to put together a case. Given Melissa was staying most nights anyway, it seemed like a formality. They still hadn't slept at Rachel and Paul's house, because they were both more comfortable in their own space. This way it would be, on a permanent basis.

"For a start, you'd need to check it was fine with V. I presume she still figures into your living arrangements?"

"Yeah, and Grace. She'd get her own bedroom, so I doubt she'll object. I wondered if it was too soon, but we'll have been together at least four months by the time it goes through, and it's not like we're strangers. I already know you'll be a nightmare."

Besides, if they both wanted this, what did it matter? Melissa could always move out again if they changed their minds. Rachel and Paul weren't short of space.

"I will consider it." Melissa stood on tiptoes to drop a kiss on Jess's nose.

"No rush, I don't need a decision now, but do you like the house? Think I should put in an offer?"

"The only question is whether you like it." Melissa prodded the centre of Jess's chest and then flicked a shirt button. "I am happy so long as I'm with you. I've got my job, my love and if you buy this house, I may even get my puppy." She shrugged, raising her eyebrows.

"Oh, I see. If I let you have a dog, you'd move in with me? Sounds a lot like bribery."

"I'd never resort to such measures. I'm saying only that the actual house doesn't matter to me. If it's covered in photos and full of my favourite people, the rest is immaterial."

Jess nodded, satisfied by her answer. She was right, although this house seemed perfect. It was close to town, which meant Melissa could walk to work and V's lack of a car wouldn't become a problem. Most important, though, it was in budget.

"Right, I'll phone and make an offer."

"Wow, who is this decisive person and what have you done with my girlfriend?"

Jess pulled her phone out and began the call. "I know. It's liberating." The agent answered, and they talked through the details before she put in a low offer. It was worth a shot. When the call ended, Jess tapped her phone against her palm. "Well, that's it. Weird how simple it is. You save for years, make tonnes of plans, and all it takes is one conversation."

It'd take more than that, but all they could do for now was wait. She still needed to double check the figures again, although David had spoken to the mortgage advisor with her at lunchtime and he'd run the rough math. It would be fine, and she knew her budget.

"We should tell Mum, she'll love to know she got her way," Melissa tugged Jess's shirt as they locked the house. "I was thinking we could have dinner at my place tonight and stay over. Feeling brave?"

Jess swung the keys around her finger. "Yeah, okay. Suppose it's only fair, I can't put it off forever. We need to go via home to tell V, though."

* * *

The news excited V but she was less thrilled than Rachel, who threw her arms around Jess's shoulders as soon as they stepped into the house. "I've made a special celebratory dinner, and Melissa's favourite ice cream for dessert."

"Wow, steady on. They haven't accepted my offer yet. I was quite cheeky."

Rachel waved a hand as she pulled away. "They expect that. You can always go in higher." She led them through to the kitchen where a stack of frozen pizza boxes sat on the breakfast bar. "I'll be sad to see Melissa go, but I'm pleased for you."

"Will you?" Jess scoffed, finding that hard to believe. "Besides, what makes you think Melissa's going anywhere?"

Rachel let out a shot of laughter, clanging knives and forks in the drawer. "I'm not an idiot. Come on, tell me I'm wrong."

"You're wrong." Melissa looked her mum dead in the eye, but then nodded and stepped away. "About lots of things, but not that. We are moving in together. Jess has also said we can get a dog."

Jess snapped her head around as she sat at the table. "Excuse me? You might have informed me of your decision first." She'd expected Melissa would drag it out at least a little longer and make her sweat before accepting. "That's good, though."

"She's too soft on you, young lady, but I'm pleased to see you both so happy. With everything that's been going on, it's a miracle." Rachel set the cutlery on the table, then clattered about with plates. "How are you getting on with Jason?"

Jess fumbled for her phone again. The past hour was about the only one this week where she'd forgotten him, and now she felt a surge of anxiety.

"He should have emailed by now." She scrolled to her

messages, not sure whether it was that or excitement. It may have been a mixture of both. "Said he wanted to send me a photo, and he's asked for one in return."

She needed to change into something more casual before they took one of her and dashed to Melissa's room to put on jeans. When she re-emerged, they were both laughing at her.

"You are so cute right now." Melissa giggled, holding up her phone and taking a photo.

Jess's mouth hung open. "What?"

"Less than two weeks since you found out you have a brother, and you're already invested. It's not a problem, far from it. He's very lucky."

Melissa was right, she was into this now. Anna needed to monitor their conversation, but they'd still been free to chat. She'd already found out he liked the same video games, and he wanted them to play at some point. The thought of hearing his voice as well gave her a thrill.

"Hurry and take a proper picture." Jess chucked her phone at Melissa, who fumbled to catch it. "One that captures my best side."

Melissa stood on a chair, angling the camera downwards. "If I've learned one thing from Instagram, it's that you need to take photos from above." She snapped the picture and turned the screen for approval. "Now I need to filter the hell out of it, and you'll look okay."

Jess grabbed the phone back and then lifted Melissa from the chair, dropping a kiss on her forehead. She opened her emails again and sat at the table to read, finding there was one from Jason, sent in the last twenty minutes. He apologised for being late, but he'd been to visit the puppies Harry had sired. There were two pictures attached and Jess opened that one first, holding it up for Melissa.

"Harry's a dad." She knew they were getting a dog the minute Melissa's face went all gooey. "Cute, right?"

"They're tiny. Look at the little brown and white one, he's my favourite."

"Hold that thought."

Jess closed the photo, and her finger hovered over the other. She tapped the icon and squinted at the screen.

Melissa peered over her shoulder. "Say what you want about Anna, she produces good looking kids."

"Can't argue with that." Jess's face screwed into a smile so wide it almost hurt. "Now when I email him, I'll know who I'm talking with. I hope he's not disappointed when he sees me."

"Don't be daft, why would you disappoint him?"

Melissa wrapped her arms across Jess's chest and kissed her cheek, while Rachel took the phone and studied it. "He's black."

They both laughed in unison, and Melissa snatched it back. "Your powers of observation astound me. Well done, Mother."

"What? He is. Did you ask anything about his dad?"

Jess nodded. "Yep. He's married to someone else now, but they all live in the same town and Jason can visit whenever he wants. They even have dinner together as one big family, sometimes. I'm glad he has that."

She took a deep breath and wondered for a second what it might have been like if she'd had it, too. There was no point dwelling, though. She had her family and Jason has his. One day, maybe they'd converge.

* * *

After dinner they relaxed in the garden, filling Rachel and Paul in on more of the progress with Jason and going over plans for the house. Then they moved inside, shouting at television game shows from the sofa and lobbing cushions at each other for ridiculous answers. When Melissa stretched and yawned at nine-thirty, making hints that she wanted to go to bed, Jess kissed her and stayed to chat with Rachel a while longer.

"Thanks for encouraging me with this house. And again, for the money offer. I know it turns out I didn't need it, but I'd love if you could help me renovate the place."

Rachel switched off the television, draining the last of her tea. "Anything you need. We'll turn it into a palace." She leant across the arm of the chair and lowered her voice. "About this dog business. Will you let me buy you a puppy as a housewarming present? Only if you're already planning to get one."

Jess smiled. She'd assumed they'd adopt, but there was room for negotiation. "I've already looked into re-homing one. V and Grace need to meet and approve any dog first, but you could help if you like? I want it to be a surprise for Melissa, so she can't know we've discussed this."

"Understood. A client of mine has connections with an organisation which helps match dogs with new owners while they're still in their previous homes. That may be a good fit, do you mind if I contact him?"

Jess agreed and hugged Rachel good night, then traipsed upstairs. As she pushed the door open, she could hear Melissa humming from the bathroom. After changing into her pyjamas, she joined in before cleaning her teeth.

"You're in a good mood." Jess dropped a kiss on Melissa's peeling shoulder and grabbed the toothbrush from her wash bag. "Any reason in particular?"

Melissa spat and rinsed, then leant against the basin while Jess finished. "Mum's supportive, you're getting on with your brother, and we're in my bedroom. These simple pleasures have made me very happy."

They'd made Jess very happy, too, but she couldn't say because her mouth was full of foam. She waited until she'd dabbed her mouth on a towel, then wrapped her arms low around Melissa's waist and carried her into the bedroom. The curtains shut out the last strains of daylight, and a candle flickered from the bedside table. She let go, taking a deep breath of the vanilla scent filling the room.

"Is that what it is, candles?" Jess took another sniff.

"No." Melissa laughed, climbing under the covers. "Well, yes, but not only that. I like for everything to be consistent, so my candles, car air freshener, body spray, shampoo and pretty much anything else you can think of is vanilla. It's quite simple."

"Will our bedroom always smell like this? I'd be grateful if you could make that happen."

It was the fragrance of home, and Jess wriggled to find a groove as she got into bed. This one was far nicer than her own, and she couldn't believe she'd been depriving them of it. She may put in a request to take that, too.

"We can give it the vanilla treatment, yes. Any other requests?"

Jess pinched the fabric of Melissa's T-shirt and drew her closer. "Only one. Take this off."

Melissa smiled and sat up, tugging at the bottom of Jess's top. "You're in my bed now, remember."

"You want me to strip for you?"

There was nothing but a nodded response and Jess complied, yanking off the T-shirt and slipping out of her shorts. She lay on her back and clasped her hands behind her head. "Now what?"

Melissa tapped Jess's right leg to show she wanted them parted and knelt in the gap. Then she placed a hand on either side of Jess's torso and grazed their lips together.

"Keep your hands where they are," she whispered, before sitting on her heels and taking off her own clothes.

Jess squirmed, unsure how long she'd hold out on that request. She entwined her fingers and tried to keep them there. "You're the boss."

"I can never hear that enough."

Melissa was back but this time she indulged in a slow kiss, stopping every so often to give a soft tug on Jess's lips that almost broke her resolve. Jess stilled a twitching hand as their breasts slipped together, her nipples hardening.

"Why am I not allowed to touch you? Seems unfair."

Melissa's hips lowered until they almost met, and all Jess wanted was to pull them tight and feel the whole of her weight. It was like needing to run when you could only walk, and her muscles tingled. All she could seek was Melissa's mouth, willing her to press harder, but she moved out of reach and smiled.

"Because this is fun. For me, anyway."

She lingered on Jess's breasts for what felt like hours, emitting mumbles of pleasure as she licked and sucked, running circles and playing with different parts of her tongue. When she added light trails with her fingers, down Jess's sides and then over the tops of her thighs, the ache between her legs fought with the will to do as instructed. Jess wrung her hands together, inching down the bed as she writhed, her entire body flushed.

"Can I touch you now?" she pleaded.

Melissa shook her head, and the action brushed a tickle

of hair across Jess's stomach that caused a moan to escape. She shut her eyes, and for a moment the sensation stopped. They were no longer in contact, and her pulse quickened waiting to see where she would land next.

When Melissa's tongue ran a line up the inside of Jess's thigh, her stomach flipped. She bent her knees so Melissa could wrap her hands around and gripped the pillow. The touches were tentative at first but sent every nerve ending firing. They built up together, and as Melissa's confidence grew, Jess rolled into her mouth.

Melissa flicked her tongue over Jess's clit, then took it into her mouth, and the hands that had shown restraint reached their limit. Jess pushed herself up on her elbows and guided Melissa to face her. She brushed away a wedge of hair, then ran her fingertips over Melissa's back.

"Not good?" Melissa once again came to rest with her elbows either side of Jess's head.

"Very good, but I want to see you now."

Placing one hand at the nape of Melissa's neck, and the other in the small of her back, Jess entwined their legs so they could slip against each other. She felt a thrill of excitement at the wet on her thigh and lowered a hand down to grasp a buttock and push them closer. With soft breasts and tongues massaging together, they rocked, and built together this time.

When she was close, Jess rolled them onto one side, creating enough space to run two teasing fingers between Melissa's legs. She rubbed up and down over her clit and opening, groaning when Melissa reciprocated, and felt her stomach flip for the second time with the gasp against her mouth.

Jess opened her eyes to find Melissa's flushed face next to hers. She kissed again, increasing the intensity and finding it matched every time until her muscles tightened and sent out waves of pleasure that crashed over her entire body. Melissa pulled them tight to still their hands and nipped lazy kisses.

They lay still while Jess stroked the hair out of Melissa's eyes with trembling fingers, smiling as she dabbed her nose and cheeks. "I love you," she whispered.

Melissa kissed her again, and her heart thudded. "Love you too."

22

The owner rejected Jess's offer on the house, but they agreed a price after a lengthy process caused by the time difference. Rachel knew someone who could do the conveyancing, and then it was just a case of sitting back and waiting for the solicitors to work their magic.

Jess wanted to be in before Grace's birthday at the start of November, which should have been possible given it was three months away. But when Melissa started her new job in September, they were stalling. Even with the house empty and no one else in the chain, having the current owner in Australia was causing problems.

They'd woken at Rachel's house, which was fortuitous because Jess was hoping to use her skills to get things moving. She'd resisted asking for too much help until now, but this was the sort of situation that required Rachel lighting a fire under someone. So far simply channelling her energy during phone calls hadn't helped, and it was time to bring in the expert.

Jess left Melissa in the shower and strode downstairs

with purpose, pulling out a chair at the kitchen table. "Can I ask a favour?"

"Of course." Rachel clicked off her phone screen and set it next to her plate. "What can I do for you?"

"I went into the estate agency on Friday to find out what's going on, but they fobbed me off. Can you tell me what I should say to get some real information?"

"I'll do one better than that. Meet me at my office for one o'clock, and we'll go in together." Rachel gripped Jess's knee and gave it a brief shake. "Don't you worry, we'll get this moving."

Jess sucked in her cheeks to hide a smile. She'd hoped Rachel would just offer to do it herself, because despite negotiating on a daily basis for work, she was appalling at asserting herself in these situations.

Melissa wandered in and poured cereal, then kissed the top of Jess's head before dropping onto a seat. "What are you two looking so pleased over?" Milk dripped off her spoon and splashed into the bowl. "Don't tell me, you're discussing my Christmas present already."

"No, although we are forming a plan, and I'm also excited about your first day. Is it okay if I come in at lunchtime?"

It felt like packing her off to school, but Melissa seemed less convinced. "It's a shop, we let the public in during all normal opening hours."

"I know, but I don't want to distract you at work."

"You're very sweet, but this isn't a big deal. It's a job. I'll get up every morning, spend the day doing book things with Kat, then come home. Visit when you like."

Melissa gave a dismissive wave of her hand, sending milk splattering from her spoon. It was rather anticlimactic, after waiting so long to start. It was her first proper, permanent job, doing something she'd enjoy. They should mark the occasion somehow.

"I guess." Jess tried to mask her disappointment. "Will you at least let me buy you dinner tonight to celebrate?"

"Nope. You told Jason you'd video call with him, remember? He wants to meet your talented and gorgeous girlfriend. Besides, we're looking after Grace so V can go on her date."

Rachel laughed over her coffee and pushed back a plate of toast crumbs. "I can't imagine why. You'll terrify him, poor lad. He'll be starting secondary school next week telling all his new friends about his sister's overbearing partner."

This was the term by which Rachel now described them. She was happy to accept everything but the word girlfriend, which she said made it sound like they were schoolchildren. Under the circumstances, she was avoiding it.

"How rude. Kids love me." Melissa was indignant, jabbing her spoon. "I intend to pursue this with the same dedication I had to show with Grace, although in this case books may not be the answer. I'll send him a video game."

"Oh yes, I'm sure Anna will love to have more excuses for procrastination land on her doormat at the start of a new school year."

Melissa took a break from her cereal as she got up and wrapped an arm around Rachel's neck. She kissed her cheek with a loud smacking noise and then sat down again. "Thank God. For a while I thought someone had replaced you with a carefree imposter. You're still in there, though, we can all relax."

"You can joke all you like, but I have my uses."

* * *

Jess looked forward to employing Rachel's uses all morning, and it was also a helpful distraction from missing Melissa. It'd become normal to have her in the office every day, and the place seemed drab without her. David was back at work, but his repartee didn't quite measure up anymore, and Jess had huffed through the first half of the day. Getting out at one o'clock was her only consolation.

"Now then." Rachel pushed through the door of her office building. She had dispensed with pleasantries, and it was an odd thrill. "Tell me who you're dealing with?"

"Martin." Jess looped her arm through Rachel's as they marched back up to the High Street.

"Oh, yes. I know Martin."

"I already knew him, too, but it doesn't seem to have helped."

When they reached the agency door, Rachel let go of Jess's arm and the widest fake smile in history broke across her face. "Martin, darling," she called, disturbing him from his baguette. "Can I have a quick word?"

Was this how she did it, killing people with kindness? Or was she luring him into a false sense of security? He set his lunch on a piece of tinfoil and wiped a hand along his suit trousers. As he approached, kissing Rachel on both cheeks, Jess could see a reassuring bead of sweat appear on his brow.

"Hello, Rachel. And you have Jess with you, so I can imagine why you're here."

He gestured for them to sit, but Rachel put out her hand. "Then this shouldn't take long. I'd like an update and don't try to tell me there's no news. If that's the case, ring a solicitor or something."

"Jess's solicitor phoned me less than an hour ago. It

looks like our vendor hadn't received his questionnaire paperwork, so we've arranged to send it again."

"Good, and you'll check in to make sure he's received it? Then let Jess or I know? We're looking for this to exchange by the last Friday in October at the very latest, and I don't see any reason why it can't so long as everyone pulls their finger out."

Jess hung back, fidgeting with her pockets and watching in awe until Rachel finished. She caught up on Martin's kids, giving V's tutoring business a quick plug, and then led her back onto the street.

"Can I buy you a cake to say thanks?" Jess squinted at the bookshop, still desperate for an excuse to go in, despite what Melissa had said. "We could take one to Melissa and Kat."

Rachel laughed, peering at her watch. "I suppose you could persuade me. I expect she'd like to know we're supporting her. Well, you. I doubt she cares a jot whether I'm there."

That wasn't true, it was all she ever wanted. Jess wasn't going there again, though. Instead, she wandered towards the bakery and ordered a selection box, then crept through the bookshop door with Rachel behind her. Kat and Melissa were both leant against the counter sipping tea, but besides that the store was empty.

"Hard at work, I see," Jess called, waving from behind a bookcase. "We came with cake, but I'm not sure you deserve it."

Melissa put her mug down and leant from the other side of the case for a kiss. "When you said you might call in, you didn't mention treats. I would have been far more enthusiastic." She swiped the box and ran back behind the counter, setting it down and passing Kat a cream horn before wedging half a doughnut in her mouth. "You can go now."

"Oh, charming. I'd like to remind you who made this introduction." Jess gestured from Kat to Melissa as they munched through the pastries.

Kat covered her mouth with a hand. "And I'd like to remind you who helped facilitate this relationship and hosted your first date."

"In that case, can I offer to buy you a car or a luxury holiday?"

"I was thinking more that you might name your first-born after me?"

Jess shook her head, taking a chocolate éclair. "Nah. Wouldn't be fair to name a dog, Kat."

While they chatted, Melissa's gaze tracked her mum around the store, watching as she pulled out and inspected a selection of books. "I can recommend something if you like?" She wiped her sugary fingers on a tissue. "We have a great self-help section."

Rachel turned to glare. "Anything about how to deal with ungrateful smart Alec children?"

"No, sorry. I have no experience with that."

"I'll take this one, then." Rachel set a guide to South America on the counter and pulled out her purse. "I've been thinking your father and I should travel more, now you lot have got your own lives. We always said we would, and I'd assumed it could wait until retirement, but I don't suppose any of us can gamble with time."

"How wise," Melissa mused, as she fiddled with the till. "I believe we're about to agree again. Someone should check hell hasn't frozen over."

* * *

Jess left work early, so she could make dinner for Grace while V got ready. She'd deliberated over this date with Stephen for weeks but decided to go, reasoning that a night out and an excuse to dress up was worthwhile even if it went nowhere. It was reassuring to see her pragmatism hadn't diminished with time.

When Melissa arrived at six, trays of chips and chicken breasts were coming out of the oven, and a pan of baked beans simmered on the hob. She let herself in and threw her bag on a chair, then wrapped her arms around Jess's waist.

"Wow, will I come home to find dinner on the table every night?" She pinched a chip, then spat it into her hand when it was too hot. "Ugh, you could have warned me."

"Why don't you do something helpful, like getting Grace a bib? Fish one out for yourself, while you're at it."

Melissa snatched a kiss then pulled the drawer open to grab out two bibs, tying one around Grace's neck and stuffing the other under her own chin. She sat at the table while Jess served the food onto plates, cutting up Grace's into little chunks. Then she did the same with Melissa's and set it down in front of her.

"I suppose you think you're funny." She peered up, her eyes glistening with amusement.

Jess shrugged. "I do, as it happens."

There was a knock at the door, and she jogged through the living room to answer it, calling up the stairs to V as she went. She'd been in the bathroom for almost an hour now, preening herself.

"Hey, is she ready?" Stephen rubbed his hands together. "I'm a bit early."

"Not yet, but come in. I was just feeding the kids."

Stephen looked puzzled as Jess stood aside to let him past, no doubt worried that V had more than one. When they reached the kitchen, Melissa whipped the bib out from around her neck and got up to take Grace's plate from the side. She blew over the top and stuck her little finger into the beans, then licked off the sauce and slid it onto Grace's highchair.

"So, where are you guys going tonight?" Melissa settled back in and speared a chip, pointing it at Stephen. "Somewhere fancy, by the looks of things."

Stephen smoothed over his shirt. "Oh, no. Just a wine bar in Oxford. I wasn't sure what she'd like."

"You're already doing better than Jess. Her idea of a romantic night in is beans and chips."

Jess set her plate down on the table and then reached an arm around Melissa's shoulder, leaning in to kiss her. "Don't forget the ice cream."

"You got me ice cream? Is that for adult time later or do I have to share it with Grace?"

Stephen shuffled, tugging on his clothes again, and Jess laughed. "Both if you like, but let's not give poor Stephen any more to worry about. He looks nervous enough as it is."

It was quite reassuring to see him this way, because she'd expected him to be a cocky little shit.

"No need." Melissa shot him a smile. "You'll be fine but remember if she brings you back here later you have to be very quiet. It's a house rule."

Jess swiped her leg, and she chuckled. "Don't listen to her. She's only winding you up."

"No, I'm not. If we have to be quiet, so do they."

The chances of V bringing Stephen home later were slim, given Grace would be asleep in her room, and Melissa knew that. She was in the sort of mood to wind people up, though, and had never been Stephen's greatest fan.

"I, um, don't think..." Stephen stuttered, but V saved

him. She was in a new black dress, and Melissa attempted a wolf whistle that didn't come off but still had the desired effect. "You look nice," he managed, unable to tear his eyes off her. "Incredible."

"Better."

Jess reached around to clamp Melissa's mouth shut. She writhed and tried to pull the hand away, but only ended up in a bear hug, half falling off her seat. "Don't listen to her. Have fun and call if you want to stay out. We can take care of Grace."

Melissa stuck up her thumb, still unable to talk.

"Thanks." V stepped across to give Grace a kiss. "Watch these two, make sure they behave," she whispered. "Pay particular attention to auntie Melissa."

Jess let her go, and she straightened out her T-shirt. "Have you upgraded me?"

"Leave, please." Jess shoved her on the shoulder. "Before I come with you."

They returned to their meals, most of Grace's beans ending up on the floor, and then hurried to clear the mess. They'd arranged a video call with Jason at half six, and Jess went to grab her laptop while Melissa fed Grace ice cream. She stumbled, almost dropping it down the stairs, and cursed under her breath.

When she got it to the table in one piece, she leant on the back of a chair. They'd only done this once before, and she was nervous, fumbling over the keys and forgetting her password, until Melissa took over and sorted it for her.

"Calm down," she soothed, dropping a kiss on Jess's forehead. "Tell me what's rattled you."

Jess clasped her hands over her head, taking a deep breath. "I'm worried about seeing Anna. He was at his dad's house last time, it was okay, but we haven't spoken in six weeks and I don't want her to use this as an excuse for us to chat."

They'd had brief contact via email to discuss Jason, but that was the extent of their interaction since meeting at David's cottage. Jess's position hadn't changed, she wasn't ready to have Anna in her life.

"Have you told her this?"

"Yeah, but what if she thinks it's worth another shot? I don't want to say something in front of Jason, it's not fair for him to end up in the middle."

"Then after the call we'll email her and reassert the boundary. You're in control here. If you're not happy with something, we'll sort it out."

Grace ran into the living room and pointed at the television when Melissa lifted her from the highchair. They didn't often let her watch it before bed, but it'd be fine this once. She settled in front of yet more Peppa Pig, then they sat and waited.

Jess slipped her hand into Melissa's, squeezing it for reassurance. "Thank you."

"What for?"

"Just... everything."

23

Rachel's meddling yielded results and on the last Friday in October Jess picked up the keys to her new house. A weekend of painting followed, with Robbie, Paul and V's mum chipping in to help. The result was a fresh coat of magnolia throughout, before the carpet fitters laid new flooring on Monday. It was amazing the transformation they'd affected in less than a week, and by Grace's birthday they had also moved in the furniture, even if a few bits remained boxed.

V enjoyed the extra space more than anyone. She sprawled flat on the double bed Jess donated her when she moved in Melissa's and claimed she was never leaving it. After months of squeezing into a single with Grace's bed cramped next to her, it was her new sanctuary. Robbie had helped make the switch on Saturday morning, and an hour before Grace's party V was still running her hands over the new duvet as she lay like a starfish on top.

Jess stood in the doorway, watching her friend indulging in the simple pleasure. "I'm so glad my old bed could bring you such joy."

V let out a satisfied groan. "Oh, it has. You have no idea how much I'm looking forward to having my own room again. There are so many things you can't do when you share with a toddler."

"Do I want to know?"

"I wasn't going there, but now you mention it." V laughed and pulled herself up to sit. "You know what feels best? Paying rent, even if it's not much." She wandered to the drawers and grabbed a sequined top, holding it against herself and pouting. "Now, what do you think? Is this the outfit of a respectable mother?"

Jess reached into the pocket of her jeans as her phone vibrated. "No, which means it's perfect." She smiled at the message from Melissa to say she was just leaving town with Grace. "You'll be the hottest mum at the party."

"You still go all goofy whenever she texts you, it's disgusting."

"Do not." Jess ducked as a pillow flew past her head. "Anyway, it's not my fault I've got the most gorgeous girlfriend in the world and you've got Stephen." With that V launched another missile and Jess laughed, slipping around the doorframe. "Touchy subject?"

"No," came the defiant reply. "I'm happy with my love life. You do the marriage part and I'll stick to kids. Between us, we're the full package of domesticity."

Jess laughed again as she wandered downstairs. Grace having her own room also meant most of the toys and other junk that cluttered the old house had somewhere to live, and it was nice not to trip over every five minutes. It almost looked like the tranquil state of her living room a year ago. The only difference was that now, it wouldn't stay that way.

Jess admired the photos in the kitchen as she flicked on the kettle. She'd sat with Melissa until late the previous evening, putting them into frames and nailing them in neat rows on the walls. David might cope with a wonky mismatch of styles, but no one else could.

She pulled mugs from the cabinet, rubbing a little remaining moving dust from the bottoms, and set them on the counter. Then she heard the door rattle open and smiled, turning to lean against the unit as Grace ran into the room wearing her new pink Converse and carrying another book. She darted into the living room, crouching on the floor and opening out the pages.

"Before you say a word, it's a birthday present from Kat," Melissa called. She appeared in the doorway, still clad in a bright yellow coat and beanie, her nose red from the cold. "Don't lecture me about spoiling her again, it wasn't my fault on this occasion."

"No, but all the other times…"

"Are irrelevant, although you're the one who insisted on buying Grace two gifts. May I refer you to the trampoline in her bedroom?" Melissa pulled the hat from her head while Jess unzipped her jacket. "Are you undressing me?" She lowered her voice to a whisper. "Because there isn't time for that."

Jess laughed. Her mind hadn't gone there, but now the idea appealed. "Are you sure?"

"Very." She narrowed her eyes, dropping a kiss on Jess's nose and hooking her coat over the back of a chair. Then she hoisted herself onto the work surface and shuffled. "I'm still not sure if this is my spot. Doesn't feel right, yet." She frowned, bouncing up and down a few times and making the units creak. "Come here a minute."

Jess put one hand on either side of her and leant forwards. "What?"

She felt a set of legs tighten around her back and two

hands caress up her shoulders, then Melissa kissed her with far more passion than she'd expected for the time of day. It took her by surprise, but she soon recovered and cupped Melissa's cheeks before running her fingers into the mess of blonde hair. Jess's heart thudded louder than the ticking clock on the wall, and she thought it might give up and explode as a tongue entered her mouth. When someone tapped on the window, it almost did.

She looked right to find Rachel and David peering at them through the window. They both waved and signalled towards the patio door, and Jess mouthed that it was already open, turning as Melissa released her grip.

"Hello, darlings," Rachel called, shivering against the cold. She stamped her feet on the mat and hugged the coat close around herself. "I hope we're not interrupting."

Melissa laughed, looping her arms across Jess's chest. "I think you can see that you were. Should we look forward to you letting yourselves in through the garden on a regular basis?"

"You may change your tone when you realise why we're here."

Rachel raised her eyebrows as she smiled, and David wore a similar grin. They looked like a couple of naughty teenagers.

"Have you come to tell us you're having a torrid affair and have left Dad?" Melissa teased.

Jess wished she hadn't, because her stomach had endured enough turmoil for one lifetime. Things were calm, for once, and she hoped to enjoy it for a while.

"No, don't be ridiculous. We've come with your house-warming gift." Rachel took off her coat and threw it onto the table. "But before we bring it in, I just want to caveat this by saying I had no idea until David phoned me yesterday. I also need you to go upstairs for a second, while we speak with Jess. Take Grace with you."

"Right..." Jess felt a sense of trepidation and turned to her dad. "What have you done?"

He only smiled, and Melissa slipped off the work surface, eying them with caution. She scooped up Grace without comment and they heard her footsteps on the stairs, followed by a door closing overhead.

"Nothing bad, sweetheart. Don't worry." David held out his hand for Rachel to pass her car keys, then raised a finger to indicate they should wait. They stood in silence while he went outside, returning a minute or so later with a puppy tucked under each arm.

"What the hell?"

David set them on the tile and they tussled with each other, while Rachel closed the doors to stop them escaping into the hallway.

"Housewarming gift. You can only keep one, mind. The other is for me, but I'll let you pick. I spent all night trying to decide."

"Explain?"

"They're Harry's puppies. Rachel told me you were adopting a dog for Melissa, and when I was in Devon this week Jason wouldn't stop blathering on about these pups. He loved the idea you should have one, so I came home with them. It'll be nice to have a companion for my retirement, dogs are therapeutic, and I've also heard they're a good way to meet women."

He'd missed the operative word: adopting. They'd already filled in an application form, and she had someone inspecting the house next week to make sure it was suitable.

"It's very sweet and Melissa will freak, but I've already started the process of adopting a dog. A puppy requires training, and V needs involvement in this. You can't bring animals into a house with kids on a whim. It's irresponsible."

"I know, which is why I had Rachel give me V's phone number. We had a chat yesterday, and she's approved."

David had phoned V? She shook her head then crouched to fuss over the dogs. They were cute, and it was lovely that Jason wanted them to have Harry's puppies.

"Can we at least donate to the re-homing centre? I feel bad."

"Don't look at me, sweetheart, I've shelled out eight hundred quid a pop on two pedigree bloody dogs. That was with a discount. And I had to agree to call mine Harry Junior."

"How much?" Jess gripped the sink with one hand and her chest with the other. "I'll donate my birthday money, then. Thank you, I'm sorry if it seems like I'm ungrateful, it's only a shock." She knelt to stroke them, the fur soft and curly around their ears. "They're gorgeous. Not sure it's wise letting Melissa see both, though, because you won't leave with one."

David bundled up a puppy and held it to his chest, turning to face away. "Noted. Get her, then."

Jess stood and opened the door, careful not to let the other dog escape, and called up the stairs. When Melissa came down the smile on her face made Jess's chest tighten.

"Dad's landed himself in a bit of trouble." She guided Melissa into the kitchen and gestured to the dog biting at David's trouser leg. "He needs to pick which one he's taking home. Do you think you can help?"

Melissa sunk to her knees, thwacking them on the tile. "Oh my gosh, they're adorable." She held a wriggling puppy, letting him lick her face. "Why are you only keeping one?"

Rachel shook her head in disbelief. "For a bright girl, that was a silly question. One of them is for you, darling, but you need to choose. Don't say both."

"You want to split them up?" Melissa pouted, snuggling into his fur. "Don't worry, I won't let the mean lady take anyone away. You're both coming to live with me."

"They'll still see each other. For goodness' sake, you make it sound so dramatic. Have that one, now you're attached."

David reached into his coat pocket, pulling out a pile of paperwork. He passed it to Jess, and she flicked through the certificate of his pedigree, his vaccination card and general info about what food he was used to eating.

"Why do they give dogs these weird names?" She squinted at his registered title. "Halcyon Spirit Wotsit... huh?"

"Hello, Hal," Melissa cooed, grasping a unit as she stood. "Welcome to your new home. Let me introduce you to everyone." She held him in front of Rachel. "This is granny. She's been looking forward to grandchildren, so expect lots of affection." Rachel pursed her lips but remained silent, and Melissa passed him to Jess. "And this is your other mummy. Always remember, I'm the fun parent, and she'll take you to the vet."

"Hal?" She frowned, setting him back on the tile. "You can't call a dog Hal."

Melissa's eyes widened. "Why the hell not?"

"While you continue this argument, someone needs to fetch his belongings. We've spent the entire morning trying to find crates, the right food and goodness knows what else." Rachel ushered Jess towards the door and waited while she carried everything in from the patio. David had supplied the lot, right down to toys and a packet of poop bags.

The dogs resumed their play fight and barrelled through the living room, with Melissa giving chase. She picked up Hal again and sat on the sofa, stroking his head with her index finger. "It feels like home now."

"Really?" Jess sat and draped an arm across her back. "I was about to say it feels like our home will be trashed now."

Melissa laughed, her head falling against Jess's shoulder. "You wait, this is only the start."

Printed in Great Britain
by Amazon

28920103R00152